Secret Lives of Mothers & Daughters

Secret Lives of Mothers & Daughters

Anita Kushwaha

HARPER**AVENUE**

Secret Lives of Mothers & Daughters
Copyright © 2020 by Anita Kushwaha.
All rights reserved.

Published by Harper Avenue, an imprint of HarperCollins Publishers Ltd

First edition

HarperCollins books may be purchased for educational, business or
sales promotional use through our Special Markets Department.

HarperCollins Publishers Ltd
Bay Adelaide Centre, East Tower
22 Adelaide Street West, 41st Floor
Toronto, Ontario, Canada
M5H 4E3

www.harpercollins.ca

Library and Archives Canada Cataloguing in Publication
information is available upon request.

ISBN 978-1-4434-5633-3

Printed and bound in the United States of America
LSC/H 9 8 7 6 5 4 3 2 1

To my dear Daniel,
you are the answer to a prayer.

I can live alone, if self-respect, and circumstances require me so to do. I need not sell my soul to buy bliss. I have an inward treasure born with me, which can keep me alive if all extraneous delights should be withheld, or offered only at a price I cannot afford to give.

—Charlotte Brontë, *Jane Eyre*

Prologue

S he checked her wristwatch again.

Stop, she ordered.

The disobedient second hand continued to tick, chipping away at the time she needed to make things ready. Ideal.

Why wasn't the second hand listening? Was it chipping faster? Seconds.

Only seconds, and they would arrive.

Nandini Shukla stood by the doorway with her fists perched on her slender hips and inspected the softly lit nursery with microscopic intensity. The walls were painted pale yellow, the colour of butter, a shade she and her husband, Prem, had decided would work whether the proverbial stork brought a girl or a boy. Adjacent to the door, to her left, against the wall, was the crib, made of sturdy oak and stained in a natural finish. Tucked in one corner and peering through the wooden bars was a caramel teddy bear with eyes like black marbles, dressed in green overalls, a replica of the toy Nandini had snuggled with when she was little.

The clerk at Toys "R" Us who sold them the crib had reassured them that it could be converted into a toddler bed in about fifteen minutes with nothing more than a screwdriver, a wrench and a little effort—twenty minutes for those who were less handy, he said, giving Nandini a presumptive grin. Apparently, he went on, many new parents were opting for convertible cribs since they grew with the child, particularly during the early years when they "sprouted like weeds." Although most parents tended to shop "while the bun was still in the oven, so to speak," he added, glancing at her flat stomach. How old was their little one? Eight months, she had told him, crossing her arms over her midsection to shield herself from the puzzlement she knew wasn't far off. Where had the little one been sleeping until now? he had asked with a chuckle. A drawer? She had forced a shy smile, felt her cheeks redden and then asked what colours the crib came in other than white.

Where had the baby been sleeping? Who could say? Maybe inside a drawer like the clerk had joked. Or on a dirty mattress tucked in the corner of an even dirtier room. Or nestled safely between its birth parents in bed while dipping into a lake of dreams.

It bothered Nandini that she didn't know, in the same way it bothered her that the nursery remained unfinished. True, the room was far from orphanage austere. They had the essentials: crib, glider, changing table. Even a tall walnut bookcase filled with toys and books they had been collecting for the past couple of years, since the adoption marathon first began: Prem's old Thomas the Train figurines, an illustrated *Ramayana* for children, her yellow-haired Cabbage Patch Kid. These heirlooms at least warmed the space with homey rays.

Still, the naked nursery walls reminded her something was missing. They had made plans for an elephant mural overlooking the crib. Sky blue, with its trunk upturned. A good-luck charm. Could its absence be what was niggling at her? Adoption limbo being what it was, Nandini had assumed they had enough time to get the mural painted. Over the past two years, it always seemed as though they had too much time, which was why she had spaced out their tasks, worried they might reach the end of their to-do list before the baby arrived, turning the nursery into a mausoleum of their unrealized dreams.

Then three short days ago, life ceased being a waiting room.

She got the call while she was at her desk composing yet another briefing note, an ordinary day.

"Are you sitting down?" asked their caseworker, Susan.

A girl.

An infant just eight months old. An adoption that left the door open a crack. Susan wouldn't elaborate any further over the phone. The rest of the details they would find out in person.

Nandini sucked in her cheeks and surveyed the nursery again, slowly periscoping between the corners of the room. Soft footsteps approached her from behind. She felt Prem's arms belt around her waist and his chin balance on her shoulder.

"Everything looks great," he said. She could tell from the encouraging tone of his voice he was trying to convince her.

It wasn't working. "The walls look so empty." She started gnawing on her thumbnail.

"We'll have time to decorate later."

Nandini force down a bump of a swallow. "Nothing feels ready." Her, least of all.

He cinched his arms around her waist another notch. "Nan, I know you're nervous. So am I. But we've waited so long for this. We're as ready as any parents."

She quit gnawing, left her rosy thumb in peace. "Parents," she echoed, a shiver of excitement tingling up her spine. She wriggled around and looked deeply into his dark eyes, which reflected the strange mix of joy and worry weltering inside her. "What if we aren't, Prem?"

He covered her with the warmth of a gentle smile. "We are, in the only way that matters."

She searched his face for signs of doubt but found not a wrinkle. She envied him. "In my mind, she's still a perfect dream and I haven't ruined anything yet."

He tipped his head to the right. "Is that what you're worried about?"

Nandini nodded, dropping her gaze. "Not being good at it," she muttered. "At being a mother."

He planted a soft kiss on the middle of her forehead, lingering. "Fear can't stop us from being good parents, Nan. We'll figure it out together. We want her. And we love her already. What else matters?"

Nandini took a deep, slow breath, knowing Prem was right. They were about to be granted everything they had ever wanted. How could she still be wrangling with these doubts?

She lifted her chin. "Do you think we've missed her first words?"

"Probably. But not her first steps."

"Or her first haircut."

"Or her first birthday. I hope she likes chocolate."

They shared a quiet, jubilant laugh.

Then the doorbell rang. Nandini's eyes widened. For a moment, she stopped breathing.

"She's here," Prem said, breathless. Their daughter. She was waiting, on the other side of the front door, for them to welcome her home.

Their lips mirrored the same broad smile. They clasped hands and hurried downstairs. Standing on the porch, covered in cool evening light, was Susan, dressed in a black trench coat and tan trousers. The petite woman was leaning over to one side, weighed down by the bulky baby carrier, her right hand gripped tight around its handle. Nestled inside was the infant, who wore a scarlet peacoat, violet leggings and white shoes. The baby was sucking on a pacifier, appearing content, as she took them in with a pair of arresting grey eyes.

"Today I play the stork," Susan said, entering the foyer. She set down the carrier, then slipped off her coat and her loafers.

Nandini led her into the living room while Prem hung the caseworker's coat in the closet. Susan placed the carrier on the coffee table and took a seat on the couch. Nandini perched beside her and, with great attention, quietly noted the baby's dark hair, knuckle-less fists, pudgy upturned nose. And her eyes. Those gem-like grey eyes. She had never seen anything like them.

The wonder of the moment was interrupted by the itch Nand-ini had felt earlier in the nursery. The pique of something miss-ing. Did their baby have her birth mother's eyes? In what other ways would their daughter take after the stranger? A hollowness bloomed below her navel. She remembered feeling the same void when, years earlier, a doctor had told her she would never carry children. She saw a windless cavern. An empty house. It occurred to Nandini that nothing of significance was missing from the nurs-ery. It was she who was lacking. She who would never be able to take credit for their baby's singular eyes, and so much more. She who wasn't blood.

Susan unsnapped the safety buckles and lifted the infant out of the carrier. "Here you go."

Nandini reached out. Her hands felt weightless as she held their baby—*theirs*—for the first time. How could she be so light? Were her bones made of twigs? Nandini realized she was holding in a breath. Holding out for cries of rejection. None, however, disturbed the still air.

Nandini cradled the baby in the crook of her arm. She didn't whimper or fuss, but rather, held Nandini in her cool, passive gaze and continued suckling. Soothing warmth radiated through the infant's wool coat. My own little hot-water bottle, she thought. My own little sunbeam.

"Her given name is Asha," Susan told them.

"Asha," Prem repeated as he knelt beside Nandini and took hold of the baby's chubby hand. "I like it."

"Asha Shukla," Nandini added. "It just sounds right, doesn't it?"

Susan smiled. "You look right together."

A few blissful moments passed in beaming and swaying and misty-eyed gazing.

"As I mentioned before, the birth family have left the door open a crack, meaning should you ever want to contact them, now or in the future, they've given us permission to share their information with you."

"Do they have any requests of us?" Nandini asked, reluctant. She knew all about open adoption rhetoric and its potential benefits. Nevertheless it frightened her. The power of blood. The loyalty it often inspired. Nandini felt the hollowness again. She couldn't compete with blood.

"No," Susan replied. "This isn't an open adoption. If you don't want to reach out to them, that's your choice. But you might feel differently someday, or Asha might want to learn more about her family history when she's older. The good thing about this arrangement is it gives you the choice, when the time is right."

If, Nandini thought. Not when.

"Like I said, though, it's one way," Susan continued. "They don't know anything about you. You don't have to worry about a stranger showing up at your door."

Nandini's shoulders slackened. What a relief. "What can you tell us about them?"

"It's a bit of a sad story, really." Susan adjusted her glasses. "The birth mother passed away and the birth father couldn't manage raising Asha alone."

"How did she die?" Prem asked.

"I don't know the details, but she was very ill."

Nandini snuggled Asha a little closer. "What kind of illness?"

"I'm not sure. Although she did leave something behind for Asha." Susan reached into her purse and pulled out a slender white envelope. "If you decide to tell Asha about her adoption someday, this letter might provide some answers." She set the envelope on the table and rose to her feet. "Now it's time for me to leave the three of you to get acquainted. I'll stop by next week to see how you're doing. If you need anything, you know how to reach me." Susan grinned at Asha one last time before politely showing herself out.

As Nandini listened to the front door shut, she peered at the envelope and her daughter's name written across it in graceful cursive—the name given to her by another woman. An unknown woman. An ill woman. A woman who had lost her sunbeam to an early death, the very sunbeam nestled warmly in Nandini's arms. This was supposed to be the happiest day of her life, but as Asha shifted, all Nandini felt was guilty for benefiting from a tragedy so profound it had destroyed her daughter's family of origin. In that moment, Nandini's fortune didn't feel like a blessing bestowed after a time of trial. Instead, she felt as undeserving as someone who had inherited a windfall from a distant, unknown relation.

A current purred along her arm, gathering in her fingertips like static. She surged with an impulse to tear up the letter. Divorce her newly formed family's unblemished present from Asha's birth mother's untimely end. Erase the proof Asha ever had another mother.

Nandini was mid-reach when Asha's pacifier popped out of her mouth.

The soother rolled off Nandini's lap and bounced on the hardwood floor, stopping against a leg of the coffee table. Asha's tiny lips smacked, expectant, like a chick anticipating an insect, but when all they found was each other, her disappointment quickly dissolved into whimpers, and whimpers into sobs.

Nandini had been waiting to hear Asha's little baby voice, and there it was, only there was nothing minute about it. Her cries funnelled upward and rained over them. Something about the urgent sound kindled urgency inside Nandini. She sprang for the plastic nub, handed it to Prem for sterilizing and asked him to hurry.

"See?" He beamed. "I told you we were ready." Then he knelt and kissed Asha's forehead before dashing to the kitchen. Asha's cries mushroomed as she watched her comfort being spirited away by a strange man.

Nandini held her daughter over her heart and rubbed her back, whispering words of reassurance. Yet underneath her docile exterior, something charged through her. Something she doubted she possessed a few moments ago.

"Shh," she cooed.

Whatever it was, she felt the force driving along her veins. Swelling inside the hollowness below her navel. Nandini hadn't known she could feel this awakened. On fire. Amber flames danced against the walls of the windless cavern now. The wails of life stirred the heart of the empty house inside her.

Whatever it was, it made Nandini want to lean in toward her daughter's cries, not run away from them.

Asha settled down. Nandini held her closer and caressed her kitten-soft hair.

Whatever it was, it was more than eye colour, more than blood. And she had it. With her dark eyes, Nandini stared down the letter. Perhaps Asha's birth mother had possessed the quality too. But Nandini was Asha's mother now. Her only mother.

"I've got you," she spoke into her daughter's little ear. "And I'm never going to leave you."

The next lullaby she hummed was "Happy Birthday."

The letter

Chapter 1

Asha woke late on Sunday. She opened her eyes to ribbons of pale sunshine pouring into her bedroom through the blinds. Her head throbbed with a dull ache like a lethargic heartbeat and she was parched, both symptoms the likely result of too much excitement the night before. She glanced at her nightstand. One of her parents had left her a glass of water before going to sleep themselves after the party. She propped herself up, emptied half the glass and rested heavily against the diamond-tufted headboard of her bed.

The memory of birthday-candle smoke lifted the corners of her mouth. Glee crept from her belly outward, like a sunburst, spreading its warm euphoria, millimetre by millimetre. She suddenly fancied a shoulder shimmy.

At last, she was eighteen.

Her parents had thrown her a surprise party. Everyone was in on it, she found out later, even her best friend, Willow, who was terrible at keeping secrets, and her boyfriend, Rowan, who was even worse.

The original plan was simple: an afternoon of shopping with her mom, followed by a family dinner with her grandparents (plus Will and Rowan, of course) at Mamma Grazzi's—her favourite Italian restaurant in the Market—and then back home for cake and presents. They had gone shopping as planned, but when they got back home, Asha remembered thinking the house was oddly quiet, expecting to hear the awful classic rock her dad usually blasted when he was on his own. Then, as startling as a confetti cannon, people burst out from behind walls and furniture and boomed "Happy Birthday!" She nearly screamed.

They hung out in the backyard under the soft glow of paper lanterns while feasting on her dad's famous barbecued chicken, her mom's extra-creamy potato salad and her favourite bakery's chocolate chai cupcakes for dessert.

As for presents, her parents and grandparents pitched in and surprised her with a MacBook Air. "To help you write all those essays on dead poets next fall," her mom said, smiling. From Will, a toffee-coloured notebook embossed with an owl on the cover, a nod to Will's nickname for her, Athena. *Fill its pages with your heroic endeavours, Goddess of Wisdom,* read the inscription. *Or at least some cringe-worthy poetry.* And from Rowan, a copy of *Alphabet Girl,* his hand-drawn comic, for which, apparently, she was the muse. She hadn't expected such a thoughtful gift after only six months together but took the gesture as thrilling confirmation things between them were starting to get serious.

Thinking back, Asha had never felt more loved. And it was all thanks to her parents, who had gathered together all her people. She had a sudden urge to squeeze them tightly. Flinging off the covers, she hopped out of bed.

She thumped downstairs and made her way to the sun-lit kitchen at the back of the house, where she found her parents seated at the table with their backs to her and their heads together. The warm, charred smell of toast flooded the air.

"Morning, oldies," she chimed, sliding into a chair across from them.

"Oh," her mom said, a bit startled. The look of surprise on her face relaxed into a smile. "Morning, sweetie."

"More like afternoon," teased her dad. "Hungry?"

Asha reached across the table and stole a crust off his plate. "Starved."

"I'll fix you a sandwich." He rose to his feet. "How does tomato and cheese on toasted pumpernickel sound?"

Asha threw her head back. "Quit with the torment and feed me already!"

Her mom smirked, shaking her head. "So dramatic."

"What can I say?" Asha shrugged. "Like mother, like daughter."

Her mom's expression flickered for a second, then restored itself. A blip so brief, Asha thought nothing of it. She reached across the table for her dad's empty glass and refilled it with Tropicana. "What were you talking about when I came in?"

"Nothing," her mom replied.

While she sipped her orange juice, Asha noticed that her mom's voice sounded unnaturally light, and she wouldn't look her in the eye, which was her mom's habit when she was hiding something.

Asha swirled the Tropicana in her glass. "It's okay. You can have your little secrets. I'd rather talk about redecorating my room, anyway."

Her parents' other present to her: a bedroom makeover befitting a young woman who was about to start university in a few short months. For weeks, she had been stopping by Chapters after school to flip through copies of *Wallpaper, House & Home* and *Elle Decor*. The other day, she came across the most perfect raven damask wallpaper in black and grey. All she needed to do now was convince her parents she wasn't depressed or going through a Goth phase.

Her dad placed a sandwich in front of her and retook his seat. "Actually, kid, there's something else we need to talk about first."

Asha was about to take a bite, but the serious tone of her dad's voice made her pause. She lowered the sandwich onto her plate and examined her parents' expressions. They both looked tense. No: afraid.

Her thoughts shot to her grandparents. "Oh God. Please tell me no one died."

"Everyone's fine," her mom reassured her. Pursing her lips, she glanced at the red day-planner beside her plate. "We have something else to give you." She opened the planner and withdrew a white envelope. Craning her neck, Asha saw her name written across the front in black ink, although she didn't recognize the handwriting.

"What's that?" she asked. *Another present maybe? Birthday money?*

"It's a letter." Her mom hesitated, then slowly pushed the envelope across the table. "For you."

Asha picked up the envelope and gave the handwriting a closer look. "Who's it from?"

Her parents stared at each other for a few long seconds, as if each were waiting for the other to speak.

"That's what we need to talk about," her dad said.

Asha couldn't understand why her parents were acting so cagey. It wasn't like them to be secretive. "What's going on?" She felt apprehensive, the lightheartedness she had wakened with turning edgy.

"Just give us a chance to explain."

Asha leaned back and crossed her arms. The backrest of the chair felt hard against her upright spine. Her hunger was gone.

"After we got married," her dad began, "your mom and I wanted to start a family almost right away. We tried for a long time. But we weren't able to conceive on our own."

"We even went to a fertility specialist," her mom continued. "Nothing worked. We still wanted to have a family, though. So we had to consider other options."

Other options? Asha thought.

"Like adoption."

Asha blinked a couple of times. "Wait. What are you saying?" Her parents didn't respond. "Is this some kind of birthday prank? Because if it is, cut it out. This isn't funny."

Her mom wouldn't look her in the eye. Her dad's face was cheerless. If they had been joking around, he, at least, would have cracked by now.

"You aren't kidding, are you?" She waited three eon-like seconds. "You're telling me I'm adopted."

Asha lowered her forehead an inch. Her heart wasn't racing. She wasn't short of breath. All she felt was stunned.

"I can't believe this is happening."

That morning, she had woken up so happy, so grateful for her parents. The same people who just explained how hard they had tried to have a biological child, only to fail and settle for adoption. Did they expect her to feel wanted? Knowing she was second-best?

"So, after everything you went through, you ended up with me. Is that right?"

Her mom picked up her gaze and looked across the table with glossy panic. "No, Asha. Our hardships led us to you. It was fate."

"Well, to me, it sounds like you ran out of options."

The once-pleasing aroma of toast now smelled repugnant. Asha held up the letter.

"Who wrote this?"

Her mom flinched like she had been pricked between the eyebrows. "Your birth mother."

"You haven't opened it."

Her mom averted her eyes back to the table. "She wrote it for you."

Asha clenched her fist around the letter, strangling the voice of the woman who had written it, a voice Asha wasn't interested in hearing. They sat in heavy silence. The telephone rang but no one answered it; no one even dared to look in the direction of the intrusive bell.

"Tell me about them," she said at last.

Her dad cleared his throat. "We don't know much. Only that your birth mother passed away when you were about six months old, and that your birth father placed you for adoption shortly after."

"She's dead?" Asha's mouth dropped open. Her chest felt oddly buoyant, as if her lungs were filled with a substance lighter than air. Was she sad? No, she couldn't miss a woman she had never known, whose existence she learned about seconds ago. What was the strange feeling, then? Something like the hollowness of disappointment, the nothingness left behind by unmet expectations. There was an open-endedness to it, as if someone had given her a biography with critical pages torn out. Pages that told her story.

Asha glared at her mom with hard grey eyes. "I've always wondered why we don't have any pregnancy photos of you."

"I told you that I didn't like having my picture taken."

And gullibly, Asha realized now, she had believed her. "What about the pictures of me as a newborn? You said the files were lost before you had the chance to get any printed."

"The truth is, we were never given any photos. Which is why our family albums start when you're eight months old. That's how old you were when you came to us. We've always told you that you're younger in the photos than you actually were."

More lies, Asha thought, her throat tightening. "How did she die?"

"All we know is that she was ill and passed away."

Asha kept still while, underneath her tough exterior, something deep inside was sinking. "And I was too much for him."

"Asha—"

"How could you keep this from me?" she snapped.

Her mom paused, a look of defeat tugging at her features, her shoulders. "A family's a fragile thing, Asha. It takes years to build and even longer to find harmony. That's what we have, though, the three of us. I didn't want to jeopardize that. I never wanted you to doubt your place in our family, when we've never doubted, not even for a second, that you were meant for us. Which is why I kept putting it off. I thought I was sheltering you. Your dad has wanted to tell you for years, but I've always convinced him to delay. Another year and you would be old enough to understand. I see now that was a mistake. There was never going to be a perfect time to tell you. This was always going to hurt."

Asha held her elbows. Yes, it hurt. Like an amputation. As if her arms had been lopped off. Arms that had never hesitated to reach for her parents—until now.

"So now what? What am I supposed to do with this?"

"We can contact the adoption agency," her dad suggested, "if you're curious about your birth family. Or maybe they have someone you can talk to."

"I don't need therapy." She pinned him with a pointed stare. "I need to know why."

Her dad's eyes shifted to the envelope still strangled in her hand. Asha guessed his thoughts. Maybe the letter had some of the answers she was looking for. It seemed to vibrate against her palm. As if the voice trapped inside the prison of paper were trying to howl a way out.

Asha shot to her feet and began marching out of the kitchen. When she sped past her parents, her mom reached out to touch her, only to pull back, as if slapped away by her birth mother's ghost, as if suddenly uncertain of her place in Asha's life. As if she and Asha were strangers.

Chapter 2

Asha darted upstairs, slammed her bedroom door and pressed her back against it. Her ears reached into the hallway, expecting the clamour of hurried footsteps, but the only sounds she heard were her own ragged breathing and the stomping of her heart.

Her knees weakened and she slid into a ball on the floor. Still clutching the envelope, she wondered what to do. Part of her wanted to shred the letter into confetti and set it on fire until there was no trace of her birth mother apart from a palmful of wispy ash. Then she wouldn't have to think about who she was and where she came from. She could carry on, a happy and carefree eighteen-year-old with adoring parents and a life she loved. A life which, as it turned out, was a complete and utter lie.

Asha wet her dry lips. She tore into the envelope and unfolded the piece of unlined paper. Row after row of the same black, slanted script as was written on the envelope filled the page. She set her eyes on the first word and read.

My dearest Asha,

As I write you this letter, I'm overcome with sadness at the thought of missing so much of your life. All the milestones yet to come. All the things I dreamed we would do together someday. At least I'm able to leave you this letter and tell you how truly sorry I am, my little bean. If anything in this life has brought me joy, it's you.

I tried. But sometimes, no matter your efforts, life still doesn't work out in the end. I hate to leave you behind. Although I trust that Sumesh will take good care of you in my absence. I know he loves you as much as I do. He'll always put you first, come what may.

I named you Asha for a reason. In Hindi, your name means hope or a wish. My hope for you—my wish on the glittering snow falling outside my window as I write this—is that you live your own life, not someone else's. That's all, Asha. Promise me.

I know it sounds simple, but even so, I found this a hard lesson to live by. Do better than I did. Stay true to yourself. Let your heart be your guide, not fear. Above all, I want you to know there's nothing you could ever do that would make me ashamed of you. You're my daughter.

Even though I'm not there with you physically, trust that I'm never far. Look up to the sky and you'll find me, always.

From your mother, with so much love.

Tears burned Asha's eyes. She was surprised the letter had moved her so much. She felt her birth mother's sadness, helplessness and regret like it was her own. Little bean, she thought. That was her nickname for me. Her gaze shimmered out of focus. She tilted her head back, blinked and blinked. *It's awful she died. And I'm sorry she got sick. But she's a stranger. I don't want to fall apart over a stranger.*

Soon, the briny waterline receded. Until then, Asha had mistakenly thought deathbed notes provided closure, even solace. A farewell that could be revisited like a bittersweet memory. What a fool.

Still, the letter had provided some answers. Clearly, her birth mother hadn't known about the adoption. She passed away believing Asha would be taken care of by a man named Sumesh—her birth father, presumably. Only he hadn't done that.

Why? she wondered, anguished. Could she really have been such a difficult baby? That unlovable?

Despite the tight squeeze of her eyelids, salty drops escaped and slipped down her cheeks, moistening the letter. The ink feathered like ice crystals on a frozen windowpane. She loosened her grip and the letter drifted to the floor. In her mind, she imagined a swift river with no end. On it, she placed the letter and the current swept it away, somewhere downriver like her birth mother's ashes.

Chapter 3

"We have to give her time," Prem said from the blue reading-nook chaise in the corner of their bedroom as he watched Nandini pace a trench in the floor.

It was already nightfall. How long were they supposed to wait? Nandini scratched the damp armpit of her pyjamas. The morning's debacle played on repeat in her mind. Her stomach cramped in a long, slow roll. What a mess. How were they going to make this better? Make Asha see? She combed one hand through her straight, dark hair, clipping it back at the crown of her head. "Things didn't go the way I expected them to."

"What did you expect?"

"When I saw that Asha was angry, part of me hoped we would . . ." Shame stopped Nandini from saying any more.

"Unite against her birth parents?"

Oh, the sound of it. "I thought she would at least see our side of things." But Asha had shown no sympathy for their efforts at protecting her from loss and confusion. Instead, all they got was the cold silence of rejection, like Nandini had always feared. Her blood felt as thin as the air in her lungs.

"I'm not sure we're entitled to understanding yet."

"Because of me."

"It's too late for this, Nandini," Prem told her, firm. "I'm not joining your pity party."

She nearly tripped. Not only over *Nandini*. But *pity party*. Her pacing lost energy, gradually easing to a halt. Was that what she was doing? Feeling sorry for herself? While her daughter grappled with the deathbed note of the woman who had changed the very course of her young life? All these years and she still felt so insecure . . .

Nandini shuffled to the end of the bed and let her body slouch under the weight she had been trying to resist since that morning. She closed her plush robe over her collarbones against a mounting shiver.

They sat in silence. Before long the air between them lost its silvery crackle. "I wonder what the letter says," she muttered.

Prem exhaled. "Me too."

What private declarations might alter their innocent daughter, as the morning's revelation certainly had? For years, Nandini had pushed the letter away. Pretended it—along with Asha's birth mother—didn't exist. Much like Nandini's underlying fear of maternal inadequacy. Her fear there would be something fundamental between Asha and her birth mother that would make their bond stronger than the bond Nandini had fostered with her daughter. Although she hadn't said so earlier, Nandini knew she had been sheltering herself by withholding the letter, as much as she had been sheltering Asha.

Nandini shuddered. She burrowed a little deeper into the warmth of her robe. Even after so many years, the threat felt as real as it had on the evening that Susan brought Asha to their home, if not more real because of her delays.

Over the years, whenever she and Prem discussed whether it was time to tell Asha the truth, Nandini would feel the threat rise again, and it was more than she could face. The possibility that, despite all her efforts to be a good mother, once Asha discovered that they weren't blood, Nandini would always come second in her daughter's heart. If only she could read the letter, Nandini reasoned, perhaps some of her fears would be put to rest.

"All I want to do is help her through this," she said. "Make up for how terribly I've handled things."

She heard the rustle of movement behind her. Prem rose from the chaise and approached the foot of the bed. The sides of their hips touched as he sat beside her.

"How terribly *we've* handled things."

He wrapped one arm around her, its mass a welcome weight against her right shoulder. Turning toward him, Nandini sought refuge in the place she had long claimed as her own, the warm crook of her husband's neck, which possessed the power to shrink the world from billions to two.

"I'm sorry," she whispered.

"I'm sorry," he echoed.

Nandini frowned. "Now if only we could convince Asha how sorry we are. What do we do?"

"How about this?" His voice brightened. "If her light's on, we see how she's doing. If it's off, we let the poor kid sleep."

With her head tilted away, Nandini wore a tiny, hidden smile of relief, comforted that, underneath, her husband was as anxious as she was.

Chapter 4

Later that night, while staring at the shapes on the ceiling that floated in the darkness like images from an electron microscope, Asha felt the phantoms surface. She flicked on her side lamp, reached for the owl journal Willow had given her and opened it to the first page, noting its new-leather smell. Gripping her pen, she started writing, hoping that if she placed the phantoms on paper, then maybe they would stop tormenting her and let her sleep.

I'm angry. But not at you. By the sound of it, you wanted to live. You said you tried, but things didn't work out for you in the end. I'm sorry about that.

I don't know Sumesh. But I know enough to be mad at him. I wonder if you're mad too. He put me up for adoption with only your letter as explanation. I'm frustrated that a man I've never met has the power to make me feel unwanted and unlovable. I have so many questions. About you, him, the little family we were before you passed away. My parents say that I can reach out to him if I want to. I can ask him my questions. Like putting myself out there is a simple thing to do, when they've been too afraid to do the same with me for eighteen years. Honestly, I can't imagine voluntarily making myself even more vulnerable than I already feel right now. Of course I want to know why he gave me up, but I'm also afraid of the answer, especially if the reason is me. I was too needy. I was too loud. I was too much for him . . .

I'm mad at my parents most of all. For keeping the truth from me for so long. I was happy. Now I don't know who I am, or even where I come from. My mom said that she's always worried you would come between us. Well, she was right about us drifting apart, but not about the reason for it. This isn't your fault. It's theirs.

I have a list of questions and no one else that I trust enough to ask. No one else who would know, except you. So here goes.

How did you die? Was it something I might have inherited?

How old were you?

Do I have grandparents? Aunties? Uncles? Any biological family at all?

Asha stopped writing. There was another question she wanted to ask, but fear froze her hand. Maybe that was best. Writing things down made them real, like naming them did. Slowly, she continued her entry.

What's your name?

Asha stared at the question. Did she really want to know? Did she really want to make her birth mother real?

Sullen, she closed her journal and turned off her lamp. The gap underneath her bedroom door glowed unexpectedly with light from the hallway. The floorboards creaked as her parents approached her room. Their shadows blotted the strip of light while they lingered. Her body went rigid. She prayed they weren't about to knock on her door. She counted to ten and their shadows finally receded.

Asha relaxed her muscles and took a deep breath, relieved.

The blackness of the ceiling poured into her eyes. She thought of her birth mother's closing line in the letter: *Look up to the sky and you'll find me, always.*

Beyond the roof of their house, Asha imagined a deep indigo

sky, winks of silver starlight, a bright half moon. This was where she sent her thoughts.

Did you ever feel out of place in your own life? she asked her birth mother, who had promised in her letter to be standing watchful guard.

Who are you?

What was your story?

A leaf stuck in the reeds

Chapter 5

Mala Sharma stepped off the crowded city bus. A surge of students spilled past her onto the campus sidewalk, trickling off in various directions, like tributaries breaking from a larger channel. Unlike theirs, her footsteps were tentative, as though she couldn't trust that she was in the right place. After eight months away, the grounds felt as foreign as they had when she started her Ph.D. four years ago.

Nervous energy prickled the air, dispersed by the sharp autumn wind. With her hands warming inside the pockets of her windbreaker, she scanned the brown buildings, crammed parking lots and bustling pedestrian paths. In the distance, she noticed that the new building made mostly of glass had been completed. And beyond it, she saw the river, the dark ribbon squeezed between verdant banks, her favourite spot.

On the surface, her surroundings appeared unchanged for the most part. Then why did she feel so strange? Almost as soon as she finished dotting the question mark in her mind, she knew: in the past two semesters, since her father's sudden death, nothing drastic about the place had changed. It was her.

Mala stood off to one side and paused. She watched the others march with studious purpose, carried by the currents of scholarly life, a rhythm she had fallen out of sync with, like a leaf stuck in the reeds.

Without thinking, she rubbed the glossy cover of her bus pass. She glanced over her shoulder and saw the Number 4 parked by the curb, its hazard lights beckoning her to board and go back home. Maybe her adviser was right. Maybe she should have taken more time off.

As she had done so often throughout graduate school, in this matter too Mala had given herself a deadline to work toward. Without deadlines, comprehensive exams were never written, proposals went undefended and dissertations dragged on like bad marriages. After taking last winter and summer off, fall seemed like an ideal time to come back, when the campus buzzed with fresh energy. For weeks, she had been psyching herself up. School was where she belonged, among the bookish and the curious. And of course, most important, her father would have wanted her to complete her studies. He had always been so proud of her following in his footsteps. She couldn't bear the thought of letting him down again.

While she loitered on the sidewalk, however, Mala didn't feel like she belonged anymore. She didn't feel like herself at all, but then she hadn't for some time. Could those around her tell she was different from them now? Could they see the black armband she imagined around her bicep like a tourniquet, or was it all in her head?

Mala lowered her eyes to the grey cement, thinking it was an appropriate reflection of her gloom, and pictured the city bus lights flashing behind her, tempting her to escape. If she climbed aboard, she could go back to bed, tell Monday she was done with it and try again another day. All she had to do was turn back.

Just then, a voice spoke plainly inside her head, low and deep, with traces of an accent, the remnants of a distant homeland. *Running isn't the answer, rani beti. You must face your fears in this life.*

Mala's eyes welled with tears. She blinked to ease their sting. A stray drop slipped down her cheek. Self-conscious, she brushed it away.

Even in death, her father had a presence, an ability to guide. She pulled her watery gaze from the pavement. Off in the distance, the river hooked her eye, the black ribbon pulling her in like the tide.

She made her way over with blinders on, barely aware of the buildings, parking lots and people she passed along the way. At the end of University Drive, she stopped, checked for cars, then crossed the street that separated the campus from the river's edge.

Maples dotted the bank, their canopies brilliant with senescing leaves; splashes of ginger and ruby, saffron and eggplant. She wiggled her toes against the soft grass underfoot and basked in a long, reflective silence, letting the current draw her into its ripples and folds. A faint sound like the trickle of rain down a waterspout tinkled in her ear.

At this time of year, river levels began to recede. Jagged rocks jutted here and there, interrupting the otherwise fluid movement of the water. Yet, undeterred by these obstacles, the river simply eddied around them and went about its course.

Mesmerized by the flow, Mala considered how throughout the seasons the water, which for the moment composed the river, travelled in an endless cycle, transforming from liquid to solid to vapour. That chameleon-like property of water—its ability to adapt and change and weather phases—amazed her. She wanted to be like that, and like the river, able to manoeuvre around the jagged rocks that obstructed her path. She wanted to free herself from the reeds and rejoin the current.

MALA UNLOCKED THE Ph.D. office door and let herself in. Her desk was located among the block to the left. As she approached, she braced herself for small talk. But no one else was around. In fact, her neighbour Celeste's desk looked like it hadn't been used in as long as Mala's. She let go of the breath caged inside her tense lungs. At least for the moment, she wouldn't have to explain where she had been to those who hadn't heard about her father, or lie if someone asked how she was doing. For now, she was safe from condolences.

Setting her bag on the floor, she peered at a map of Nunavut hanging on the wall, which she had picked up at a northern studies conference in Iqaluit last fall. Circled in orange highlighter was her case study area, a small hamlet located at the southern tip of Baffin Island. Hit by a sudden rush of longing, Mala pictured the earthy tones of the rolling tundra like beached walrus, the cobalt-blue water of the inlet, the clear open sky. She had spent two summers in the coastal community conducting environmental research, yet somehow her memories of that time seemed to belong to some Other Mala. She blinked at the map. She wished she was there now, out on the land with the cleansing wind, free. How she envied that Other Mala.

She surveyed her desk, which was as she remembered it—cluttered with photocopied journal articles, books and hastily written Post-it notes.

Lab meeting Tues 1:30
Return library books by Friday
Eat!

Another note, stuck to the middle of the desk, written by someone else, caught her attention:

Mala,
I borrowed a pen.
Promise to give this one back.
Eventually . . .

A scant grin lifted one corner of her mouth. She traced his hand-writing, lingering on the way he had written her name. She felt a strong *whoosh* right below her diaphragm, then panicked a little. She had thought all that was behind her.

Although Mala tried in vain to stop it, she drifted into a memory from before the winter break last year, the last time she had seen him. It was a snowy afternoon. They meandered from the departmental holiday party to the grad student pub to toast the end of term. They talked about many things, but at one point he confessed he wasn't looking forward to the holidays. It was hard to keep up appearances when he and his partner weren't getting along. In fact, they'd had a terrible fight earlier that week and they weren't speaking. Another terrible fight, Mala thought. Ever since, he had been questioning whether they should stay together. But they had been a couple since undergrad. They lived together. Their families expected them to get married someday. It was a lot to walk away from. He wasn't sure what to do. But his sense was that things were going to come to a head over the holidays.

Mala recalled the strength of her racing heart, which had been secretly beating his name for some time. She felt for him. His situation seemed common enough. Sometimes things ended and it was no one's fault. Sometimes they had to end to make way for life's next surprise. Even so, she kept those thoughts to herself. It wasn't her place to interfere in matters of fate.

For the first part of the holidays, she couldn't escape the feeling that she was on the cusp of something life-changing. While she couldn't define it yet, she dared to hope that a new beginning awaited her with the arrival of the new year.

Then her father passed away and her life did start over, only not in the way she had dreamed.

An unexpected sound ended her dismal recollections. She heard the familiar shuffle of sneakers brushing against tiles—lazy heels—followed by a cold feeling of doom. As it drew closer, her stomach wrung itself out. She regretted pushing him away after her father had passed, but she'd had her reasons. Now, it seemed, she couldn't hide from him any longer.

"Mala," he said with a touch of awe.

A wave of heat rolled over her as his voice kissed the inside of her ear. Slowly, she turned around.

"Hi, Ash." She smiled shyly.

He wore a red-and-black lumberjack shirt and brown corduroys. His hands were tucked inside his pockets, giving him an easy-going manner. His mop of wavy auburn hair was as shaggy as she remembered. The chunky black-framed glasses were new. Mala reached through the slight shine reflecting off his lenses for the singular gaze she had missed. But there was no warmth in his eyes, only steel.

"It's been a while," he said, unsmiling.

"I know." She swallowed, squeezing a quiver in her stomach. "I'm sorry for being hard to reach." Hours after her father had passed, he was the first person she told, in a rambling, tearful email. He wrote back right away, full of sympathy and comfort, as ever, offering to take care of anything school-related—covering her TA duties, marking, returning library books—whatever she needed. And, he added, he wanted to be there for her outside of school too. That was how he phrased it, yet Mala couldn't help but wonder if he was alluding to something more. Maybe he and his girlfriend had ended things over the holidays, she thought in passing. Then sickening guilt befell her for thinking even fleetingly about herself at a time when her sole focus should have been on comforting her mother and mourning her father. So she took a long step back, the appropriate thing to do under the circumstances.

Of course, that was only part of the reason. The whole truth was although they knew each other well, she couldn't bear the thought of him seeing her that way, so undone, deboned by grief. In an act of self-protection, she replied to him with cool politeness, treating him like an acquaintance rather than one of her closest friends, telling him she was fine, she was handling things. He wrote to her a few times after that, but she hadn't replied. She planned on writing him back once she started feeling like herself again, only that day had never come. Even now, she wondered if the person standing in front of him was a Mala he would recognize.

"When I didn't hear back from you, I figured you wanted to be left alone. Sorry it took a while for me to get the message."

Mala could tell by his flat tone and the stiff line of his mouth how much she had hurt him with her distance. "I appreciated your emails." She offered him a sincere smile. "I just needed space. It was wrong of me not to write you back, though. I meant to, but I kept putting it off because I didn't know what to say to anyone at that point. Grief really is like a fog. Then one day it starts lifting and you ask yourself where you've been and for how long. Anyway, no excuses. I'm sorry."

He jingled the change in his pocket and glanced away as if both resisting and considering her apology.

"So," she said, nudging them along, "where is everybody? I was hoping to run into some familiar faces." Three other students made up their cohort, a little support system they had relied upon to get through the stresses of coursework, comps and proposal defences. Much like with him, Mala had gradually fallen out of touch with them too.

"Celeste is in Kenya on fieldwork," he replied, monotone. "She won't be back until the spring, I think. Oscar got lured away by a government job. Linh's lab moved to the new building on the other side of campus, so she's been using the fancy new offices over there."

Her mouth twisted into a grimace. "Oscar's working for the government now?"

He looked at her again, his expression a shade lighter. "I had coffee with him the other day. He's doing well."

She blinked at the space between them. "I feel so out of touch."

"Some people graduated while you were away too. The academic conveyor belt stops for no one." He shifted his weight, readjusting his stance. He hesitated before asking, "How does it feel to be back?"

She took a moment to consider. "Strange. Everything's different."

He nodded, grim. "I guess it is."

A few uncomfortable moments passed. Mala wasn't sure where to set her eyes, or what to do with her hands.

"But it might feel less strange if I fill you in."

She raised her head and their eyes met. He watched her with a slight frown. Yet Mala thought she detected an old affinity peeking through the coarseness.

"We could grab a coffee later, if you want, and I can tell you all the departmental gossip. After that, maybe you can let me know what's been going on with you all these months."

Her heart contracted. Talk, like they used to. Well no, not exactly, and not right away. At least it was a start. At least he was giving her a chance to make up for ignoring him. "I'd like that." She smiled, grateful. "Thanks."

He regarded her for a long moment. "It's okay, Mala," he told her, like a pardon. Then he gave her his crooked grin, the same crooked grin she had pictured for months. "I'm glad you're back."

Mala couldn't speak. She was too overcome with relief. Instead, she held her grateful smile until he returned to his desk. Once she was alone again, she let her cheeks fall and pressed a hand against her sparring stomach. At least the hardest part—the part she had been reluctant to acknowledge—was over.

Chapter 6

For the rest of the morning, Ash Groves couldn't focus. Before Mala arrived, he had been slogging his way through a dull article about carbon sequestration in wetlands. Now his eyes drifted over the same sentence without absorbing any of its meaning, like water spilling over ice. He blew out a sigh and thrust the paper away.

Finally, after months of absence—of silence—Mala was back. Or was she? She looked so different. Her skin, sunless. Her cheeks, hollow, scooped out by grief. Most startling of all, though, was how she had changed in the eyes. Her eyes—the ones that each used to hold a tiny full moon—had lost their light.

He winced to think of her loss. He had glimpsed her pain once, gotten a rough idea of it, like reading an abstract. The email was fragmented, unfiltered. As soon as he finished it, he remembered wanting to run to her side, only to realize he didn't know where she lived, which was odd, given how close they were. It struck him then that they were school friends, their relationship confined to campus. But the loss Mala had suffered wouldn't be contained. It would bleed over the lines, over everything.

In that moment, he knew something concretely. He wanted to be there for her while she weathered that season of pain, and afterward, when the rains moved on. It was the final confirmation he needed about the depth of his feelings for her, which he was ready to confront at last. The next thing he planned on doing was ending things with Laine.

Then something he hadn't anticipated happened. Mala pushed him away. She rejected, albeit politely, his offer of support, which at the time felt like a rejection of himself personally. Eventually she stopped replying to his emails altogether.

After that, he stopped trusting his emotions. He gave over control to his cold, analytical brain. The right thing to do, he convinced himself, was to commit to Laine and figure out their issues. They had a long history together. No relationship was perfect. But at least they had each other. So they reconciled for the hundredth time.

He stopped writing Mala emails. He told himself he was respecting her wishes, giving her space. But really, he was hurt. The cave she had left in his life hurt. And he had to get over it. He had to accept she didn't care about him that way. And in time he did.

Now, remembering the traits of her doppelganger—ashen, hollow, rayless—he wondered if he had let himself off the hook too easily. Let his ego get the better of him. A true friend wouldn't have given up on her. A true friend would have found a way to be there for her, regardless of pride.

And if he had managed to push his conceit aside and reached out to her from time to time, maybe then Mala wouldn't be as altered as she was now . . .

Months had passed by in a mess of obligations—work, home and more work. Yet now time condensed, reducing the long, lonely months they had spent apart into days. Until seeing her again, he hadn't fully realized how long, or how lonely, those months had been for him without his friend. He could only imagine what they must have been like for her, without her father, whom he knew she loved so deeply.

He swivelled his chair, peered in her direction and quietly promised to make it up to her. This time, he would be the friend she deserved.

Chapter 7

After another poor sleep, Veena Sharma let light into her eyes. For thirty-six years, she had slept on the right side of the bed. Grown accustomed to this pattern. Even found solace in it lately. This morning, however, she woke as sprawled as a starfish in the middle of the mattress. Sunken by a leaden feeling, she pictured her husband, Pavan, frowning down on her, clothed in white shrouds and wreathed in pale light. She heard his deep voice, whispering in her ear like a waft through the feathery leaves of a tamarind tree: "You've forgotten me already, champakali."

A sudden chill ran through her like a trickle of melting ice along her spine. Named after the Hindu god of wind, eight months ago her husband's spirit had been carried away by a ruthless polar gust. Now he existed in that mystical place of the atman and rebirth. Now he was too far.

Some mornings, she expected to turn over and find him snoring beside her. Thought she heard his heavy-heeled footsteps thudding across the creaky floorboards in the hallway. Woke with her head fuddled by dreams in which he spoke and moved and touched. Phantoms. After a few bleary-eyed winks, the spells of sleep would clear, only to be replaced by grief's heavy murk. Blanketed as a shoreline, she would remember with a stricken sigh. *He's gone.*

Rolling onto her side, she gazed upon his memorial portrait, which hung on the wall in a gilded frame, wreathed in garlands of silken marigolds. Below the black-and-white photograph was a small mahogany table where she kept certain items for daily pujas—steel diyas like small birdbaths, sandalwood incense, a brass urn that she filled daily with fresh water.

The portrait had been taken more than thirty years ago, with their first camera, a Canon 35mm. He wore a light-coloured collared shirt. He favoured his left side. He peered into the distance without a smile. Back then, his hair grew full and dark. A thin mustache traced his upper lip. No lines creased his deep complexion.

Was it my fault? she wondered. Am I to blame for his death? In Canada, she had let go of so many customs—smearing vermillion on the part in her hair, wearing glass bangles on her wrists and silver rings on the second toe of each foot—these marks of a married woman, which each in its own way was meant to bring luck, like a charm. Certain customs she had never bothered with at all, such as the Savitri Brata, a fasting day observed by married Hindu women to bless their husbands with long life. When in Rome, she had reasoned without lamentation. Or in my case, the Great White North.

Now she wondered if this mute loneliness was her penance. Perhaps if she had been an ideal wife, like Savitri, then Yama would not have taken Pavan away. Could a month's worth of sacrifice have added years to his life? Or was it all superstition and myth?

Veena shifted onto her back. Beams of dusty light filtered into the bedroom through the spaces between the blinds, casting pale yellow ripples on the white duvet. Outside her window, perched on a telephone line, a mourning dove cooed its melancholy song. She wondered for whom it sang.

Before he had passed, Veena would wake to the sound of her husband making tea, to the bell-like chime of a spoon tapping against the side of a cup. (How many times had she let those cups of tea go cold?) Now, as she stared expressionless at the ceiling fan, simultaneously looking at everything and nothing, she listened for other sounds, other traces of life to coax her out of bed.

The house was as lifeless as an urn full of ashes. Earlier that morning, her daughter, Mala, had left for school. While Veena was pleased she had resumed her studies, the months they had spent brooding around the house had buffered against the chill of solitude she faced now.

This is nonsense, she thought. Get up. Her weighty limbs seemed to sink deeper into the mattress, as spiritless as a marionette without a master. *Get up*, she repeated. Yet she could not find the interest to follow through with her own demands. *What has happened to me?* Her will, drier than a Rajasthani desert—desiccated, cracked, degrees away from barren. *All this foolish feeling sorry for myself.*

Veena hadn't felt this inertia in many years. She tended to think of herself as a practical woman, and practical women didn't waste their time lying in bed when there were things to be done. Even during her lowest spells, when she was a young wife and life was at times a living hell, she had always managed to function, pretend she was fine, especially in front of Pavan. Once she was alone, however, the pit would be there waiting for her to settle inside its gaping mouth, until the performance of daily life called upon her again. But that shame was between her and God.

When Mala got home that evening, she would get back to her practical ways, back to feeling like herself. For the morning, though, Veena allowed the past to cover her like a blanket of lead and memories.

Pragmatism, after all, was what had led her to marry Pavan in the first place. Although theirs was not a love match, Veena grew to love her husband in due course.

At their first meeting—in the late sixties, when she was twenty-one and he was twenty-nine—she remembered feeling so nervous she spent most of the time staring at the hand-knotted rug that covered the marble floor of her family's sitting room, as demure as the wooden dolls she had played with as a girl, their stiff bodies draped in colourful saris, their vacant eyes lined with black. What was she so afraid of finding? Bald patches? An oversized mole? Hungry eyes?

Veena listened as Pavan explained how a journal article he had published during his doctorate caught the eye of a professor in Canada, who offered to sponsor him for a postdoctoral fellowship. That spring, he would immigrate to Canada, to a faraway city named Ottawa. The immigration laws in Canada were changing; in time he would be able to apply for citizenship. His family didn't like the idea of him being on his own so far away from home. Since he was finished his education and he had secured a good job, it seemed like the right time for him to take the next inevitable step. He hoped to start his new life in an exotic land with a bride.

All of this sounded very logical to Veena. From this brief introduction, she was able to ascertain that she and Pavan shared a few key values: they prized education (she herself had recently completed a teaching degree); they were pragmatic (she too was at the right age to be considering marriage); and, above all, when it came to life-changing decisions like marriage—an act that created a family while simultaneously altering the ones that preceded it—they counted on their parents' loving concern and good judgment to steer them in the right direction, a direction that would benefit not only them but also the family as a whole. Family, after all, was what life was about. It needed to be carefully planned and constructed, like a bungalow built to shelter multiple generations.

When Veena asked for her mother's advice, she told her that everyone coveted the plumpest laddu in the box of mithai—her mother's way of saying that if Veena didn't choose Pavan, someone else surely would. Such a well-educated man. And one who didn't believe in accepting dowries; well, he was a rare find indeed.

The prospect of moving to the other side of the world was captivating and terrifying, like listening to her dadiji tell old tales. *If you pull out one grey hair, ten will grow in its place. Walking over someone's feet will shorten their life . . .*

Veena knew she would miss living at home, four generations laughing and fighting under one roof. On the other hand, she would have the opportunity to travel to a foreign country, fly in an airplane, explore the wider world beyond her family's concrete walls.

They consulted a pandit, who determined an auspicious day for them to wed the following month. A few weeks later, she boarded a plane from Delhi to Amsterdam, then another from Amsterdam to Ottawa.

Together, she and Pavan built a life, a family. And over time, love grew. It grew from strife—the loneliness, the otherness. It grew from heartbreak—the miscarriages, the threat of divorce. It grew from unforeseen blessings—the eventual birth of their Mala. It grew from home—the place they made for themselves, in a land that wasn't accustomed to them at the start but welcomed them eventually.

Then, eight months ago, the life they had built crumbled around them like a mud hut. The attack happened shortly after Christmas. Snow had fallen, wet and heavy, for three days straight, blanketing the ground up to their knees. She begged Pavan to call a snowplow or tempt one of the neighbourhood children with five dollars or at least wait for Mala to get home from brunch, if he insisted on clearing the driveway himself.

"How could anything so beautiful be deadly?" he told her.

Anxious, she watched from the front window, expecting him to hunch over panting after shovelling the first few scoops. Only he didn't. In fact, he seemed spry, tossing the snow with their bright yellow shovel.

Perhaps he was right. She tended to worry. She felt a draft as she stood by the window and shivered, which gave her the idea to make some garam chai to warm them up.

When she returned, she found his body collapsed on the snow-bank. He looked like a doll tossed aside by a careless child. She ran out into the snow wearing nothing but her chappals.

Now, as she lay in bed, Veena shuddered at the memory of shouting his name, the echo of which seemed to carve a tunnel through the cold. By then, he had drifted away on the icy wind. She wriggled her toes under the blanket, recalling the frosty touch of winter that had bitten her almost-naked feet. The only other time she had run outside without shoes was during her first November in Canada, on the day of her first snowfall. At the time, she had been watching television to distract from her nausea when a white flutter caught the periphery of her eye. She remembered the sound of her chappals clacking against the wooden stairs that led from their duplex to the street, the grace of the flakes as they fell like crabapple blossoms loosened by a gust of wind, the shiver of wonder as they melted on her cheeks and eyelashes. *How could anything so beautiful be deadly?* And that same night, how all wonder had faded from the world when her first pregnancy slipped from her womb like an egg from its shell. That was the first time she experienced the pit, with its black, hungry mouth, although it wouldn't be the last, nor the worst. After her loss, the first of too many, the initial wonder of the snow faded. The world outside their apartment turned as stark white as her grief. Veena stayed indoors, waiting for spring and its resuscitating rays to melt the frostbite from her bones. Much the same way she felt now.

As a young bride, she could never have guessed the trials she and Pavan would face, and how those trials would bind them together. She knew better than most how love could grow with the right person. She only hoped Mala would be so blessed.

Before Pavan passed, they had agreed to postpone any conversations about marriage until after Mala completed her studies. But circumstances had changed. Veena worried something might happen to her before she had the chance to secure Mala's future. Now that Pavan was gone, and almost a year of mourning had passed, the matter seemed more urgent than ever. Veena knew she would have to broach the subject of marriage with her daughter soon.

She only hoped Mala would understand her reasons.

Letters to the dead

Chapter 8

It was Thursday night. Asha lay on her bed, propped up on her elbows, with a pen in hand and her biology binder open. Finals were a few weeks away. Her last high school exams, ever. But she couldn't focus on the notes in front of her.

A couple of weeks had passed since she first read the letter. The next day after school, she ran off to Willow's and stayed with her for a few days until her parents finally came and gently abducted her. While she was at Will's, Rowan picked her up after dinner in his dad's vintage rusty-red Mustang and took her to Mooney's Bay, where they sat on the beach and talked, or she simply crawled into his arms, breathing in his fabric-softener scent, while they watched the dragon boats on the water, the volleyball players spiking in the sand.

Since then, Asha mostly kept to her room or worked late at the school library, needing no better excuse for being alone than having to study for finals. The summer vacation she had been looking forward to all year—sleeping in, lazing around the house, spending hours with her nose in a book—now seemed like nine weeks of detention. Thank God for my job at the library, she thought. She had impressed her boss, Agnes, during her co-op term. But the library was only open for so many hours a day. She wondered if Willow's parents would let her stay with them on the weekends. Could a person be adopted twice?

Asha closed her binder with a sigh. It was impossible to concentrate on the impact of climate change on marine life when her head was crammed with other things. She sat up, fetched her journal from the drawer of her nightstand and flipped to a fresh page.

Mom blames your letter for the distance between us. Not to mention the "change in my attitude." Well, she's obviously in denial and you're an easy target. It's the secret. That's what hurts and makes me feel like I don't know them anymore. How can I ever trust them again? What else are they hiding? She keeps hoping I'll drop hints about what you wrote to me, but I haven't given her any. It's only a matter of time before she starts snooping around my room for the letter. Part of me hopes I catch her in the act.

To me, your letter is like a catalyst. Everything's changing. Not only with my parents, but inside me too. I can feel it like a storm. It hurts like the growing pains that used to keep me up at night. I still get them sometimes. I guess I'm not as grown up as I think.

When I think of you, I feel awful. I find myself wondering how you got sick, what it was like to know you were going to die, how hard it was to accept, knowing you had no choice but to leave me behind. Did that break your heart? What were we like together? Does it hurt to hear me call another woman Mom?

I have so many questions for you.

The dead don't write letters, though, do they?

Asha

Asha put her journal away and reopened her binder, ready to give reviewing her notes another try. But emptying herself onto the page had only left her drained. She assumed a position of surrender, flopping on her back with her arms outstretched to either side like a cross and closed her rubbery eyes. Fatigue was gently tugging her away from the waking shore when her cellphone buzzed.

She groped for it groggily and half smiled at the white glow of the screen.

Thinking of you

Three little words and the storm clouds inside her parted for one perfect stream of dusty light. Her parents might have forgotten to consider her feelings, her birth parents might have forgotten about her altogether, but at least she had Rowan. He was thinking of her. For him, she was enough.

Thinking of you too. Sweet dreams xx

When she finally drifted off, sometime after two o'clock, Asha dreamed of driving along an endless coastline, the scent of crisp linen on the wind and Rowan at her side, with only new roads ahead of them.

Chapter 9

Nandini stood at the counter in front of a trio of blue Ziploc containers, portioning out leftover shepherd's pie for tomorrow's lunches, while Prem washed the dishes. Dinner had been another quiet meal. It seemed like her worst fears were coming true.

Panic always made her want to lash out. "I'm not sure how much more of the silent treatment I can take," she said. Asha appeared to enjoy the power that came from withholding. Nandini sensed it in every slam of her daughter's bedroom door, the *thwack* a message: they were on the outside. How long was the banishment going to last? It was agony. "How are we supposed to clear the air if she keeps shutting us out?"

Prem rinsed and lathered, rinsed and lathered. "We're her parents. We keep trying."

Nandini sealed the containers with a snap and spun around. "I have been trying, Prem. But she's impossible. It's like she's a different girl."

Prem shut off the tap and faced her. "She's angry, Nan. It's natural."

Of course, she knew that, but Nandini suspected there was more to it. "Her attitude really started changing after she read that letter, you know." Nandini cursed herself for not destroying it years ago. She should have trusted her instincts.

He squinted, puzzled. "The letter?"

"Don't you think?"

"Her attitude started changing after we told her she was *adopted*."

"Well, yes. All I'm saying is, I think there's more to it." She tapped her front teeth in a staccato rhythm, a bad habit when she was plotting. "I wish I could read it. Asha doesn't have to know."

"This again? I thought we settled that. It's Asha's letter, not ours. Leave it alone."

"Yes, but—"

"No, Nandini." He enunciated. "Enough of this. We have more important things to talk about."

She jerked her head back and crossed her arms. She was accustomed to him giving her more leeway. "Such as?" Blink. Blink.

Prem held his rib cage in a one-armed hug and stroked his lips with his free hand. "I've been thinking it's time we had an honest conversation with her. I know we've been trying to give her space so she can process everything, but it's backfired on us. Maybe if she knew more about what we went through to adopt her, she'd start to understand how much we wanted her. And why, after all that, you felt the need to keep the truth from her."

Nandini's breath caught. "Me?" She glowered. "So much for presenting a united front."

"I'd never say anything in front of Asha, you know that. But the truth is, we wouldn't be in this situation if we'd done what I wanted from the beginning."

"How many times am I going to have to apologize for this?"

He held a neutral expression. "Once would be a start."

"On the morning we told her she was adopted, I admitted that waiting had been a mistake, didn't I?"

He turned his back to her. "Never mind." The sound of rushing water filled the silence as he poured himself a glass of water.

"Don't be like that, Prem. You have no idea how hard this has been on me. I've carried the burden of this secret for the past eighteen years. I've worried myself sick over what it might do to our family."

His elbow froze, the drink partway to his mouth. "You didn't carry the secret alone. This has been hard on all of us. You make everything about you."

She gawped, speechless.

Water sloshed around the walls of the sink as he dumped out the untouched glass with an angry flourish. "Never mind all that for now," he said. "Our issues can wait. Asha's struggling. We need to figure out how to reach her. That's what matters. Not finding the letter and betraying her trust all over again."

Nandini clenched her teeth. "Fine. What do you have in mind, since you seem to have all the answers?"

He turned back around, gripping the counter ledge behind him. "If we open up to her, she might start opening up to us. To be honest, we could all use a little normalcy. An evening of us at least trying to act like a family again. Maybe then we'll remember how to be one."

Her cheeks began to cool as anger diminished to remorse. "That's a good idea."

He blew out a weary exhale. "Okay, then. I'll make a reservation at Mamma Grazzi's for tomorrow night."

He exited the kitchen without another word and went out to the back deck. Nandini picked at the dry skin of her lips. It wasn't like them to snap at each other. She wished she had done a better job of controlling herself, but she felt so vulnerable these days. Hopefully Prem was right and tomorrow's dinner would get their family life back on track.

Chords of a familiar song drifted into the kitchen through the open window as Prem strummed "Summertime," the song he taught himself to play the month Asha had blessed their home. Nandini quit torturing her lip and with a gentle sway hummed along, so weak with nostalgia anyone else might have mistaken the bout for sickness.

Chapter 10

The hallway was a tunnel of end-of-the-day sounds—lockers slamming, giddy chatter, sneakers squeaking against the soon-to-be-mopped tiles—a noisy bluster that curved up and over Asha as she gathered her things at her locker. Every book she slid into her backpack felt three times as heavy as she remembered. That was the strange physics of insomnia, or at least she was learning. How lack in one area could amplify in another.

Thank God it was Friday. Maybe she would have more luck coaxing the Sandman with her heavy eyelids over the weekend. First, she had to survive dinner with her parents. The thought of it made her intestines feel like they were being knit and purled. She didn't want to go out with them, not even to her favourite restaurant, and she definitely wasn't ready to talk. Not that it mattered. They were forcing her to go anyway. Still making decisions without truly considering her feelings.

Asha closed her combination lock with a click and went to pick up Willow at her locker so they could walk out to the buses together, as usual. When she didn't find her there, though, Asha had a good idea of where her best friend might be. It was Friday afternoon, after all.

Asha exited the side doors, turned a corner and was smacked by the thick musk of pot.

Willow grinned as she leisurely exhaled a thin stream of smoke.

"Athena," she said, drawing out the last vowel. "What are you doing visiting stoners' corner?"

Asha poked her side. "Looking for you."

"Ouch!" Willow flinched. "I think you punctured my kidney."

"Your kidneys are at the back, genius." Asha tucked a strand of her best friend's long red hair behind one ear. She wore her mom's old teal dashiki and Birkenstocks, but thankfully without socks now that it was spring.

"Excited for the weekend?" Willow asked.

Asha looked off into the yard and shrugged.

Willow pulled a face. "Are you okay? You've been spacey all day."

"I'm just tired."

"Still can't sleep?"

Asha shook her weary head.

"Well, let's do something tonight to cheer you up. I'll even let your lame boyfriend tag along."

"Rowan's at his mom's this weekend." Rowan had transferred to their school at the beginning of the year, after his parents' divorce. While he lived with his dad most of the time, he spent a couple of weekends a month at his mom's, on the other side of town. Before catching the city bus, he had stopped by her locker for a long good-bye kiss she had wanted to last and last.

"Even better!"

Asha tossed Willow a playful look that told her to behave. Willow wasn't a fan of Rowan. Not since she had heard a rumour that he still hung out with his ex sometimes. When Asha asked him about it, he said they were over, and she believed him. She didn't care about gossip, or who Rowan had dated at his old school. He was her first serious boyfriend and she trusted him. Besides, she needed every bit of his attention right now. The warmth she felt when they were together was the only thing that tamed the cold beast of loneliness she had been carrying inside since finding out she was adopted.

"I can't. My parents are forcing me to spend time with them."

"Are you still freezing them out?"

"It's not like that, Will. Sure, part of me wants to punish them for keeping me in the dark. But honestly, I've been keeping my distance because ever since they dropped that bomb on me, I've been scared about what else they might be hiding. I don't trust them. I feel like I have to protect myself." Asha's chin started to tremble. "I'm dealing with as much as I can right now."

Willow's pink eyes sobered from dull to sharp. "Hey, are you all right? You look like you're going to cry."

Asha clasped her elbows. "I'm sick to my stomach about tonight. That's why I've been so out of it. Apparently, they want to have a big talk. I have no idea what to expect. I got so nervous about it, I couldn't sleep last night. And I haven't been sleeping as it is." She sniffled. "I don't know how much more of this I can take. They think I like giving them the silent treatment, but it's just as awkward for me living in that house, if not more. I always feel like I'm walking on eggshells. I can't concentrate. I can't sleep. How am I supposed to focus on my exams with all this going on? I'm probably going to fail."

"Whoa, whoa, whoa, Athena." Willow gripped Asha by the arm, curbing her spiral from getting any worse. "Take a deep breath. Good. And another. Well, look at that! You're breathing again!"

A subdued laugh, Asha's first lighthearted feeling of the day. Thank goodness for her Willow. She wondered if her birth mother had had a best friend too. Someone she could confide in. Someone who understood what she was going through. Could it have been "him"?

"Maybe what you need tonight is a little moral support. Any chance I can tag along?"

Asha's mild grin faded. "I already asked. They said no."

Willowed sighed. "In that case." She proffered the joint, raising her eyebrows. "Maybe this'll take the edge off."

The lower lid of Asha's right eye skittered. Normally, she would have passed. She hated the rank smell of pot and the way the smoke singed the back of her throat. But she was desperate for a little relief, a little break, from the near-constant rattle of her nerves, the howl of the phantoms, the fierce throb of the hurt. She licked her lips, pinched the joint and brought it to her open mouth. As she held in a sooty lungful, fighting not to cough or gag, off in the distance, the rev of yellow buses summoned them home.

Chapter 11

They must have looked like the saddest Friday-night diners in Mamma Grazzi's history. It was a warm evening and the courtyard looked inviting, but they chose a corner table indoors because her mom said it would be more private and conducive to conversation. Laughter spilled into the dining room from a large gathering outside. The strange physics of insomnia seemed to have something in common with the strange physics of silence. The cheer from outside made the hush at their table seem all the quieter.

Asha peered past her dad's ear at a string of little white lights wrapped loosely around a maple tree that shone a soft gleam of whimsy over plates of pasta and tartufo. She couldn't take her eyes off them. The lights were mesmerizing.

"Asha?" her father said somewhere in the distance.

If only they twinkled like Christmas lights. No, like starlight. Then they would be perfect. Magical.

"Asha?"

"Hmm?" She pulled her dozy eyes from the glow. Her parents stared at her with worried faces. She glanced between them. "Sorry, what?"

"I was asking how exam prep's going."

"Oh." She picked up her fork and stuffed a twirl of fettuccine carbonara into her mouth. "I got distracted by the lights," she mumbled.

Her parents looked over their shoulders, then at each other and finally back at Asha.

"Are you okay?" her mom asked.

Asha's mouth felt gluey. "Yeah, why?" She reached for her water and glugged.

"You seem a little off tonight."

Asha lowered her empty glass. Why was she still so thirsty? "Are you going to drink that?" she asked her dad, pointing at his water. She grabbed his glass and started drinking before he had a chance to answer. Once she finished, she set it back down in front of his plate. "What were you saying?"

There was a silence. "You seem distracted," her mom said.

Asha adopted a thinking posture, slanting her head to one side, raising her nose, her bottom lip pouting. "Do I?"

Then it hit her: she must still be a little high from earlier. She felt overly self-conscious all of a sudden. She lengthened her spine, cleared her throat and smoothed out her napkin. "Sorry. I've . . . had a lot on my mind lately."

"Of course you have," her dad said. "Which is what we wanted to talk about. We want to respect your personal space, but we can't keep living like strangers in the house. The sooner we clear the air, the better. Your mom and I wanted to tell you more about what it was like for us when we were trying to conceive and about the adoption process, not to make you feel uncomfortable, but just the opposite. Hopefully by the end you'll realize how much we wanted you."

"And how much we went through to build this family," her mom said, cutting in. "Maybe then you'll understand why we were reluctant to tell you about your adoption."

"Not that that excuses anything," her dad added quickly. "But if you knew the whole story, you might see that we never did any of this to hurt you. At least, not on purpose." He studied her, dubious. "But now I'm not sure if tonight's the best time to talk about this, after all." He frowned. "Asha?"

"What?"

"Are you sure you're okay?"

"Yeah, why?"

There was another silence. "You haven't blinked."

Damn it. She was trying too hard. She batted her eyelashes at what she thought was a normal tempo. "I'm . . . just taking it all in, that's all." Was she blinking too much? Too fast?

Her parents exchanged another anxious look.

"You might be coming down with something," her mom said. "You always act funny when you catch a fever."

Asha partially veiled her eyes. "I do feel a bit lightheaded." It wasn't a lie. If her parents wanted to assume she was getting sick, and that assumption ended their awkward dinner sooner than expected, Asha wasn't about to interfere. Besides, she wasn't interested in hearing their explanations or excuses. Not until they told her something else first.

"Let's go home," her dad said, balling up his napkin and tossing it aside. "We can talk again when you're feeling better."

Her mom nodded. "You'll want to be rested for your grandparents' visit."

Asha's eyes flashed open. "They're coming over?"

"For dinner. Tomorrow night."

Asha fumed. "Thanks for telling me." She hadn't seen her grandparents since she had found out about her adoption. It was still difficult to think of them, knowing they weren't blood relatives. But that wasn't the only thing bothering her. "It would've been nice to be asked." She worked her jaw. "I'm not ready to see them."

"They're still your grandparents, Asha," her mom said. "There's nothing to be embarrassed about."

Asha scowled. Yet again, they didn't understand what she needed to hear or what she felt. Asha wasn't embarrassed: she was angry.

"They've always known I'm adopted?"

"Well, yes."

"Which makes them no better than you."

"Don't talk about your grandparents like that."

"They could've told me the truth, but they didn't."

"Only because we asked them not to. It isn't their fault."

Asha irradiated her parents with a disapproving glare. "I know it isn't."

Her mom broke eye contact. "They love you so much. We all do. You know that."

Asha's throat ached. In that moment, she realized that anger wasn't the only emotion she felt when it came to her grandparents and their involvement in the adoption secret.

Yes, she was furious. But she was also terrified. Everything was different now. And it chilled her to think that things might be different with her beloved grandparents too. Given the choice, she would rather keep them away, keep their love for each other perfect in her memory.

WHEN THEY GOT home, Asha rushed to her room and picked up her journal.

They still don't get it. They're still making choices without consulting me. They're still keeping me in the dark. This time about my grandparents coming over, but that isn't the point. They could have come to me, asked me how I felt, tried to start rebuilding the trust between us in some small, symbolic way. Only they didn't. Instead, they did what they always do. They'll never change.

Can you believe they expected me to sit through their bullshit excuses at dinner tonight when they still haven't even apologized to me? They've said it was wrong to wait, they've said they want to explain their reasons for keeping the secret, but the one thing I need to hear before anything else is, "Asha, we're sorry." That's the place to start. But they don't listen.

Asha

Chapter 12

Asha carried an armful of dishes to the sink. On the surface, the first dinner with her grandparents in weeks had gone like any other. They had sat around the dining table, talking over each other—well, the adults had—and eating too much—again, them. Now that dinner was over would come the games, many hands of cards and matches of chess. She had waited the entire meal for someone to mention the adoption, but no one had. She was about to go to her room when she heard her name.

"Asha?!" her naniji called from the living room. "Come, beti, I need your eyes. I forgot my glasses. And your dadi has the foolish notion that she is going to beat me at crazy eights this time." Asha couldn't help but grin. Her grandmothers were so competitive. She entered the living room.

"Nonsense!" her dadiji said. "She was on your team last time. Come, Asha, sit beside me."

"Why should she be on either of your teams?" Nana said from the dining table. Sitting across from him, her dadaji was drawing the chessboard and its piece from the box. "Aaja beti, you're too intelligent for cards. Come play chess with us."

Four sets of deep, dark, loving eyes upon her. At that precise moment, Asha burst into tears.

She sprinted to the washroom and locked the door behind her. As she dabbed her eyes with toilet paper, she realized her tears weren't angry or mournful. They were tears of relief. She had really needed to be fought over just then.

Once the pink had left the whites of her eyes, she rejoined everyone in the living room. Her mom and dad were seated on the loveseat, watching their mothers play cards. For the moment, no one mentioned her tearful outburst.

Instead, her dadaji motioned to the chair beside him. "I need to confer with my partner about our next move."

She crossed the room and took a seat.

"Don't let on," Dada whispered. "But your less-clever grandfather's bishop is a goner." He winked at her, then lingered on her face, his eyes moving from forehead to cheek to chin, checking to see that his Asha was still there, his Asha was still his Asha. She winked back as if to say, *Yes.*

A little while later, her grandmothers carried out trays of tea and mithai.

"Asha beti," her naniji said. "You wouldn't remember this, but I made kheer for you to celebrate our first meeting. This very same recipe. I fed you with a tiny spoon and you ate an entire bowl. That was when I knew I was your favourite."

"Such nonsense!" her dadiji scoffed. "Asha, I made you besan laddu, so buttery and sweet, you ate them right out of my hand. Now tell me, who's the favourite?"

An unexpected chuckle floated through the gathering.

Her naniji's smile dimmed and she turned misty-eyed. "It was one of the best days of my life." She touched Asha's chin. "I always wanted to be a grandparent. That's what you made me, beti. That's what you made all of us."

Her other grandparents nodded, each looking dewy in the eyes.

"To think we might have hurt our precious Asha," her dadiji continued. "Well, that is truly an unbearable thought. We're so sorry, sunder beti."

Asha thought for a few moments. Her grandparents had done

what they were asked to do. She could forgive them for that. If she resented anyone, it was her parents, for placing her grandparents in that impossible position to begin with.

"It's okay," she told them. "And thank you for saying sorry." The words she had been waiting to hear, which, despite all her parents' backtracking and excuses, they had yet to utter.

Each of her grandparents rose to their feet and made their way over to her, pausing, one at a time, to kiss her forehead in a lingering way that told her everything she needed to know: They loved her. Nothing had changed. They were sorry she was in pain. They were sorry for their part in causing it. And they loved her.

Tears crested the rims of Asha's eyes, like they had earlier in the washroom, only this time they shimmered with the relief of knowing that she still loved her grandparents too, as unconditionally as before.

Chapter 13

Later that evening, as she huddled in bed under the covers with her journal, Asha wrote:

Then why isn't it enough? Why do I still feel so lonely inside? So unloved?

In your letter, you told me you loved me, and you said "he" loved me too. That "he" would take care of me and always put me first. Instead, "he" got rid of me.

I don't understand why. Wasn't I good enough? To keep? To love?

Yes, my family loves me. But they aren't the ones who created me. They aren't the ones who raised me for the first eight months of my life. They aren't the ones who left me behind, by choice or not.

I need to know how it all came together and how it all fell apart. Was it a fling? A mistake? Is that all I am?

Or did you love "him"?

Doesn't everyone want to know that they come from love?

Asha

Fools, fancies and fate

Chapter 14

Mala glowered at the cursor as it blinked once every second, taunting her. She counted along: one Mississippi, two Mississippi, three Mississippi. In five weeks, she was scheduled to give a paper at a conference in Saskatoon. So far, her work progressed at a pre-industrial pace.

"Writer's block?" asked a familiar voice from behind her.

She savoured a private smile, then swivelled her chair a quarter-turn to face him. Ash stood at the opening of her cubicle with his hands in his pockets, grinning his lopsided grin. He wore a navy fleece, dark jeans and bright red Converse. And, she quietly noted, he was letting his stubble grow out in rusty bristles.

"I'm getting nowhere with this paper," she told him.

"The good news is it's almost time to quit. Are you going to the talk?" The departmental seminar, a Friday-afternoon institution. Researchers from within the department and beyond were invited to present their work. Although it wasn't strictly enforced, attendance was expected.

"I'm looking forward to it. It's my first since coming back. How about you?"

"I'll be there. Want to grab a drink after? You can tell me all about your paper woes."

She grinned on the inside. Before her absence, going out for a post-seminar pint had been one of their rituals, and she had missed it, perhaps too much.

They made plans to meet later. As he went back to his desk, Mala clenched her stomach, quelling a sudden frisson of delight.

DULL AND JARGON-FILLED, the seminar had dragged on like a dead limb. The speaker, a postdoc who was being considered for a position within the department, droned on about atmospheric modelling. Yet despite the yawn-inducing topic, Mala envied the researcher for being further along in her career than she was.

Afterward, while she walked along the custard hallway wallpapered with posters, Mala found herself envious again, and disconcerted, as she considered how bizarre it was to have years of work distilled into a three-by-four-foot sheet of glossy paper, knowing there was so much of the process missing from the tidy paragraphs and diagrams. Where were the late nights, the trial and error, the failures? And in her case, the loss, the semesters away, the frustration of finding her rhythm again? Nothing was as it seemed. There was the surface level of things, the properness that could be displayed to the world, and the mess of everything else underneath. Ash fell in step with her and she looked at him, sidelong. Mala wondered if the same could be said of life.

He rubbed the back of his neck, massaging away a crick. "Please tell me that was as rough for you as it was for me." They followed a small group of seminar-goers who were making their way to the grad student pub.

"I almost fell asleep," she said, stifling a yawn.

They continued to discuss the seminar and split from the group, opting to cut across the quadrangle rather than travel along the mine-like tunnels that snaked beneath the campus. The sharpness of the wind pierced Mala's sweatshirt, signalling the harsher months to come. They quickened their pace.

Inside the Unicentre, they descended to the second floor and entered the dimly lit pub, reuniting with their group, who had secured a few tables to the right of the mahogany bar. They pirated a pair of stray chairs and Mala took a seat.

"First round's on me," he said.

"Wait—" She tried to stop him, but he was already making his way to the back of the line.

Mala sat uncomfortably at the table. She still didn't know many of the new students. Of those she was acquainted with, some had graduated during her absence, while others were busy in their labs or writing their dissertations and were less inclined to socialize. It was unfortunate how her cohort had splintered. Mala meant to reach out to Linh, but she had been so preoccupied with making up for lost time, she hadn't gotten around to it yet and, frankly, she doubted whether she would. Ash had gone to the trouble of introducing her to a couple of people, though. One of whom was sitting across from her now, making conversation. What was his name?

She chatted with half her attention at best, glancing at Ash every now and then. He stood in line with his hands ruffling inside his pockets, surveying the beer menu above the register written in coloured chalk. She quietly chuckled to herself about how he mouthed the menu items as he read them. There was something endearing, almost childlike, about it. The student asked her why she was laughing.

"No reason," she said brightly. "How's your research going?"

The student went on about habitat fragmentation and Mala resumed her covert watch. Just then, Ash glanced at her. Their gazes touched for an instant. A look she felt, like a pinprick through her navel, like a gasp. She inched her sightline to the left and refocused on the student. Her belly flooded with dread. Had he caught her staring? She could see in the background that he was ordering. She sighed discreetly. He probably hadn't noticed.

What was it about him? she wondered. They were so different. Then again, maybe that was the appeal. She had wanted to be his kind of different her whole life. The kind of different that fit in. The kind people admired.

Or maybe what distinguished him was that he never made her feel awkward or embarrassed about their differences, where others had. Like when she had told him about her parents' arranged marriage. Rather than make a judgment about the origins of her family, question her parents' choice in the matter or doubt their love for each other, he had approached it with an open mind and a desire to understand the nuances of a custom he was unfamiliar with, knowing he had no basis or right to criticize.

That, she realized, was the root of their connection: she could be herself with him, whereas with others she had learned there were parts of her life she would always have to hide. He knew her like no one else.

Something inside her fell away. Or at least he used to know her, before she rejected him and disappeared from his life.

With a half-hearted smile, she watched him approach the table. He set down the pitcher and glasses, then took a seat.

"So," he said as he poured, "did you break through that writer's block in the end?"

She shook her head. "I haven't presented in so long, I wanted to get a head start. So much for that."

"You still have lots of time to prepare."

She crossed her toes. "Are you going to the conference?"

He slid her pint across the table. "Can't wait to see the Prairies."

She did her best to dim her delight, pinching the inside of her cheek between her teeth. "I wonder if they're as flat as everyone says."

He raised and lowered his drink. "According to Laine, they are."

Mala felt the warm glow of happiness slowly drain from her face at the mere mention of Laine. *Plain Laine*, as Mala secretly teased. Anyone else would have called her Helen.

Mala hid her disappointment behind the rim of her glass and took a deep sip. Their relationship hadn't ended, after all.

"Are you okay?" he asked.

Mala's lips cracked into a plastic grin. "Of course," she blurted. "How's Laine?" She cursed herself for pursuing the very subject she wanted to avoid.

He tapped the side of his glass, expressionless. "Fine, I think."

Was that a touch of guardedness she detected in his eye? "Are you sure about that?"

He scratched his stubble. "Actually, she hasn't been feeling well. Not for a while."

"The flu's going around."

"The flu's on fixed rotation in elementary school." He paused, pensive. "That's what I thought too, at first. Now I'm starting to worry it's something more serious."

"Has she seen a doctor yet?"

He shook his head. "She won't go. She says she's just over-worked. I keep telling her to slow down, but she spends most nights either correcting homework or making lesson plans." He let out a laugh of poorly masked insecurity. "Sometimes I think she's trying to avoid me."

"She's probably just a little rundown, that's all." Or was there more to it? Mala wondered. Was the pressure of discord mounting in their relationship again?

He didn't seem convinced. "Maybe." He stared into the middle distance for a lengthy moment, then checked his watch.

"Late for dinner?" she joked. Anything to coax a smile out of him.

He looked up, straight-faced. "Laine hasn't had much of an appetite lately, except for this carrot ginger soup they make at the Wild Oat. I was thinking of picking some up before they close."

Mala was touched by his thoughtfulness. "That's a nice idea. It's okay if you have to go."

He glanced at his watch again. "We have enough time to finish our pints." He grinned, regretful. "Sorry for rushing our catch-up."

"There's nothing to be sorry about."

Mala swallowed another mouthful while strongly praying that he didn't feel obligated to reciprocate and ask about her social life. Conjuring one up was always so humiliating.

"How's your research going?" he said instead. "Has it been tough getting back in the flow of things?"

The tight cords across her chest released with an inner sigh. She was relieved he had redirected their conversation back to school, the realm that made her truly happy.

"It's slow going. I've been frustrated lately."

He topped up their glasses. "About what?"

She frowned into the foam. "Sometimes it feels like I'm never going to finish. I'm so far behind. Before my dad passed away, though, I was in such a good place." She lifted her gaze. "Everything was. I guess it's hard to imagine getting that back." *Could he guess the unspoken meaning she was trying to convey?*

His eyes were soft with sympathy. "You'll get there, Mala. You've been through a lot. It takes time to find your stride again. But it'll happen. Just be patient. Keep going."

She hooded her eyes. *No, he hadn't understood.* She shrugged, watching the bubbles in her glass fizz to the top.

He leaned forward on his elbows. "Is there something I can do to help?"

Mala peered at him across the table, remembering the times he had offered to help her in the past, and how she had rejected him, and the distance that had resulted from that thrust. An unbridgeable distance, she feared, until a moment ago.

"You know you only need to ask."

Gratitude bloomed inside her chest like sparks of light, and relief brought a smile to her lips.

"I will," she told him.

Next time, no matter how vulnerable she felt, she wouldn't push him away. She would go to him, talk to him. Prove to him she was worthy of this second chance at friendship.

Chapter 15

For the past month, Veena had found herself in an unexpected yet familiar position. Without Pavan for company, or the insulating effects of Mala's presence, the daytime stretched out like a ribbon of pock-marked asphalt, starting at her toes and reaching to an unknown locale ahead. She was reminded of the isolation she had felt as a newcomer, back when the depth of her complexion and the thickness of her accent made her shy away from people.

That was then, of course. Now she had friends. And she had been speaking to them more often recently, and had even had a few over for tea the other day. What Veena lacked was the desire to actively socialize the way she used to. The ladies from temple kept leaving her messages on the answering machine, asking when they might see her at community events, if she planned on rejoining their weekly game of rummy. She wasn't back in India, they insisted. She didn't have to give up everything because Pavan was gone. None of them had lost their husbands, of course. They didn't understand how the loss of one person could empty the world of joy and the soul of will. Still, Mala seemed to be thriving in her old routine. Perhaps it was time for Veena to emerge from her cave too. She resolved to think about it.

Thankfully, she still had Mala to look after, at least for the time being, and this gave her purpose. Her daughter's arrival was the event around which she structured her day.

Now, as she sipped a cup of ginger tea that didn't taste quite right, she stirred a pot of dahl on the stove. The warm scent of cumin and curry powder, of fried garlic and onions, spiced the air. Even if she did nothing fruitful all day, she never went without cooking for Mala. Somehow, while she chopped and fried, following recipes written only in her head, she felt at least a tiny bit necessary. Lifting the steel spoon to her mouth, she tasted the dahl and declared, "Needs salt."

She pinched a generous amount from her spice thali and sprinkled the fine grains into the lentil soup, yellow as the petals of a sunflower. Although it had taken her years to master the art of cooking, after a while she began to understand its alchemy—how much turmeric turned a dish bitter, how many chilies were too many. Pavan had always been an obliging test subject, never pushing away any plate she set down in front of him, even when she knew what she had prepared was close to indigestible, perhaps because he felt guilty that she had to cook at all, servants not being part of everyday life in Canada. After each meal, while chewing on a handful of candy-coated saunf, the licorice-tasting fennel seeds that helped his digestion, he would say, "Annapurna herself could not have done better," invoking the goddess of food and cooking. How supportive he had turned out to be about the matters of life, both big and small.

Satisfied, she set down the spoon on an inverted pot lid. There was still time to change out of her cooking-smell clothes before Mala got home. On the way, she stopped at the altar in the living room, lit two sticks of rose incense, then made her way to her bedroom at the end of the hall. Without turning on the lights, she unbuttoned her blouse, tossed it at the end of the bed and perused her closet for another. She chose a rayon blouse with a floral pattern, her shoulders groaning with a dull ache as she put it on. Too much idleness, she thought. Too much time spent watching silly soap operas.

Veena buttoned her blouse and reassured herself that this limbo wouldn't last forever. Soon, Mala would get married and start a family. Soon, Veena would be a grandmother, a privilege her own mother was denied due to the uncrossed oceans that chopped between them. Life would renew itself, as samsara assured, and this in-between phase would be nothing more than the necessary pause that preceded a new beginning. For a moment, Veena's spirits lifted, as they would every year back in India with the arrival of the cool monsoon rains.

Then, the downward pull of gravity. First, she would have to broach the subject of marriage with Mala, earlier than they had agreed, and her daughter wasn't going to like it.

Nevertheless, it seemed like fate that Chitra Shah, her oldest friend, should mention the Mishras to Veena when they had tea together the other day. How they were looking for a suitable girl for their son, Sumesh. Chitra thought Mala might be a good match, knowing how anxious Veena had grown about her daughter's future.

Really though, what did Veena know about this Mrs. Mishra? An image of her own mother-in-law flashed inside her head, with her laddu-fed hips, her lumbering side-to-side gait and the look of permanent disapproval she must have perfected by watching too many Bollywood films. Veena respected her elders, as she had been raised to do, but even now, years after the old woman's death, her memory was enough to stir smoke from the old fires.

Strange, Veena considered, how she had let go of so many customs in Canada. Yet others had travelled with her across the oceans, as though packed in her suitcase beside her sari blouses and petticoats. Perhaps her conservative Indian upbringing was responsible for her belief that it was unsafe for a young woman like Mala not to have a man in her life, someone to look after her, whether it be a father, brother or husband. Under the circumstances, Veena would have even settled for a cousin, but the closest lived in Delhi.

Veena sat on the edge of the bed, fiddling with the blouse she had changed out of. She knew Mala wanted to postpone any discussion of marriage until after she graduated, and Veena wanted to respect her daughter's wishes. If only she could quieten her fears. They doubled with every passing day. The same questions hounded her: What if something happened to her? What if she disappeared in a blink like Pavan had? What would become of Mala? With their entire family living in India, and mostly unknown to her, who would her daughter have to rely on? Veena pictured Mala as helpless as a calf separated from its mother, bewildered and vulnerable to predators. She had raised her daughter to be modest, careful. But that very upbringing seemed like a disadvantage now. Mala was such an innocent girl. She didn't even consume alcohol. What could she possibly know about men? She was too naive, too trusting. She needed someone to take care of her.

Veena stopped fiddling with her blouse. No, she couldn't delay any longer, even if raising the subject might cause an argument, or some deeper clash between them in the short-term. She rose and tossed her blouse into the hamper. Veena's eyes were set on Mala's future. It was the motherly thing to do.

VEENA SAT ACROSS from Mala at the kitchen table. Laid out in front of them were several white Corningware dishes filled with her daughter's favourites: dahl and rice, stuffed okra, matar paneer and aloo parathas. For dessert, kheer, the rice tender and fragrant with rose water and sprinkled with pistachios. Granted, the menu was more elaborate than Veena tended to prepare of late, but the meal was tactical. Mala was always more pliable with a full belly.

Veena lifted one of the pot lids, a slide of condensation pouring into the sabji.

"More paneer?" she asked.

Mala leaned back and rested one hand over her stomach. "Where would I put it?"

"How about another paratha?"

"I'm leaving room for dessert."

"What am I going to do with all these leftovers, hein?" Veena sucked her teeth. "You need to keep your strength up, my doctoral candidate."

"That's funny coming from the woman who survives on toast and tea."

"Arré, I'm an old woman. It doesn't matter what I eat, as long as it keeps me going. Life is nearly done with me, but yours has just begun."

"You won't be happy until I gain twenty pounds."

"I would be satisfied with ten." Veena smiled. "Now, challo, make your old mother some chai."

While Mala cleared the table and prepared tea, Veena served the creamy rice pudding. She had left it to simmer on the stove until the milk formed an indulgent crust. Veena skimmed off the delicacy and folded it into her daughter's bowl.

"I left you the malai," she said. As a child, Mala had loved eating the thick skin with a crunchy layer of sugar on top.

"Let's share it."

Veena tilted her head to one side. "No, it's for you."

Mala placed the steaming cups of tea on the table.

"Do you have more marking to do?" Veena asked.

"Even I need a break sometimes. Feel like watching a movie?"

"Sure, beti." Veena circled the bowl of rice pudding with her spoon, doubting Mala would want to watch a film with her by the end of their conversation.

"Why aren't you eating?"

"Too much thinking."

Mala lowered her spoon. "What's on your mind? Is it about Papa?"

"Yes and no."

"What is it?"

Veena gazed across the table into her daughter's bloodshot eyes and lost her nerve. She reached for Mala's half-full bowl and served her another scoop of kheer.

Mala took the heavy bowl. "Thanks," she said. "Now out with it."

Veena silently summoned Pavan, praying that he was with them in spirit. You always had a way with her, she thought. Knew how to cool her quick temper. "You know that nearly a year has passed since Papa left us," she said.

"Yes."

"Well, it's got me thinking about your future."

"My future?"

"I've been wondering about your plans."

"What plans?"

Veena paused. "About marriage."

"Marriage?" Mala's face contorted. "Mom, I haven't finished school yet. We agreed to wait until after I graduate to talk about this. I have so much work to catch up on. Marriage is the last thing on my mind right now."

"By the time I was your age—"

"That isn't the point." Mala pushed the kheer away, finally seeing the elaborate meal for what it was. "You promised me. You and Papa."

Veena pressed on. "Chitra Auntie told me about a good family. The Mishras. They have a son about your age. His name is Sumesh. He's looking for someone."

"Mom, you aren't listening to me."

"He's a medical student. I've seen his picture. He's very handsome."

Mala huffed a small, unpleasant laugh. "Of course, he's a doctor."

"Don't you want to get married, Mala? Raise a family?"

Mala thought. "I think I do. Someday."

"How do you expect to meet someone?"

"Oh, I don't know, Mom. Maybe the old-fashioned way?" A piercing look. "At a bar?"

"A bar?" Veena gaped. There were her worst fears, coming out of her daughter's mouth. What kind of man would Mala meet at a bar? Only the disreputable kind of man who went to bars to begin with. "Mala, what nonsense! You don't even drink!" Mala averted her eyes. What Veena needed to find for her daughter was a man who went to temple, to school, to visit his parents every week, if he didn't still live with them. A good boy meant a good match. "That might be the old-fashioned way here, Mala, but not for us. I know you have reservations. But remember, Papa and I had an arranged marriage, and we were very happy together."

"Not everyone's as lucky as you were."

"Lucky?"

"Mom, you were the most well-suited couple I've ever met, arranged marriage or otherwise. Trust me, most people don't find that."

"Not everything is as it seems." Veena heard a younger version of her husband's voice echoing from the past: *If I go against her wishes, she has threatened to disown me.* "We had our troubles." *How can I disobey my own mother?*

"What are you talking about?"

Veena hesitated. "I've never told you about this because I would rather forget. But I will, if only to prove to you that it isn't the lack of trouble, rather how you handle it, that makes a marriage strong." Veena chose a beginning. "Before you came along, you know there were many losses."

Mala nodded.

Veena quashed the memory of the pit, the darkness. Mala could never know about that. It was too shameful. "We would try, and I would lose, but your papa never blamed me. His family was another story. Five years into our marriage, his mother demanded that we buy her a plane ticket. She was going to fix me."

"How?"

"I was expecting the usual overstepping. Maybe she would change my diet or my clothing or ask a pandit to bless our home.

I wouldn't have been surprised if she'd asked to see my doctor."

"And instead?"

"When she arrived, I knew from her coldness that she had washed her hands of me. The only time she spoke to me was either to bark an order or criticize. Then one night, I overheard them talking."

"About you?"

Pavan, she is a disgrace. "In my own house." *Why should you pay the price for her bad karma? God has cursed her womb. Otherwise, you would have had three children by now.*

"What did she say?"

I'm telling you, you must rid the family of this curse. If you don't, we will be ruined, do you hear me? Divorce her, Pavan. "She wanted Papa to remarry." *I will find you a new wife, younger, prettier. A wife who will bring more to our family than shame.*

"You're joking."

"It's what she knew. People marry, have children and the children take care of their elders when the time comes. It's tradition. What good is a wife who can't perform her duty?" *I told you to take her dowry. At least then the useless girl would have given us something.*

"That's unbelievable."

"My life would have been over. Your papa would have been able to remarry, while I returned to my parents' home, a disgrace."

"Obviously Dad didn't go along with it."

"He was under a great deal of pressure. He didn't want to cut ties with his family, like his mother threatened to do if he disobeyed her. You don't understand these things because you were raised here, but Papa and I were raised there, surrounded by a certain mentality. It doesn't vanish when you immigrate. Those were early days for us in Canada too. We still didn't know if we were going to make it, or if we would have to go back to India. This country was still foreign to us, we didn't belong, so we clung to what home we had back in India. Losing that connection would have been like severing another arm because, of course, we had already severed one when we left. All of that was going through your papa's mind while he was thinking about what do."

"He actually considered divorcing you?"

Veena pictured herself kneeling in the nursery, picking through a box of unused baby things they had accumulated over the years, each item purchased during the highest highs and stowed away during lows that had no bottom. "I was sure he was going to leave me." Veena didn't tell Mala about the dismal thoughts she had contemplated that night. That if Pavan obeyed his mother, then her life was as good as over, in which case she might as well be dead. Not even after the miscarriages, when the darkness visited her for weeks at a time, had Veena ever plunged so deeply into the pit. That night, however, she remembered feeling as though her time had run out: she would never fulfill her dream of having a family, and it was her own fault.

"But he chose you in the end."

Veena's eyes smarted with tears. "He did." *I don't care what she says. I'll never leave you.* "Do you see now? How troubles can make you stronger?" *Even if we never have children. It is God's will.* "We loved each other, very much." *It was written for us to be together. Meri pyar, please don't cry.* Yes, after years of pain, they finally got to be happy.

"Your story proves my point, at least in part. Would you really want me to go through the same thing? End up with a mother-in-law like her? You can't blame me for having reservations."

"You shouldn't assume that things would turn out badly. You could meet someone as devoted as Papa. You could end up as happy. Anyway, that's getting ahead."

Mala fell silent and gazed into her cup. Veena watched her daughter turn inward, like a tulip at dusk.

"I just want what's best for you, beti."

"If you wanted what's best for me, you wouldn't rush me. And you wouldn't go back on your word. You're acting like you want to get rid of me."

"How can you say that?" This was Veena's second-worst fear: that Mala would misunderstand her loving intentions. Eyes glistening, she said, "You're all I have." Veena shuddered as she beheld her daughter, who, even in anger, still possessed the most beautiful face of any she had ever seen. A face that might never have existed had she given in to her dark, desperate heart back then. This secret shame, above all, Veena had to protect Mala from knowing. She quietly thanked God for helping her overcome the darkness, and still deeming her worthy of motherhood, despite her weaknesses.

"Why else would you bring this up before the time we agreed?"

"As your mother, it's my duty to guide you. To help you get to the next step in life. While I can." Veena's throat constricted. "Since Papa passed away, I've been worried that something might happen to me and then you would be left on your own. For me, there is no greater fear, beti."

"Mom." Mala's voice was sympathetic. "Nothing bad's going to happen to either of us."

"You can't understand these worries. You aren't a mother. Please, Mala, won't you at least meet the boy? It's just an introduction. That doesn't sound so bad, does it?"

Mala was silent for several moments. Then she looked across the table beseechingly, as if invoking clairvoyance. "What if I meet someone on my own? I mean, what if I've met someone already?"

Veena stared, astonished. Her quiet daughter, full of secrets. "If you've made a love match, you must tell me, beti. I'm not as old-fashioned as you think."

Veena waited patiently for her daughter to reveal, in detail, the bio data of her potential suitor. But Mala kept silent. This worried Veena. She knew that not all Indian boys who were raised in Canada ended up being good boys. Some shamed their families by drinking and smoking and dating girls from outside the community. Some even had sex before marriage. The type of boys who lied to their parents, led double lives and would inevitably lie to their future wives. The type of boys who couldn't be trusted. Was it any wonder that introductions were so important?

Mala had yet to speak. "Tell me about his family. How long have they lived in Canada?" Still no reply. "They're Hindu, yes? There's a chance we've crossed paths at temple."

Mala's face tensed. "Never mind," she said, dropping her gaze to the table. "I was speaking hypothetically."

Veena sighed. "Then I'm not sure what else to do. Unless, of course, you want to try one of those online matchmaker sites? Chitra Auntie told me they're quite popular with the younger generation."

Mala gave her a flat stare.

"Mala, beti, can you at least think about meeting Sumesh?" She faltered for a moment. "For Papa's sake?" A tactic as strategic as the meal. "If I'm this worried about you, can you imagine how worried he must be?" Ten seconds passed. Then twenty. Veena had pushed her daughter too far. "Mala?" Thirty seconds. The silence between them might stretch on for minutes, years.

Mala rose to her feet. "I'll think about it," she said, dour.

Veena nearly gasped. She sent her gratitude skyward. "Thank you, beti. You've made Papa happy and me too. You've always been a good daughter."

Mala carried her dishes to the sink.

"You haven't finished your kheer."

"I'm full."

"Shall we watch a film now?" Veena scrambled to keep Mala from storming out of the kitchen. "We can get some of that caramel popcorn you like."

Mala gazed a gazeless stare outside the kitchen window. "I'm tired," she said. Then she turned on her heel and took herself out of the kitchen without glancing at Veena or kissing her good night.

Veena listened to the thud of her daughter's brisk footsteps echo through the hall with a heavy heart. She winced at the sound of Mala's bedroom door shutting. She felt guilty for ruining Mala's night, especially when she was already so tired. But she had no choice. In the long run, one ruined evening, one disagreement, wouldn't matter.

She just needs time to settle down, Veena thought to her husband. *One day, when her future is secure, and she's happily married and as in love with her children as I am with her, she will thank me. She will realize that I did all of this for her.*

Sipping her lukewarm tea, overwhelmed by the vastness of the silence, Veena felt a chill as she glimpsed a future of how soulless the house would be once Mala was married, the way the world had been before she arrived.

Chapter 16

The teaching assistants' office was barely wider than the length of Mala's arms outstretched, and modestly furnished with a desk, two chairs and a trash can. She had heard her peers call it a shoebox, a closet, a hole in the wall. Mala tended to think of it as a cell, a place where she did her time, awaiting parole.

Students rarely stopped by during her office hours. Most picked up their assignments in class or lab. Those who teetered between passing and failing, the ones she wanted to help the most, were often too shy or embarrassed to seek her out. Every now and then, a keener might tiptoe in with a winsome smile, only to start arguing a second later about marks they were sure they were entitled to—the keeners were always the most work.

She was battling her way through an electronic journal article on the reduced body condition of polar bears in the Hudson Bay area. She rubbed her sore eyes, wishing she hadn't worn her contacts that day, and sighed at her laptop. She missed reading non-academic things. Losing time in someone else's story was the one positive about her grief hermitage last year. At her local branch, she had befriended a librarian named Agnes, who recommended she read *Jane Eyre*. Whenever Mala felt lonely, she reminded herself: At least you have Mom. Think of Jane. How long it took her to find a place to call home. A person to call home. Then, that was the difficulty, wasn't it? How her life seemed void of shelter now, as if it had been spirited away along with her father, plucked into the afterlife. Would she ever find that kind of refuge again?

A figure appeared in the doorway. Mala expected to see one of her students. Instead, there was Ash, holding two cups of coffee.

"I thought you might need a pick-me-up," he said with a weak grin as he entered the office. He was wearing her favourite shirt, red-and-green plaid, which reminded her of Christmas ribbons. "Two milks and one raw sugar." He held out her cup.

She smiled. "Thanks." Taking the coffee, Mala noted the pinkish tint of his drowsy eyes. "I'm not the only one who looks like they could use a shot of caffeine. How was lab?" Their TA duties overlapped that day.

He lowered himself onto the chair across from her, rumbling a low groan, and made himself comfortable, crossing one ankle over the opposite knee. "Awful," he said. He twisted the lid off his travel mug, blew over the coffee and took a tentative sip. "I wasn't prepared. And the students kept freaking out about the roaches."

Mala wriggled as if one of the insects had scurried across her collarbone. "I remember that lab. Just thinking about it makes my skin crawl. Dissecting live cockroaches is pretty inhumane, don't you think?"

"They're anesthetized."

"On a block of ice? You don't actually think that works?"

"Well, if it makes you feel any better, think about all the insects that have died on the windshield of your car. At least in the lab they die in the name of science."

She blinked. "You have a point."

Ash sighed. "I'm just glad lab's over for another week. How about you? Any students drop by today?"

Mala shook her head. "Another no-show. I tried to catch up on some reading." She shut her laptop. "But I can't seem to focus."

He eyed her. "Is something on your mind?"

"You could say that." She kept her gaze on her laptop. "I haven't been sleeping well, I guess."

Not since the conversation she'd had with her mother last Friday. Instead, when she lay in bed, Mala peered into the darkness, wondering what the future held: her mother's vision for her life, or her own. Even now, it was almost impossible to push her mother's request out of her mind entirely. It lurked in the background, as threatening as a creature. She knew she would have to face it soon.

"Same here." He massaged his temples. "I've had a splitting headache all morning."

Mala wished she had some pain medicine to offer him. "What's been keeping you up?"

Even the blink of his eye carried weight. "Things at home are a little tense."

Mala's stomach contracted the way it did whenever Ash alluded to Laine even slightly. "Is Laine feeling any better?"

"A bit worse, actually." He paused. "She'll be fine, though."

"She finally went to the doctor?"

"Mm-hmm." He didn't elaborate.

Mala sensed that something else was bothering him. She could see it in the wilt of his shoulders, the creases of his forehead. She wondered what he was holding back. Could they have had another argument? "Is everything okay?"

He swallowed, his mouth a taut line. "I don't know." He fell silent, lost in thought for several moments. Then he forced a dim half smile, like someone who was trying to at least appear optimistic despite their worries.

Mala waited to see if he might share what was on his mind, but when it became obvious that he wasn't ready, she didn't want to deepen his unease by pestering him with another question. "Well," she offered instead, "if it makes you feel any better, I didn't have a great weekend either."

He dropped his half smile. "That only makes me feel worse. What happened?"

Mala cradled her cup. "It's my mom. She surprised me with something on Friday. I wasn't expecting it."

"Not a good surprise, I gather."

"No," she said, long-faced. "Whatever the opposite of that is."

He raised his eyebrows a fraction. "What did she say?"

Mala paused. She often encountered confusion, if not disdain, from her non-Indian friends—although less so if they were also children of immigrants—when she tried to explain to them certain realities of her life, which many deemed insupportable. She tended to fail at impressing the importance of respect over rebellion. The group over the individual. Responsibility over want. Which was why she was willing to follow certain rules—studying what her parents wanted her to, going to university close to home, living at home until she was married. And also why she was willing to entertain certain ideas, if only for show.

Unlike the others, Ash had always been understanding. She hoped this time would be no exception. "Do you remember how I told you that my parents had an arranged marriage?"

He nodded, then drank from his cup.

"Well, it's always been understood I would at least entertain the idea when the time came. At least, that's what I've led my parents to believe. I've never seriously considered it, to be honest. But I respect them too much to refuse them outright. When I started my Ph.D., I managed to convince them to wait until after I graduated to talk any more about it. They wanted me to do well in school and not get distracted, so they agreed."

"Kind of like buying yourself time?"

"Something like that."

"So, that's what your mom brought up?"

Mala nodded, sombre. "Out of the blue. She wants to set up an introduction. She said she's worried something might happen to her, like it did with my dad, and I'll have no one to look after me. I tried reasoning with her, but she's determined to keep pushing."

"Oh." He blinked. "Jesus, that's a lot. No wonder you haven't been sleeping. What are you going to do?"

Mala swallowed a mouthful of coffee. "I told her I would think about it."

His eyes were large and alert. "And are you?"

She glanced at the TA office door as someone scuttled past. "If I'm thinking about anything, it's how to get out of it. Don't be shy if you have any ideas."

A touch more at ease, he thought quietly for a few moments. "Well, it sounds like your mom's shaken up. Maybe since losing your dad, she's struggled to find a way to make things feel safe again, for both of you. Eventually it'll pass, though. Don't you think?"

"I keep hoping if I humour her for a little longer, she'll snap out of it somehow. I know the rug was pulled out from under us when my dad died, and life will never be the same without him, but we're still here. And we're going to be okay. I just don't know how to convince her that there's nothing to be afraid of."

"Maybe that's hard to remember when you've lost your whole world. It might take a while to get through to her, that's all. I feel for your mom. I can't imagine what it's like to have to go on living without your partner. It's hard enough to find one."

"They were too Indian to ever call themselves soulmates." Mala grinned tenderly, sadly. "But they were made for each other. Or as my dad would have said, *It was written*."

"It was written," Ash repeated, straight-faced.

The grin slipped from Mala's lips. She nodded, self-conscious, sensing a subtle charge mounting in the air.

"That's what it must feel like." He paused, unblinking. "Inevitable."

They held each other in a powerful stare. The space in the office seemed to shrink. He felt no more than a few inches away.

Then he blinked, quick and sharp like a snap of the fingers, and whatever unspoken connection had passed between them was severed. He reared back as if he had felt the contraction too. "I didn't realize you were dealing with so much. I'm sorry."

Mala averted her eyes and commanded her heart in vain to stop pounding. "It's not your fault. It's just distracting. All I want to do is focus on my work. But life seems determined to keep throwing me off track."

He drummed his fingernails on his metal cup, a tinny sound like bells. "The fact that you're back at school less than a year after your dad's passing speaks to how strong you are, Mala. The next time your mom starts worrying about you, remind her of that."

If only it were that simple, she thought. She enjoyed a sip from her perfect cup of coffee. When she looked up, she caught him watching her with a thoughtful expression. Her heartbeat quickened again and she became hyperaware of the silence.

"I mean it. You shouldn't doubt yourself." He shifted his hips. "And I've been meaning to apologize for not keeping in touch after your dad passed."

"You have nothing to apologize for. I'm the one who pushed you away."

"And I should've realized why instead of taking it personally. But I thought about you." He peered at her nakedly. "I worried about you."

The room seemed to shrink another foot. Mala lost track of seconds, sounds, breaths. There was only them.

Then he shot to his feet, like there was danger in staying any longer.

"I'm glad you stopped by," she rushed to say, fearing he might dash out the door before she had the chance. "You were right. I needed a pick-me-up. And thanks for listening. Next time the coffees are on me."

His crooked grin creased the corner of his eye, yet he still looked as sullen as when he had arrived.

"We'll see," he said, his gaze lingering on the shape of her mouth for a moment too long before he left the office.

Chapter 17

Mala arrived home late that evening. After evading her mother, she locked herself in the washroom, the drone of the fan insulating her from any intrusions and ran a steaming bath. As she waited for the water level to rise, she perched on the edge of the tub, dressed in her blue terrycloth robe, and watched the sink faucet drip. *Tap, tap, tap.* Her father had planned on fixing the leak that weekend. She swept away the saltwater streams from her cheeks, embarrassed by how the thought of such a mundane task could overwhelm her. What was the leaky tap but a small, unfinished chore that would remain that way? Mala realized it wasn't the banality of the task that upset her. It was the finality of the word *forever*. It went on and on. She would never catch up to it.

The tub was nearly full. She shut off the taps, let her robe drop to the floor and stepped into the bath. The first touch of scalding water sent a shivery wave from her toes to her crown. Leaning back, she rested her head on the rim of the tub. Her temples throbbed. She blew out a long sigh, closed her eyes and waited for the heat of the bathwater to sear hotter than her anger or her grief or her lust. She imagined the things she didn't want any more seeping from her pores like flecks of lead: her sorrow, her mother's expectations, her growing need for Ash's attention. She saw them settle on the bottom of the tub, where they would stay until she pulled the stopper. Then they would slip down the drain and finally leave her in peace. For now, while the bathwater was still hot, all she wanted to do was submerge these torments, soak them away, and in some small manner free herself from their collective ache.

AFTER BATHING, MALA returned to her room, flicked on her side lamp and climbed into bed. Unable to settle the chaos of her thoughts, she reached for *Jane Eyre*. Her thumb grazed a notch in the front cover of the paperback she had borrowed from the library. The notch tore into Jane's grey dress. How long before the notch would grow and maim Jane's lovely face? Gingerly, Mala lifted the cover and reunited with the story: "With *Bewick* on my knee, I was then happy: happy at least in my way. I feared nothing but interruption, and that came too soon."

She heard a gentle tap on her bedroom door. Mala closed the book, resting it on her lap with a sigh.

Her mother peeked through the slit in the doorway. She was holding a silver tray. "I thought you might be hungry." She waited for permission to enter.

I can't be mad at her when she's being so sweet, Mala thought. "Come in."

Her mother approached the bed, careful not to upset the tray, and took a seat beside Mala, the mattress dipping under her weight. With the tray balanced on her lap, she tore into a warm paratha glistening with ghee and dipped a triangular piece into the pool of saag at the centre of the plate. She held the morsel up to Mala's mouth with her hand cupped underneath to catch any drips. "Khana, meri beti," she said, warm with love. Eat, my dear daughter.

Mala hesitated. For most of her life, she had complained that her parents infantilized her, treated her like she was excessively naive, helpless and unworldly. But as Mala stared at the tantalizing offering in her mother's hand, all complaints and resistance dissolved into the sudden spring below her tongue. Perhaps it was her tiredness, or her loneliness, or her increasingly toxic desire for Ash that made her want to regress, just a little, for just a little while. She opened her mouth. Relishing the familiar taste, she felt small, sheltered from adult decisions and, for the moment, unconcerned about the nebulous future. The saag tasted especially delicious that night.

A pang of loss needled her navel. "Papa would've loved this."

"It was his favourite. He would make these perfect little balls of saag and rice. The way he licked it off his fingers always made it look so appetizing." A bittersweet smile raised the apples of her mother's cheeks. "So, beti, tell me about your day."

Mala thought of the time she had spent with Ash and felt a warm glow. "It was fine. Nothing special."

"You look tired. You're going to get sick if you go on like this."

"I told you, I have a lot of catching up to do."

"Well, you can't do a year's worth of work in a day, haan?" Her mother held out another parcel of food. "I miss having you around."

Mala chewed, waiting for her throat to open. She hated that her mother was home alone all day, that she was lonely, that she couldn't restart her father's heart and make her mother happy again. She forced down a swallow, then asked, "When are you getting together with the temple ladies?"

"Chitra Auntie came over today for tea. We had a nice visit. She's trying to convince me to join the rummy game next week. I'm considering it." Her mother circled another triangle of paratha through the puddle of saag. "Have you thought about what we discussed the other day?"

"A bit," Mala lied. She had thought of little else.

"And?"

Mala turned away, rejecting the food held at her mouth. "I haven't changed my mind. I want to finish school before I start thinking about marriage. Like we agreed."

Her mother lowered her hand, hovering it over the plate. "I wish our circumstances hadn't changed either, but they have. Remember, Mala, I'm not asking you to marry the boy. Just meet him. Papa would—"

"Please, Mom. Don't drag Dad into this. You know how guilty I feel about his death already." If she hadn't gone to brunch that day, if she had been home to clear the driveway, Mala was certain her father would still be alive. She felt her guilt like a rising tide, a cold line creeping up from her belly toward her lungs; it was getting harder to breathe. "Please don't make me feel any worse. Like I'm disappointing him if I don't go along with what you want."

"I'm not trying to make you feel guilty. It's my job to speak for Papa now that he's gone. Leaving you behind, with no one to look after you, terrifies me. Every night when I close my eyes, I worry that I might not wake up. Then what would happen to you?"

"I don't need looking after, Mom. Heaven forbid, if something did happen to you, I would be able to look after myself. Why can't you believe that? I know things were different for you. But that's not my reality. I have other choices."

"Just meet with him. That's all I ask. At least then I'll know I've done what I can." She placed a hand atop Mala's. "You're my good girl. I know you'll do what's right."

"Can I at least think about it for a little longer?"

Her mother squeezed her hand as if preempting her retraction. "Mrs. Mishra called this afternoon. Apparently, there's another girl interested in meeting Sumesh. A girl from a *very* good family, she made sure to emphasize." She paused. "She would like to have our answer by tomorrow."

Mala balked, snatching her hand back. "Tomorrow?"

"I'm sorry to rush you. But from what I hear, Sumesh is a nice boy. It would be a shame for you to miss your chance to at least meet him."

Mala's body started to feel heavy, tired. The length of the day had caught up with her. All she wanted was to be alone with her book, but she knew that her mother wouldn't leave until she was told what she wanted to hear.

"Please, Mala."

"All right," she said, toneless. "I'll meet him." That was all. Then she would refuse him and get back to her life, her work.

Her mother's anxious face relaxed.

"I'm tired," Mala went on. "I'd like to go to sleep now."

"Accha, accha. You've had a long day." Her mother hastily wiped her fingers on a napkin, carried the tray to the door and paused. "I know you have your reservations, beti. But you've made us proud. And you never know, maybe Sumesh will be as good a match for you as your papa was for me. Some things are written." She beamed one last parting smile before closing the door.

Fate, Mala thought. Her mother believed Sumesh Mishra was her destiny, or at least *might* be her destiny, going so far as to compare him with her father. To Mala, however, he was nothing but a stranger, a distraction who had stolen enough of her time these past several days.

She placed the book aside, turned off the light and pulled the covers over her nose. As her eyes widened in the darkness hovering over her, which seemed to extend infinitely, she pictured Ash— his careless hair, his striking eyes, his crooked smile. In her mind, she replayed their conversation, skipping to the best parts, as if fast-forwarding to her favourite songs on a mixed tape. She went over the things she loved the most about him, like the way his eyes crinkled when he smiled, the way he made her laugh. The way he listened to her. She recalled, rather breathlessly, how, for a moment in the office, her world had paused for him. No one else possessed that power, to stop everything with merely a look.

Flooded with these glowing thoughts, the darkness that surrounded Mala no longer seemed so opaque, nor her life so devoid of starlight.

Collisions

Chapter 18

Asha closed her eyes and enjoyed the rush of the breeze as she swayed in the swing. Around her, the frenzy of her classmates filled the public park next to the high school. It was tradition for seniors to gather there and celebrate the end of exams. The smell of cigarettes and pot hit her in pungent waves. She opened her eyes and immediately started smiling, or maybe she had never stopped. Rowan and Willow were on either side of her, swinging and laughing, while their classmates swarmed the playground, unapologetically obnoxious in their occupation of the slide and monkey bars. Asha's head swam from the spiked cranberry juice she had been sipping, but never mind, it was a party. She toasted the sky and knocked back another swig from her Thermos.

Willow taunted Rowan with a joint. He didn't smoke or drink. All he gave her in return was a sneer. When Willow offered the joint to Asha, she passed on having another toke. Now that exams were over, she had promised herself to find a better way of falling asleep at night. That reminded her, she wanted to give Willow the rest of the stash, which was hidden in her backpack. Given how snoopy her mom had been lately, it was a miracle she hadn't found the Baggie already.

"This is getting boring," Rowan said. He hopped off his swing and turned around to face her. "Let me take you somewhere." He reached into his pocket and jangled the keys of his dad's Mustang.

Asha looked him over leisurely. She loved the way he hitched his thumb in his pocket, stood with his hip dropped, like nothing was ever a big deal. *Let me take you somewhere.* She jumped off her swing into his arms. *Yes.*

"Be good," she warned Willow, slipping the Thermos into her backpack.

Then she slung her bag over her shoulder, kissed Rowan with her eyes open and, pulling back an inch from his still-pouting mouth, whispered, "Let's go."

IT WAS A scorching afternoon and the beach was packed. People were stretched out on towels, splashing in the water, playing volleyball. Rowan treated them to Drumsticks, which they ate while sunbathing on the hot sand and dipping their feet in the cool water of the bay. They chatted about how their exams went, what they were looking forward to that summer, how happy they were to finally be done with high school. Asha felt bad that Rowan wasn't going to graduate with his friends from his other school, but he said he didn't care; chances were he wasn't going to graduation anyway, it was too complicated with his parents' divorce.

"I can't wait to get out of here," he said, digging a twig into the sand. In September, he was going to study game development at Sheridan, but Asha didn't want to think about it, or about what might happen to their relationship once he moved away. Not today anyway. Unlike him, she was staying in Ottawa. Going to Carleton and living at home, like her parents wanted her to, the compromise for them paying her tuition. Now she wished she had taken on student debt like everyone else and chosen freedom instead. She took a swig from her Thermos and looked sideways at Rowan. How was she going to cope without him? How was she going to escape?

She was sagging with these gloomy thoughts when Rowan popped to his feet, whipped off his T-shirt and tossed it at her head.

Asha squealed in surprise. By the time she uncovered her flushed face, he was standing in front of her wearing only his boxers.

She traced the length of his body, inching her gaze from his sandy feet to the teasing glint in his dark eyes. "No. Way." She tossed his shirt at the bull's eye of his chest.

"Come on," he tried to persuade her, nudging her with his big toe. She pretended to ignore him, looking in the opposite direction, lifting her nose in the air. He reached down for her hands, helped her up and held her waist the way she loved—sure, solid. She felt lightheaded and wobbly, like all her blood had rushed to her feet. She was tipsier than she thought. She giggled. "It's the last day of high school," he said. He curled his lips into a mischievous grin. "Be a little reckless." He dragged his fingers along the curve of her hips, which sent a feather-like shiver down the back of her legs.

Oh, how she wanted to let it all go. She held his playful gaze and, with a smirk, snatched his T-shirt from his hands. She changed fast, swapping their shirts. Then she kicked off her shorts and chased after him, shrieking as she splashed through the cold water. The bay felt fresh and cleansing. Asha called out to Rowan to wait for her, but he had already started breast-stroking to the centre of the bay. He was treading water comfortably by the time she finally caught up to him, out of breath.

Dog-paddling in place, she panted. "I won't be able to keep this up for long."

He reached through the water and cuffed her legs around his waist. "Better?" he asked, quirking an eyebrow. Asha draped her arms around his neck, intrigued by the slippery texture of his skin. A current ran up her spine.

"Better," she told him, exhilarated, her heart thumping. While they bobbed, the noise from the shoreline seemed far away, like the problems that awaited her there. She hated to think about going home soon. The nerves she couldn't manage to shake from her belly made her shudder. She held Rowan closer—he was her warmth, her antidote to the hungry beast.

"Do you want to go back?" he asked.

Asha shook her head no. If she could stay with him at the centre of the bay forever, that was what she would choose. Without a word, she caught a drop of water off the end of his chin in her mouth and savoured it like nectar. Then she kissed him deeply and forgot about everything else.

Chapter 19

Nandini slumped on Asha's bed with her journal open. After another fruitless search for the letter, she had stumbled upon it in the drawer of Asha's nightstand. Desperate for some insight into her reticent daughter's innermost thoughts, Nandini found herself picking up the notebook, opening it, reading it.

Now she wished she hadn't. When she came across the first entry Asha had written to her birth mother, all the warm blood seemed to seep from Nandini's heart, replaced by shards of cold confirmation of her worst fears.

. . . I'm angry. But not at you . . .

That despite never knowing the woman, Asha would have a natural connection to her birth mother, a closeness Nandini couldn't compete with.

. . . My mom said that she's always worried you would come between us. Well, she was right . . .

And there it was, recorded in the journal, Asha's one-way conversation with her confidante.

. . . they don't listen . . .

> *. . . It's only a matter of time before she starts snooping around my room for the letter. Part of me hopes I catch her in the act . . .*

Nandini swallowed the oversized clot of shame massing in her throat. What was she doing? Prem was right. Betraying Asha's trust again wasn't the answer. How had she allowed herself to become this desperate? The journal felt hot in her hands, like a brand, like sin. Nandini closed it with a slap. She was reaching out to return it to the nightstand drawer when she heard a voice behind her and froze.

"I knew I would catch you."

Her head jerked toward Asha. Her daughter's face was contorted by rage. Nandini was further startled by her bulging red eyes. Why was her hair wet?

Asha dropped her backpack on the floor, bolted over and snatched the journal from Nandini's stiff hands.

"What do you think you're doing?"

"Asha, I—"

"I knew you were snooping around for the letter, but this is so much worse. You have no right!"

Prem hastened into the room, his nervous eyes bouncing between them. "What's going on?"

"Mom's just invasion my privacy." Asha paused, scowling. "I mean, invading."

"Asha, let me ex—"

"No! I'm through with your bullshit excuses!"

"Don't talk to your mother like that."

"Heaven forbid I offend your accomplice!"

"I didn't know about this." Prem flashed Nandini an angry look. "At least not about her reading your journal. I've been trying to get her to stop looking for the letter."

"Like all the times you stood up to her about telling me I'm adopted? Stop fooling yourself! You go along with whatever she wants. I don't trust either of you anymore. And I hate living in this house! I wish you'd never adopted me! I wish I had parents who were honest with me from the beginning instead of being stuck with liars!"

Prem fell silent, his expression like a deep open wound.

"Asha," Nandini said, stern. "Calm down. We can't talk to you when you're like this." In fact, Nandini realized, she had never seen her daughter act like this before, out of control, irrational. Something wasn't right. She stopped to examine her. Asha's eyes were sickly red, and her cheeks were flushed. Earlier she had mispronounced a word. It was almost like she was . . .

Nandini huffed a sharp sigh of frustration as it dawned on her. She could recognize a drunken diatribe, having performed several in her time.

She narrowed her eyes. "Have you been drinking?"

Asha reared back. "No."

"Come here." She curled her finger. Asha didn't budge. Nandini stepped forward. Asha took a step back. Nandini spotted Asha's backpack on the floor. Before her daughter could stop her, she snatched it.

"Don't!" Asha shouted.

Nandini unzipped the backpack and pulled out the Thermos. "What's this?"

Setting her jaw, Asha stared at the floor, unspeaking.

Nandini unscrewed the lid and sniffed. It smelled like fruit punch, but she had to be sure. She took a shallow sip and grimaced. Vodka. From their liquor cabinet, she surmised. Asha had always been such a rule-abiding child that they'd never thought it necessary to keep what little alcohol they had locked away. Clearly, they were going to have to make some changes around the house. She passed the Thermos to Prem, then went back to rooting around in the backpack to see what else her daughter might be hiding. She found the last thing she would have expected.

Nandini held up the Baggie containing a small amount of pot. "This is how you decide to rebel against us?" Her voice was frighteningly controlled. "By coming home drunk and high?"

Asha crossed her arms and jutted her chin out, defiant. "I don't drink."

"Don't lie to us, Asha. We have the proof right here."

"I mean, I don't, normally. It's just this stupid tradition for seniors. Everybody goes to the park off school grounds and gets drunk. Kind of like giving the finger to the administration. It was a one-time thing. I didn't want to be left out."

Nandini knew about the tradition; she had participated in it herself as a teen. Although it was reckless and immature, she could excuse it, if only once. "Well then, how do you explain the pot? And don't even think about telling us you're holding it for a friend."

Asha's features softened. "It's not what you think," she muttered, tucking her chin. "I wasn't even going to smoke the rest. I'm stopping."

"How did you ever start?" Nandini asked, appalled. "You know we don't approve of this kind of behaviour. I can't even begin to understand what's gotten into you lately." She shook her head, disillusioned.

Asha's rigid body lost its hard line. She uncrossed her arms, letting them hang limp at her sides. Then she dragged her heels over to her desk and flopped into her chair, as if giving in to a weight she could no longer resist. Her sickly red eyes began to shine. She pressed her trembling lips together, like she was gathering her broken voice.

Nandini's disdain dissolved as she watched her daughter struggle on the verge of tears. "Asha?"

"I . . ." she stammered. "I can't sleep."

"What do you mean you can't sleep?"

Asha held her head and the dam broke. "I try. But I can't. Not since I found out about the adoption. Most nights, I just stare at the ceiling until I'm tired enough to drop off. It's like there's too much on my mind. I can't stop thinking about everything, especially when I'm alone. It all comes up." She bit her bottom lip. "There's so much tension in the house. I feel like I'm always walking on eggshells. I'm so anxious. On top of that, I had finals to study for. But I've been too exhausted to concentrate. I was terrified about failing and not graduating on time. The pot helped me relax and get some sleep. But I never planned on using it any longer than I had to. I just needed to get through exams. After that, I promised myself I would stop." She paused, looking incredibly sad. "I don't expect you to believe me, but that's the truth. I was desperate. I didn't know what else to do."

"Why didn't you come to us?" Prem asked.

Asha's chin quivered. "Because nothing's the same between us anymore." She folded her hands into a pillow, lowered her forehead and finally burst into tears.

The awful sound of their daughter's weeping overtook the room. Nandini stared at Prem, bewildered, wondering how their close little family could have split into so many jagged, ill-fitting pieces.

Chapter 20

Nandini was pouring herself a large glass of pinot noir when her cellphone chimed. She set down the bottle to see who was calling her. Prem, like she expected. He had left half an hour ago, needing to clear his head with a drive after they settled Asha down for the night, an old habit of his from back when they were battling through the war of infertility treatments. He liked cruising on Highway 50 out to Wakefield, parking alongside the mighty Gatineau and losing himself in the steady course of the river. During the summer, he might catch some of the local kids jumping off the iconic, red covered bridge. Before they had Asha, he had daydreamed of having a child brave enough to take the leap that he never could. Two years ago, on Asha's sixteenth birthday, they had brought her there. She had jumped without a second thought, freefalling without a care. Nandini felt a stitch in her chest. Such a different daughter than the one who broke down a short while ago.

She held her wine in one hand and with the other raised the phone to her ear. "How was the drive?" she asked. "Is the ice cream shop still open?"

"Hello, madame," said a man with a strong French-Canadian accent. "My name is Constable Giroux. I'm with the SQ." The Sûreté du Québec. The provincial police.

Nandini slowly lowered her untouched glass of wine onto the counter. "Why are you calling me from my husband's phone?" she asked, unnaturally calm.

"Monsieur Prem Shukla is your husband, madame?" The constable mispronounced their surname. Normally, she would have corrected him—*shook*, like the past tense of *shake*, not *shuck* as in shucking an oyster.

"Yes."

"Madame, your husband has been in an accident." Nandini would reflect on this moment—when her knees began to shake and she thought this was what it must feel like to have them give out—specifically about how wrong she had been, because it was only later, as she watched Prem being pulled from their deer-impaled car, unconscious, and put onto a stretcher, that terror turned her joints to water and she fell.

"Is he okay?"

"The damage to his vehicle was severe. He has lost consciousness, madame."

"But he's alive?"

"Oui."

"Where are you?" She would find out the rest when she got there.

"Along Autoroute 50. But, madame, it would be better for you to meet us at the hospital in Wakefield."

"Will you be there for much longer?"

"Oui, madame. We have not been able to remove him from the vehicle yet."

Nandini gripped the counter. "I'll be there soon."

Chapter 21

Asha waded through a pool of uneasy dreams. A clatter wakened her. She batted her eyes open to the bright light of her room. She squinted, groggy. "What's going on?" she asked her mom, who was rifling through a pile of clothes on the dresser.

Her mom tossed a pair of jeans and a top onto the end of the bed. "Get dressed. We have to go."

"Where? What's going on?" Asha's eyes adjusted to the light and she saw the look of horror on her mom's face.

"It's your dad," her mom said, wooden. "He went for a drive. He's been in an accident."

Asha's daze cleared in an instant. She sat upright, alert and filled with dread. "Is he okay?"

Her mom's chest heaved. "I don't know. The police officer said he's unconscious."

Despite the need to rush, neither of them moved as the gravity of the situation seeped into their marrow. They stared at each other, pale, and as they did, Asha was sure the same terrible thought was whispering inside both of their heads. *If something happened to him, what would become of them?*

Chapter 22

Asha waited beside her dad's hospital bed on the edge of her seat, watching the heart monitor with intensity. The emergency call button was poised in her hand, ready to summon help at the slightest change in her dad's vitals.

His right arm was broken. Several of his ribs too. His pelvis was badly bruised but thankfully not fractured. His head was covered in a turban of bandages.

He still hadn't woken from the coma. The impact of the crash had caused swelling in his brain. The doctor said once the swelling went down, he might wake up. He *might*.

Asha's breathing became beleaguered, and her vision blurred, but she kept her back rigid and her eyes fiercely pointed at the monitor. She counted along with the audible beat of her dad's heart, beeped by the machine, and blinked away the tears she had no sympathy for.

No sympathy. Not for her. If it weren't for the awful things she had said, her dad wouldn't have needed to clear his head in the first place. He would still be at home, in his own bed, safe and unharmed.

A monster of grief tried to scratch its way out through her skin. It wanted her to scream, to lose it. But she had as much right to emotion as she did sympathy. The time of her coddling was over, like her childhood and its belief that her family was untouchable.

That was how good her parents were at being parents. The home they built her was so stable she had never felt its foundation quake, not like this, not until now. The adoption secret had shaken her, but she'd had the freedom to be shaken because she never doubted the ground beneath her feet or the integrity of the walls that kept her safe. As she peered at her dad from the corner of her eye, only able to stomach the damage she had caused a sliver at a time, Asha knew that even if their house crumbled to dust, it wouldn't matter because her mom and dad were her true shelter.

And she had pushed them away. Punished them. Stressed them out with her silly problems and teenage acting out. Well, no more. She wasn't going to make as much as an unpleasant sound from now on. She would be quiet and good and help her dad get better again. Covering her eyes, she reached out with everything in her and meekly asked that he be saved.

If he didn't wake from the coma, if he had to live out the rest of his life in a vegetative state or, worse—if he died—Asha would never forgive herself.

Her mom entered the room with crossed arms, hugging herself for warmth. "How are you holding up?" she asked.

Asha commanded herself to give her mom her best resilient smile. "I'm good. Keeping an eye on his vitals. Everything's looking stable."

Her mom patted her shoulder. "That's what the monitors are for, Asha. Come on, let's get you home."

Asha dropped her fake smile. "I want to stay with Dad."

"They only let one family member stay overnight. I'm going to split the watch with Dadi."

"Please, Mom, don't send me home."

"Dada's going to stay at our place tonight. You won't be alone."

"I want to be here when he wakes up."

"I promise to call you the second he does."

A question throbbed in her throat. "What if something happens to him while I'm away?"

"Nothing's going to happen."

"You can't know that."

"He's gone from critical to stable. That's a good sign. But there's no telling when he'll wake up. It could be in an hour or a couple of days from now."

Or never, Asha thought, bleak.

The sight of her mom's quivering chin made Asha's chin quiver too. A stray tear traced her mom's cheek and dropped onto Asha's shoulder with a faint tap. She felt like breaking down but ordered herself to keep calm until she was alone in her bedroom, where she could yield to the sadness that was slowly drowning her from the inside.

"Please stop crying, Mom. I'll do whatever you want. Just please don't get upset."

Her mom reached for a tissue and dried her eyes. "Thanks, sweetie. For not fighting me on this." She opened her arms for a hug.

Asha collapsed into her mom's embrace and swore to any unseen powers that she wouldn't fight or cause trouble or be anything but good, so please, please, open her dad's eyes and wake them all from this nightmare.

Between holidays

Chapter 23

Mala sat at her desk in the nearly deserted Ph.D. office, hunched over a pile of quizzes. It was the Friday before Thanksgiving and most people had taken the day off. Even the departmental seminar was cancelled. She heard Ash rustling papers at his desk. Apparently, they were the only ones who would rather hang around the campus than go home.

At least marking diverted her attention away from thinking about the upcoming holiday, yet another day of family togetherness that jutted from the calendar like a rusted nail. Whenever Mala stopped for long enough to think about pumpkin pie and stuffing, all she saw in her mind was a haunting image of her father's empty chair at their dining table, all she felt was the wounded morphology of her family, a hand missing a thumb. But the holiday wasn't the only matter preoccupying her.

"Working hard?" Ash asked. His voice drew her out of her ruminating. She hadn't even heard him come over.

She swivelled her chair around and offered him a tired grin. He leaned against the opening of her cubicle with his hands in his pockets. Today he wore a cream-coloured cable-knit sweater and khakis.

"Just marking quizzes," she said.

He smirked, widening his eyes. *"Thrilling."*

"Endlessly. So far, the highlight's been catching a couple of cheaters. They had the exact same answers, right down to the spelling mistakes."

"Lazy on multiple levels." He shook his head. "Have a little finesse, people."

"Mmm." She pursed her lips. "How about you? How's your work going?"

"My brain's already on vacation." He sighed, glancing over his shoulder out the window. "The sun's been calling my name all day. Want to join me for a quick stroll? That is, if you can bear to tear yourself away from the excitement for a whole ten minutes."

"You're always *hassling* me," she teased with a roll of her eyes. Then she rose and followed him out of the office.

The air was as sharp and bright as the foliage that clung to the branches and littered the slowly freezing ground. The frothy clouds dotting the sky were reminiscent of the toppings on fancy coffees. For a while, they walked in silence next to the rush of the river. As they followed the path, Mala kicked at leaves and listened to the pleasing sound of them crackling underfoot.

She regarded him sidelong. In the office, he had seemed lighthearted enough, if not a little tired. Now, he appeared burdened with thought, his shoulders hunched, his eyes low and dim.

"Are you okay?" she asked. "You seem down."

He stooped over, picked up an oak leaf and twirled it between his fingers. "I'm not looking forward to Thanksgiving, I guess."

"Why not?"

"Laine and I are hosting this year." He tossed the leaf aside. "Our families are coming down from Toronto. We've never done it before. There's lots to plan. I guess I'm just hoping it goes well."

"*Hosting.* That's a big deal. Why bother if you're so nervous about it?"

He gave her an unreadable look. "Call it a truce," he said. He glanced away. "What about you? What are your plans for turkey day?"

She kicked an acorn into the grass. "No plans."

"But it's the best holiday of the year."

"I'm a vegetarian."

"It's not about the—" He stopped mid-sentence, regret wrenching his features. "Mala, I'm such an idiot."

She walked a few paces with a bruise in her heart. "Don't worry about it."

His voice was full of remorse. "It's the first Thanksgiving without your dad and I should've remembered. I've been so preoccupied with my own shit." He shook his head, disappointed in himself. "I'm sorry."

"Stop beating yourself up."

He peeked at her profile, trying to read her mood. Finally mustering the courage, he asked, "How are you feeling about it? The holiday, I mean."

The base of her throat squeezed. "Thanksgiving used to be our favourite. Somehow that makes it worse." The bruise in her heart felt like it was being pressed by a thumb.

They continued their quiet stroll. Mala's secret weighed upon her. Now would be the time to make good on her promise. Bending forward, she grabbed a dried leaf, crumbled its desiccated body to pieces, then littered the ground with a rain of rusted confetti.

"What I told you before wasn't entirely true. I do have plans this weekend. Only not for Thanksgiving." She wavered. "Remember that introduction I told you about the other day?"

"What about it?"

She stepped over a crack in the asphalt. "It's happening this Sunday."

Out of the corner of her eye, she could see his shock bloom. "Are you serious?"

"Unfortunately."

"I thought you were going to get out of it."

"I tried."

"Okay," he said, blinking quickly. "So, then what?"

Mala set her gaze far along the path. "Then nothing. I'm only going to please my mom. Believe me, I have no intention of impressing the Mishras."

"Good. I mean, good for you, Mala," he was swift to add. "For finding a way to respect your mom's wishes while also standing your ground." He hesitated. "So it's not like you're getting engaged or anything?" The lightness of his voice gave something away.

"Not a chance." She kicked at another acorn. Even though she considered the outcome of the introduction predetermined, the looming obligation kept taking up space in her mind, kept draining energy she would rather spend on her work. While she was dreading the meeting, she also couldn't wait to put it behind her.

"Well," he said, studying her frown again, "since we're both dreading the weekend, I think we've earned a longer break, don't you?"

She narrowed her eyes at him. "What do you have in mind?"

He stopped and pointed his nose at the sky. "You know what I don't do enough anymore?"

She scanned the sky too, wondering what he was looking at. "What's that?"

He lowered his chin and grinned. "Stare at the clouds. I bet you don't either."

She wasn't expecting that. Her chilled cheeks slowly lifted. "You're right." She appreciated what he was trying to do. The least she could do in return was play along.

They strayed from the path and stretched out on a welcoming patch of grass. Mala leaned back on her hands, the ground uneven beneath her palms. The midday sun beamed down with summer-like vigour. She closed her eyes and raised her chin, wishing she could dilate her pores like pupils in the dark and soak up even more of its warmth. The wind rustled through the leaves, a whisper like the sea haunting the treetops. She hadn't felt so at ease in days.

"I used to do this for hours when I was a kid," Ash said.

She opened her eyes to the bright sky. The world felt still, apart from the gentle coast of the clouds overhead.

"What do you see?" he asked.

She chose a downy cluster that was gliding past, illuminated by a fine tracing of golden sun.

"A face" she said, lit with sudden wonder. "It's smiling."

Mala followed the path of the clouds, thinking of her father. She pictured his glimmering soul watching over her. She wondered if he could read her earnest heart and knew its furtive wish. If he, above all others, understood that Sumesh Mishra couldn't be her destiny because her destiny was right beside her, trying so sweetly to ease her troubles.

Maybe it's a sign, she dared to whisper to herself, luminous as the sky above. Perhaps the face in the clouds was telling her to survive the weekend because afterward the bad weather would move on, leaving in its wake the promise of fairer days thereafter.

Chapter 24

Mala frowned at the mass of unmarked quizzes in front of her. She had intended on completing them over the long weekend, but meeting the Mishras thwarted her plans.

After Sunday, she assumed the matchmaking ordeal was finished. Based on the glacial indifference she had shown Sumesh, she was confident he would be the first to refuse pursuing a relationship, bringing the failed introduction to an end.

On Monday morning, she discovered differently.

The telephone rang during breakfast.

"Let the machine take care of it," she told her mother, her mouth full of aloo tikki slathered in tamarind sauce.

"It might be the man I've hired to clean the eavestroughs," her mother replied. "Ek minute."

The caller wasn't the handyman. It was Mrs. Mishra. Mala had met people like her before, people who wore masks of politeness to disguise their agendas. Although they had spoken only briefly, Mala had felt the cold woman's critical eye scanning her, evaluating her worth. Mala couldn't imagine calling her Auntie, let alone Mother.

While she spooned yogurt over her potato cutlets, Mala imagined that the clever woman was partway through telling her mother a backhanded excuse. *Your daughter is very lovely, but . . .* A smile washed over Mala's face at the thought of it.

When her mother returned to the kitchen, Mala was surprised by her hopeful air.

"I have good news," she said. And Mala shivered as though touched by a breath of February.

Now, as she rubbed her forehead, Mala thought, Everything is going to be fine. I will get myself out of this. I have to.

Gripping her red pen, she focused on the answer key. You know your life's not quite right, she told herself, when you take refuge in a pile of marking.

She sank into a trance-like rhythm. Every red scratch of her pen drew her further away from her vague future. Just as she finished tallying the grade of one quiz—a meagre fifteen out of twenty—she heard a familiar brush of heels in the hallway outside the TA office.

Looking up, she found Ash standing at the threshold, holding two cups of coffee. He wore a grey cardigan, black corduroys and a white T-shirt.

"You're becoming a little predictable," she said. She touched her hair, self-conscious. That morning, she had thrown on an oversized sweatshirt and jeans and tied her hair back in a hasty ponytail. Her worrying left no energy for contacts or makeup. "I was supposed to get the coffees this time, remember?"

He entered the office and set down the cups. "I know. But you weren't around when I bought them. How convenient."

Mala smiled, her first honest smile in days. "Thank you." She drew her cup closer. "How was Thanksgiving? Did hosting turn out better than you expected?"

He took a seat, his level expression faltering, if only for a moment. "It was fine," he said, toneless. Then he gave the pile in front of her a puzzled look. "You're still marking those quizzes?"

Mala blinked at the stack, disheartened. "I meant to finish them over the weekend." Instead, she spent the extra day off reeling. Trying to think of ways to stop what should have only been an introduction from becoming anything more.

"Mala?"

She looked up. His forehead was scrunched with concern.

"Is everything okay?"

She fixed her eyes on the quizzes again. "Not really."

After a short pause, he asked, tentative, "How did Sunday go?"

Mala considered, still baffled by how things were playing out. "It was as boring as I thought it would be. I made sure to come across as uninterested as possible. I figured no self-respecting man would think twice about a woman who was actively rejecting him."

"And instead?"

Mala swallowed with effort. "He wants us to get to know each other," she said, disbelieving. When her mother had told her, in that moment Mala saw Jane Eyre locked in the red room. Then she saw the walls of her own prison rising from the kitchen floor, threatening to seal her in, with her mother and the Mishras guarding the door.

"You told him no, right?"

"It's not that simple. If he wasn't interested, I could've blamed him for things not working out. That's what I was hoping for. Then I planned on persuading my mom to stop all this until after I graduate, like we originally agreed. Not that it matters now."

He watched her warily. "What are you going to do?"

If indifference hadn't worked, Mala was sure a delay would encourage Sumesh Mishra to reconsider his interest in her. "I'm going to tell my mom I'm too preoccupied with school to focus on anything else right now."

He lifted his eyebrows. "And you think that'll work?"

Mala gnawed her lower lip. "I don't know. I think so. I'll tell her I have to put all my energy into my conference presentation. That if I seem unprepared, I'll look bad in front of my professors. With any luck, she'll be convinced and pass the message on to the Mishras. I can't imagine they'll wait around for me." Mala knew Mrs. Mishra, in particular, wouldn't like to be kept waiting, especially with other girls in line to meet Sumesh. Mala was hopeful this lack of eagerness on her part would provide the Mishras with the extra nudge they needed to carry on with their search for the perfect bride elsewhere.

A deep scowl settled into the corners of his mouth. "I'm frustrated you have to deal with this. Like you said the other day, all you want to do is focus on your work." He shook his head, irritated. "I haven't even had the chance to ask you how Thanksgiving was without your dad yet."

Mala's insides turned to liquid for a second, then she commanded them into stone. "I miss him more than ever." *None of this would be happening if he were alive.*

Ash exhaled. "Why does everything have to be so complicated? Why is it always one fire after another?"

Mala regarded him, wondering what unruly fires of his own he was trying to control.

Her body felt saturated with exhaustion. "All I want to do is finish my marking. Then I'll probably go home. I didn't get much sleep over the weekend. I think it's catching up with me."

Without a word, he reached across the desk, grabbed about half the quizzes and took a pen out of his pocket. "Is blue ink all right, Professor Sharma?"

"I wasn't fishing for help, honestly."

Leaning forward with his elbows bent to either side, he drew the answer key between them and got started.

She smiled at him softly. "Thank you."

They worked in easy silence. From time to time, Mala glanced at his hands, noting the rose undertone of his skin, the ginger hairs over his knuckles, the clusters of freckles like pointillism. In them she saw shapes—a sickle moon, a teardrop, a sunburst. A faint sadness overshadowed her. She knew that with every marked quiz their time together was coming to an end, and soon she would have to go back to a life she didn't want to go back to any longer.

Chapter 25

The cramped pub was decorated with clusters of balloons and twists of streamers in orange and black. "Thriller" blared over the speakers, and the floor was littered with candy wrappers. Around them, as expected, was a mundane abundance of ghosts in white sheets, witches with pointy hats and vampires gnashing plastic monster teeth.

Not that Ash could claim his costume was any better. Frankenstein's monster, the same character he dressed as every year. What could be simpler than shoving a cushion between your shoulders and hiding behind a mask from the dollar store?

"We kind of match," he said to Mala. Her hair was tucked under a bright red clown wig that reminded him of Ronald McDonald. An oversized pair of neon-green novelty glasses overwhelmed her face. Completing the ensemble was her lab coat. A mad scientist, he thought with a grin.

"I guess we do. Although I'm not sure this is the look Shelley had in mind for Victor Frankenstein." She smiled, fluffing her wig.

He laughed. "It's good to see you out enjoying yourself." She had seemed so unhappy lately.

"You too."

He looked at her, confused. "What do you mean?"

"I don't know." She shrugged. "You seem more preoccupied than usual, I guess."

"Oh." He blinked, surprised. Maybe he hadn't been masking his worries as well as he thought. "Well," he went on, "my supervisor wanted our lab to spend some family time together, so I decided to show my face for a bit. How about you? What had the power to drag you away from the *thrills* of marking?" He smirked.

"I wanted to blow off a little steam. And, to be honest, I didn't feel like being home alone. My mom's at temple tonight. She's helping with Diwali preparations. It's next week."

"She went out again?"

Mala nodded, smiling. "I'm proud of her. I know it isn't easy. Part of her still feels guilty about socializing, but she's doing it. I figured I should at least try. But really, I think we were both looking for reasons to get out of the house. My dad loved Halloween. He never got over the novelty of people dressing up and going door to door. The thought of passing out candy without him was too hard to face this year. It's the small things."

Ash wished he had more to offer her than the useless sympathetic grin on his face, something substantial that would not only ease her heartache but also change her circumstances. He wondered where things stood with her mom and the introduction business and was about to ask when he was interrupted by the high-pitched screech of a microphone. Turning toward the sound with pinched lips, he saw a woman dressed as a belly dancer standing on a chair. She proceeded to announce that karaoke was about to start and shimmied her coin scarf in anticipation to the whooping delight of the horde.

He groaned. "I think I'm done with this. Are you going to hang around for a while?"

She pulled off her wig and glasses. "I've had my fun." She tousled her hair loose. "I'll walk out with you."

They entered the fresh autumn night and cut through a group of people who were smoking in the glow of the building. He stuffed his hands into his pockets and raised his shoulders instinctively. Off to the right, the river glimmered in the silvery moonlight.

He checked his watch and moaned. "I think I just missed my bus."

"When's the next one?"

"Twenty minutes."

"Same here."

"I really don't feel like going back inside."

She looked in the direction of the river. "It's nice out. Why don't we sit by the water while we wait?"

He agreed. They crossed the parking lot and made their way to the riverside.

"The sky's so clear tonight," he said, lifting his gaze. He peered at the pinpricks of light scattered across the inky sky, and the yellow bow of a moon. They let a few quiet moments slip away, stilled by the tranquil sound of water trickling over rocks.

"Do you know any of the constellations?" she asked.

"Only the basic ones." He pointed. "There's the Little Dipper."

"And Orion's Belt."

"And the Big Dipper."

"In Hindi it's called Saptarshi."

"What does it mean?"

"Each star represents one of the Seven Sages. My dad told me they're the guardians of divine law."

"Much more impressive than a giant ladle. Do you know any others?"

"I used to," she said, wistful. "But that's the only one I remember." Her chin sank to her chest. She stared at the river, reflective.

"Mala?" he asked. "Is everything okay?"

She slowly shook her head.

"What's wrong?"

She pressed her lips together. A few tense moments passed. "It didn't work," she muttered.

He wasn't sure what she was talking about. "What didn't work?"

As he waited for her to reply, he felt like Mala wasn't there with him at all, her body was so still, her expression so expressionless.

"Sumesh doesn't mind waiting," she said at last. "He's busy with med school too, apparently. He still wants us to get to know each other. So much so, he's decided not to meet anyone else."

While Ash absorbed the news, a prickle crept up his neck. "Well, he sounds a bit too eager, if you ask me." His mouth felt drier than normal. He wriggled his tongue, then swallowed a slimy trail of saliva. "What now?"

She filled and emptied her lungs. "I think I'll have to see him at least once more."

Ash was flustered—exasperated. He could feel the red of his cheeks. "This is ridiculous. You can't let this go on, Mala. Tell your mom you're not interested in him. Have that difficult conversation now. Stop this before it goes any further." Even he was surprised by the force of his tone.

Covered by the night, she turned and examined him without a hint of shyness. "I can see you feel strongly about it."

His heart hammered against his breastbone. "I guess I do."

She took a step forward and probed deeply into his eyes. "Why?"

He fidgeted. "What do you mean, why? You're my friend, Mala. You clearly don't want to go through with this. I hate seeing you go through it too. I understand how important it is that you respect your mom's wishes. But it's just as important that you respect your-self. It's *your* life. You should do what you want to do."

She didn't respond, only held him with a stare he couldn't deci-pher, that told him nothing about whether he had overstepped his boundaries.

Just as he was about to fumble his way through an awkward apology, she took another step forward. "What I want to do?" she said, her steady gaze shifting between his startled eyes.

Ash felt like he was barely breathing. He was about to reiterate that yes, it was her life, her decision and . . .

Then she kissed him.

Overhead, a shooting star traced the night sky, its tail an arc of light that dazzled for an instant before disappearing into the blackness.

A promise made

Chapter 26

Despite the cups of coffee Asha guzzled when she got home from the hospital to keep herself awake, she nodded off around three o'clock, unable to hold back the boulder of exhaustion any longer.

Her cellphone rang a couple of hours later. When Asha asked her mom if everything was all right, she didn't answer right away.

"He's awake," she said eventually. Asha detected something off about her mom's voice. *Wasn't that great news? Where were the quivers of joy? The cracks of relief?*

"That's good, isn't it?"

"He has a bad concussion, Asha." Her mom's voice was gentle. "He doesn't remember the accident."

Asha jumped out of bed. "I'll wake up Dada. We'll be there in half an hour."

"Asha, I don't think that's a good idea, sweetie. He's in a delicate state. The doctor says he needs rest. He's . . . very confused."

Asha compressed her trembling lips.

"Maybe around dinnertime. You could come by for a quick visit then?"

"Mm-hmm," Asha mumbled. She couldn't speak. Her throat was filling with tears.

"At least he's conscious. If he gets enough rest, his memory might come back."

Might. There was that word again. If it was possible that he might get his memory back, it was possible that he might not. That he might bear the scars of the accident for the rest of his life. Maybe life's real intention was to bring him back to them in a damaged state, as a punishment for Asha, so she would always remember the cost of taking him for granted.

They said their goodbyes and Asha hung up. She checked her messages. Rowan still hadn't replied. What was going on with him? she wondered. Where was he?

She paced and called him again. Her call went to voicemail. She remembered the early hour and left him another message updating him on her dad's condition and asking him to call her as soon as possible. She really needed to talk to him.

Then she collapsed on the edge of her bed, missing Willow. Her parents wanted her to keep her distance for a while, since finding out it was Willow who had supplied her with the pot. That much, at least, they had settled after their fight, agreeing to talk about the rest when everyone was calmer.

Asha stared at the good night text Willow had sent last night.

Sweet dreams, Athena. No more teachers, no more books! xo

Asha frowned at the message, thrown by how much had happened in less than a day. The last time they saw each other, they were celebrating the end of the school year at the park. Willow didn't even know about her dad yet. Asha wanted to keep the promise she had made to her parents, especially now that she felt like her every action was being weighed. But she had to at least tell Willow about the accident.

She typed quickly and tapped send. A minute later, her cellphone started ringing. It was Willow.

Asha shoved her phone into the drawer of her nightstand before the answer button tempted her any more. If she was going to talk to Willow, she would have to ask her parents for permission first.

Chapter 27

The lights in the hospital room were dim. Asha entered and saw her dad holding the side of his bandaged head, his face strained with pain. She passed her mom, who was on her way out. They paused, standing shoulder to shoulder, and her mom placed a hand over Asha's heart, wordlessly communicating that it was time to steel herself for what was coming.

Asha approached her dad's bedside, each step making barely a sound.

"Hi, Dad," she said in a low voice.

Despite her whisper, he was startled by her presence. He stared at her with a complete and utter lack of recognition for a few very long seconds, his dilated pupils like a pair of black holes—she couldn't tell what was on the other side of them. The blood clots that stained the whites of his eyes made her whole body wince. She wondered if his concussed brain looked the same.

"Asha?" His arm floated down to his side.

"Should I get the nurse?"

"No." He made the mistake of shaking his head. She hated seeing him like this, a statue, frozen in pain. When the spell passed, he apologized, explaining how his migraine hadn't lessened any. The slightest movement or sound or flicker of light and it lashed out in paralyzing jabs.

Asha fidgeted. She wanted to sit beside him in bed, stroke his hand, but he seemed so fragile that she just stood there, looming, instead.

"Can you sit down?" he asked. "It . . . hurts to look up."

"Of course." She lowered herself onto the chair at his bedside, feeling clumsy and cursed. Even when she did nothing, somehow she still managed to cause harm. "Sorry."

The silence made Asha more aware of the ruckus rattling inside of her. Her mom had warned her not to burden him with questions, but questions were all she could think of. Was he in pain? Did he remember anything about the accident? Was he angry with her?

"I don't want you to . . ." He exhaled forcefully, like speaking was hard labour. "See me like this."

"Don't worry about it, Dad. Just rest."

"I don't remember."

"Nothing at all?"

"It was dark." He squinted, as if trying to see through his cloudy memory. "I don't know."

Then he made a face like he was supressing a cough. He pointed at the bowl on the side table. Asha passed it to him and he threw up. When the fit was over, she cleaned away the mess in the washroom and rejoined him. He looked more exhausted than before— blanched, haggard. His eyes were closed. He was trying to catch his breath.

A groan rumbled at the back of his throat and Asha worried he might vomit again.

He opened his eyes lazily and asked for some ice water. As she filled a plastic cup from the jug at his bedside, the apology she had been reciting since the night before came to the front of her mind. She handed him the cup. He raised an unsteady hand to his chapped lips and took a sip. "Thanks, kid." He forced a weak grin.

Hearing her nickname made her weak with remorse. She was about to ramble a messy apology when he threw up the few sips of water he had swallowed. He looked down at himself in horror and started to cry.

"I wanted to see the bridge."

"The covered bridge?"

"I wanted to remember good times." His breathing grew ragged. "Didn't get there. Can't get there now."

"We'll go when you're feeling better."

He clenched his eyes, cringing in pain. "It hurts so . . ." He was panting, more upset by the second.

Her heart tilted with sorrow. "Oh, Dad." Her voice quavered. She felt something wet on her chest. Her grief was so great she hadn't realized it had started overflowing and dripping from her chin. "Please, calm down." His body shook and shook. "Hang on," she told him, rising to her feet. "I'll get Mom."

Somehow her feverish legs carried her into the hall and the startling light.

ONCE HER DAD was stable, her mom found her in the hallway, in the same spot, leaning with her back against the wall, staring at nothing. Her mom told her not to blame herself. Reiterated that everything her dad was experiencing was typical for the brain trauma he had suffered. Her next visit would be better, and the one after better still, until one day they wouldn't even realize it but he would be back to himself again. That was the goal they needed to focus on. Hope was their torchlight. After this quick pep talk, she sent Asha home with her grandfather.

None of the comfort her mom had tried to impart was able to reach Asha. On the drive home, as droplets of rain tapped against the windshield, she wrestled with the haunting images that kept rising in her head, of her dad's bludgeoned vision, slowed speech, body so frail it couldn't hold a sip of water, mind so cracked it misplaced memories. Her worries ran rampant: that her mom secretly blamed her, that their family would never be the same, that her punishment for taking her parents for granted was losing them both. If her dad didn't recover, Asha knew that her mom would end up resenting her eventually, despite the understanding she had shown tonight.

By the time they got home, the drizzle had swollen to a downpour, falling in sheets, streaming like a shower. Asha waited for her grandfather to close the guest room door, then she walked out onto the back deck, lifted her face toward the black clouds and let the rain weep all over her, as she wept with the rain.

Chapter 28

For the first week of her dad's hospital stay, Asha and her mom got into the habit of meeting her grandparents there, taking turns to sit with him while he mostly slept. They brought books, embroidery, newspapers and crossword puzzles to occupy themselves. Asha lost herself in *Jane Eyre*, which she had borrowed from the library before her dad's accident, a paperback with a tear in the front cover, thinking there could be no world more different from hers than mid-1800s northern England. The book she was reading in the waiting room, on the Thursday before prom, when her mom sat beside her and patted her knee.

"Can we talk for a minute?" she asked.

Asha sat up straighter and closed the book over her thumb. "Is everything okay?"

"Your dad's fine. I wanted to talk about you. About prom." Now that her dad was stable, Asha had been expecting this conversation. That her mom would tell her she wasn't allowed to go, not after her rule-breaking and their fight, still unresolved. None of which Asha could disagree with. "I want you to go," her mom said and smiled.

Asha blinked, astonished. "You do?"

Her mom nodded. "We had a long talk with your dad's doctor. He's going to stay at the hospital for a bit longer, and then they're going to transfer him to a rehab centre."

"What does that have to do with prom?"

"Your dad's recovery is going to be a long road. It's going to disrupt our lives. So we have to maintain what normalcy we can. You've earned this time with your friends. It isn't something you should let pass you by." She squeezed Asha's forearm and kept her hand there. "You shouldn't feel guilty about going either. Your dad wants you to. He only wishes he could drive you and Rowan himself."

Asha felt all caught up inside. Even after everything she had put him through, her dad still wanted to be her chariot.

"But we have one condition," her mom continued. "We want you to stay away from Willow."

"I have, Mom. I promise. I've only texted her a couple of times. I haven't even spoken to her, not since you told me not to. But she's going to prom and after-grad. How am I supposed to avoid her?"

"As much as you can, then."

"But she's my best friend."

"I know, Asha. And you know we love Willow. She's like a part of our family. Which makes what she did so hard to forgive."

"It isn't her fault, Mom. She didn't force me."

"But she encouraged it. Your dad and I want you to distance yourself from her for now, not forever. Just until we get a handle on your situation. Okay? Can I trust you?"

Asha frowned at the book in her lap, tracing the tear in the cover with her thumb. "To be honest, I don't even want to go anymore."

"Why not?"

Asha gnawed the corner of her mouth. She was desperate to talk to her mom about Rowan and the doubts she was having because of his recent disappearing act. In the past week, she hadn't even seen or spoken to him, only gotten a couple of short texts. She peered at her mom sideways. But she had promised not to add to her mom's worries, so she kept quiet.

"If I can't hang out with Willow, I'd rather stay at the hospital with you and Dad. Please, Mom."

Her mom pressed on. "The other thing I wanted to mention is the library."

Asha was supposed to start her summer job next week. "I've already told Agnes I have to quit because I'll be looking after Dad." Helping him recover was how she was going to make up for the trouble she had caused. She had been waiting for this chance to ease her conscience. Maybe then she would be able to sleep again.

"Well, you're going to have to call her back and hope she hasn't given the position to someone else."

"Mom—"

"You were looking forward to it, weren't you?"

Asha nodded. But that was before the accident, when all she wanted to do was to get away from them. Now all she wanted was to keep an eye on her dad and make sure he never slipped away from them again.

"Good." Her mom nodded to herself. "Routine. That's how we're going to get through this. We'll keep living our lives, so your dad has something to ease back into when he's feeling better. Right?"

No complaining, she had promised. Not so much as an unpleasant sound. Asha gave her mom a brave smile. "Right," she echoed.

BACK AT HOME, Asha stretched out on her bed with her journal. For a second, she hesitated.

I feel like I'm betraying my mom by writing you. But then, she betrayed me by violating my privacy, so maybe this makes us even.

I feel like I'm losing everyone. I'm forbidden to talk to Willow. My dad's in the hospital. I don't want to add to my mom's stress. Rowan's never been harder to find . . .

It's so confusing. Before my dad's accident, things were getting serious between us. He was so understanding about my adoption. I felt closer to him than ever. Which was what I wanted to talk to my mom about today, but I couldn't. The thing is, we've decided to be together on prom night. He's been with another girl, his ex. But I haven't yet. I wanted it to be Rowan.

Now I'm not sure. The night of my dad's accident, he didn't answer any of my calls or messages. He said his phone died and he didn't have a charger at his mom's place, where he slept that night, apparently.

Maybe all of this is too much for him. First my adoption, now my dad's accident. Or maybe my worst fears are coming true and he wants to break up now that university is only a couple of months away.

Listen to me. I sound so paranoid. I'm probably overreacting because I'm stressed and exhausted.

And lonely. I miss Willow. How does my mom expect me to avoid her at prom and after-grad? She's overreacting, the way she did about the letter, and we know how that turned out. Can you feel guilty about something and mad at someone at the same time? My mom says I broke her trust by doing pot and I know that's true, but she broke my trust too when she read my journal. Why am I the only one being punished? I don't suppose I'll get any justice now. That issue has conveniently slipped off the table along with everything else.

Of course, none of this will matter if my dad's condition doesn't improve. My mom says she doesn't blame me for what happened, but I'm worried if he doesn't get better, deep down she'll end up resenting me. Then I'll lose them both.

I'm scared that soon all I'll have is this journal, and you.

Asha

Touching the fire

Chapter 29

Stooped over the small library desk, Ash exhaled, irritated, as he jiggled his leg under his chair. He couldn't concentrate over the chatter of the people sitting behind him. And his nose itched. He never liked the air in the library, musty and dusty. Well, it served him right. Instead of working in the grad office, he had been hiding in the library to avoid colliding with Mala. But they had collided already. What he was avoiding now was the ashen fallout.

All weekend, his thoughts had circled back to their kiss. The gentle pressure of her full lips. How he held his breath, unmoving. And afterward, the lingering taste of mint left behind to haunt him.

Most unsettling was how the kiss seemed to have raised the latch, opened the box and released his affection in a way he worried might not be contained again. Even now, as he tried to do the right thing and stay away, he was in pieces for her, an uproar.

Nevertheless, those dreams were impossible. He had other responsibilities now. He had made other promises.

He wasn't sure how much to tell Mala. But he knew he had to tell her something. Just like he knew he would have to split himself in half, work hard and in time learn to shut his secret heart back inside the box, this time vaulting it up for good.

He checked his watch. There was a chance she might still be in the office. He had to set things right between them. He gathered his belongings and descended to the main floor.

As he exited the stairwell, he saw her, standing at the circulation desk, wearing a red sweater. He stopped, as if the connection between his brain and his legs had been severed, as if seeing her made everything pause.

His heart thudded strongly in his chest. He stood to one side and waited while she checked out her books. Once the librarian returned her student card, she veered in the direction of the photocopiers with a couple of large hardcovers in tow. He contemplated letting her go, skulking away unnnoticed. Then he pushed past the sickly feeling in his stomach and caught up to her, interrupting her swift stride.

He raised one hand in a wave. "Hi," he said, unsmiling.

She clutched her books like a shield over her heart. "I didn't think you were in today." She scrutinized him with her large, dark eyes.

He hesitated. "I had some research to do in the library."

She dropped her gaze to the off-white tiles. "Right."

He felt transparent, like she could see through his thin excuse, even while she peered at the floor. "Can we talk for a second?" he said. "About what happened the other night?"

She looked up at him. Her face was smooth—too smooth. "These books are on reserve."

"It'll only take a minute. I just want to clear—"

"I'm sorry." She started walking away. "I only have them for a couple of hours."

"Mala . . ." he called after her, but his plea only doubled her speed.

He watched her march past the photocopiers to the elevator, disappearing behind the rumble of its sliding doors. Stunned, he stared at the empty space she left behind, the memory of her image haunting the air. Which triggered another memory in Ash, as he remembered the last time Mala had pulled away from him, eventually vanishing from his life. Powerless, he felt the deep, old wound of her absence. How was he going to reach her now?

Chapter 30

Mala sped toward the elevator doors as quickly as her wobbly legs allowed without breaking into a sprint. She waited for it to descend, gasping. She hoped Ash hadn't followed her, but she didn't dare to look back and check. The metal doors creaked open and she stepped inside. They rolled shut and she sighed with relief.

Ash's words made her cringe: *Can we talk for a second? About what happened the other night?*

She closed her eyes, mortified. How? When all she wanted was to forget.

The elevator stopped on the sixth floor and she exited. At the photocopiers, she opened her first book and mechanically started copying the second chapter. Her eyes glossed over and she fell into a rhythm—flip, press, scan; flip, press, scan.

What had gotten into her that night? She remembered thinking of her father as they star-gazed, then telling Ash about Sumesh, then feeling the red room rise around her again, that feeling of being trapped.

When Ash spoke with such outrage, trying to convince her to end things with Sumesh before they went any further, telling her with such passion that it was her life and she should do whatever she wanted, what could she say—she heard what she wanted to hear.

So she kissed him.

And it lit up the dark matter of loneliness within her, with all the sparkle of the night sky. For a fleeting moment, while their lips touched, it felt like more than a kiss to her. It felt like a convergence, as though her loneliness found his, fused together and formed something whole.

Afterward, she reopened her eyes and saw the look of terror on his face. She realized what she had done, the trespass she had made. Without a word, she hurried all the way to the bus stop, climbing onto the wrong bus, but she didn't care, she needed to get away from that look of terror.

Her shame, however, wasn't so easy to escape. Panic soured her insides as she agonized over her bad karma. She wasn't that kind of woman. She wouldn't be that kind of woman. Worst of all, she hated to think of her father watching over her and what he must have seen.

All weekend, she tortured herself with slavish thoughts of impeccable Laine—tall, slender, fairy-like Laine. She reminded herself of Ash and Laine's sepia-tinted history, their grown-up plans, their solid partnership, which could surely withstand something as mercurial as a kiss. It barely existed. Like Mala.

Which was why, when Sumesh called on Saturday unexpectedly and invited her for coffee, she accepted, taking it as a penance, a remedy.

And Mala had to admit, while they chatted over lattes, that Sumesh turned out to be more charming than she remembered from the introduction. More handsome, with his dark, refined features. More interesting, especially with regards to his hopes of working with Médecins Sans Frontières one day, and how he approached health with a holistic perspective, studying Ayurveda in his spare time.

At one point, Mala was surprised to find herself comfortable enough with him to ask why he was considering an arranged marriage.

"The same reason you are," he replied, straightforward. "Basically, it simplifies things." He sat quietly for a moment with a resigned look in his eye. "When you meet the right person, you'll do anything to keep them."

Mala hadn't understood his last remark, nor had she asked for clarification, because it didn't matter, she wasn't the right person for him. She left their first and only date thinking that Sumesh was going to make someone a good husband someday, just not her.

Her penance for the kiss was over. Like her duty to her mother. Tonight, Mala would tell her she had tried, but she and Sumesh were a poor match, and she didn't want to see him again. Then she would convince her mother to go back to their original agreement somehow. Mala would stand up to her mother once and for all. Ash was right—it was her life and she needed to decide how she wanted to live it. She needed to bring this distraction to an end.

The photocopier beeped, drawing her back to the present. Mala glanced at the control panel. Her copy card had run out of credit. Annoyed, she gave a frustrated sigh. She would have to descend all the way to the basement to refill it. Languidly, she collected her things and headed toward the stairwell. She knew she wasn't going to be able to avoid Ash forever. Just like she knew what he was going to say. She felt a pang pierce her middle as she imagined him kissing Laine hello when he got home. A sharper pang as she saw them cooking dinner side by side and, later, cuddling on the couch while they watched television. And the sharpest pang—the one that sent her groping for the banister—as they slipped into the darkness of their bedroom, of each other, and came together.

Chapter 31

Mala glanced at her watch. Only ten minutes left and her office hours would be over for another week. The momentary relief she enjoyed at the thought of her impending freedom was soon flattened as a thick wave of sadness rolled over her. This was the first time she had spent her office hours alone in weeks. She wasn't used to that anymore. She had grown accustomed to Ash's visits—to the perfectly made cups of coffee, the easy banter, the deeper conversations. To the way time passed when they were together, too quickly sometimes.

A soft tap on the door drew her out of her thoughts. Ash loomed in the doorway with his hands inside his pockets, his face long and grim. Her heart hovered with relief. He came, she thought. Thank goodness, he came.

"Mind if I join you for a second?" he asked.

She nodded for him to enter.

He stepped inside and took a seat. "Sorry, I forgot the coffees this time."

The schism between them was palpable. Fruitlessly, Mala searched for something clever to say. Of course, whenever she tried to sound witty, she failed. With her eyes on the desk, she gently cleared her throat. "I've been meaning to cut back anyway. I haven't been sleeping very well lately."

He joined her in staring vacantly at the midpoint between them. "Me neither."

For a few vast moments, they sat without speaking until Mala couldn't bear the yowl of the silence any longer. "I'm sorry," she said above a whisper. "I crossed a line that shouldn't have been crossed. I feel terrible about it. I'm so embarrassed."

"If I did something to—"

"It wasn't you. It was me. I was missing my dad, then we started talking about Sumesh and I don't know. I just felt . . . trapped. I reacted on impulse." Her throat felt sticky as she swallowed.

"I know I talk about my problems with Laine, but I'm committed to her. We're trying to work things out." He waited a beat. "I have to believe that we can."

Mala nodded, solemn. She felt like giving in to the tears gathering behind her eyes, although less so than she felt like a fool. For ever thinking, even for a minute, that their kiss might have lit up the darkness within him too. "I understand," she managed to utter.

"No, you don't," he clipped. He stopped to take a slow, deep breath. Mala thought she saw a twinge of pain tighten the corners of his mouth, as though there was more to say but the words were like brambles caught around his tongue. "I don't think we should spend as much time together. At least for now."

Mala smiled as kindly as she could while quaking inside. Her humiliation was cresting to the surface. She wouldn't be able to hold the banks for much longer. "That makes sense." She prayed her veil-thin façade was enough to conceal her shame, her mangled hopes. *Now go*, she begged him silently. *Please.*

He rose to his feet. She watched him—his downcast gaze, the pain in the ridges of his creased brow. She felt weak with foreboding, like he might be stepping out of her life forever and it was her own reckless fault. Then he turned away and left.

And Mala gripped the desk until her fingers ached, to stop the feeling of falling.

Lovesick

Chapter 32

Asha lolled by the bonfire, licking the best melted chocolate she had ever tasted off her fingertips. The cool night air weaved through the trees with the smoky smell of burning wood. After all the stress and formality of the day, it felt good to be in the country, under starlight, surrounded by her friends and classmates.

Rowan was on the other side of the fire, building a s'more at the snack table. A mix of nerves and excitement—and a smidgen of doubt—swirled through her as she watched him. Asha thought back to earlier that evening. Prom was prom: beautiful dresses, corny couples' portraits, music, dancing. Altogether more fun than she expected, although way less without Willow to celebrate with.

"You looked pretty tonight," Willow said to her.

Asha's head jerked to the left. She was so focused on the nerves snaking inside her belly, she hadn't heard Willow come over. Her heart twinged at having her best friend near.

"So did you." She eyed Willow uneasily.

Willow wiped her hands on her jeans, marking them with streaks of molten marshmallow.

"Don't look so worried, Athena. I'm not going to make you hang out with me."

"*Will*, you know that's not what this is about."

"I know." Willow frowned. "I'm just bitter." She sulked at the fire, its pop and crackle filling the silence. "Anyway, that isn't what

I came over to talk to you about." She tossed a glance over their shoulders. "I see you've pitched your tent."

Asha raised an eyebrow. "And?"

"Don't give me that. I've noticed the looks you two have been giving each other all night."

"Just spit it out, Will."

"I want to make sure you're being careful, that's all."

"We talked about it. We're prepared. Okay, Mom?"

Willow paused, flattening her lips. "Just one more thing, then," she said. "Are you sure about this?"

Asha peered over the fire at Rowan, who was helping a pretty girl she didn't know build a s'more. She chewed her top lip. Was she sure? No, not entirely, if she was honest with herself. She still felt sore about Rowan's evasiveness after her dad's accident. But once they had talked, he started being more attentive again. And tonight, while they danced, their connection felt the way it used to. Asha reasoned that the distance between them was partly her fault. She had been distracted lately. No wonder their relationship was suffering. After tonight, though, they would be closer than ever.

"I'm sure," she said.

A warm gust of air blew over her. She shivered. Even the fire wasn't enough to soothe the cold beast of loneliness, which had grown even colder since her dad's accident. The frigidness only lessened when she was with Rowan. The rest of the time, it felt like she was carrying a shiver in her belly, all day long and all night.

The fire sparked. Tonight, with Rowan, she would find comfort.

THE PARTY WAS starting to get rowdy.

"I swear, she's going to fall into the fire," Rowan said as they watched Willow hippie-dance around and around.

"I think she's trying to commune with Gaia."

They laughed. He threaded their fingers together. "Want to get some space?"

Were her eyes as wide as they felt? "Sure."

They walked to their tent, the heat of the fire and the sounds of the party tapering with their every step over the uneven ground.

Through the roof of their tent, Asha could see the almost-full moon, its cool grey light falling on her like the disinterested gaze of a distant mother. Things moved quickly. Her entire body felt alert. Rowan seemed like he was in a trance. She kept her eyes on the moon.

Leading up to tonight, Asha knew to prepare herself for certain realities. What she hadn't expected was the stark duality between her body and her thoughts. Her body and Rowan's. Their experiences. She expected oneness.

Then she saw, out of the corner of her eye, the red plastic wrapper in his hand, split, but—unless her eyes were fooling her—not empty. He had paused to open the wrapper earlier, and although she had averted her eyes, she assumed he had put on the condom. Now, as she tried to focus on the wrapper in the dark, she thought she could see the beige-coloured disc still in his hand.

A spasm of fear ripped through her core.

It must be a spare, she thought. Maybe he wanted to be extra careful and took out more than one.

Rowan suddenly groaned like he had been speared, every muscle in his body stiffening. He rolled over to her side and kissed her forehead. She cast a panicked look at the parts of them she had been embarrassed to see, despite the closeness they had shared, but it was too dark to tell.

Straining to sound casual, she asked, "You used one, right?"

He held up the unused condom and gave a little smirk. "I guess I got lost in the moment." He ran his forefinger along her jawline. "You're just too hot."

Nothing, for a second. No motion, no thought.

Then, a cascade, as Asha felt something dribble along her inner thigh.

Sitting up, she started the self-conscious process of groping for her clothes and dressing under an unwelcome gaze.

"What's wrong?"

"How can you ask me that?" While things were in motion, she hadn't thought to check, or suspected him of deviating from their plan, especially after he had paused and made it seem like he was following through. Now she felt stupid for looking away and trusting him. "We talked about it. You were supposed to use one."

She found her jeans near the tent door. She rolled onto her back and wriggled them on. But where was her bra? Her shirt?

"You're overreacting."

She curled back up to sitting. Her eyes darted around the tent and stopped. Both items were on the other side of Rowan. She crossed her arms, covering her breasts, as if only just realizing she was topless. Between the skin of her arms and chest was the recent memory of his broad palms, long fingers. She suppressed a chill. "Pass me my clothes," she ordered.

"You're acting crazy."

"*Now*, Rowan."

"Just relax." He reached up and pulled on her shoulder. "Lie down."

"Stop it!" she yelled. She dipped her shoulder, releasing herself. Before he had time to react, she leaned over him and grabbed her clothes.

Then she unzipped the tent and sprinted into the woods, hiding behind the shelter of a tree where she finished getting dressed, quicker than anyone could ogle her. As she pulled on her clothes, she listened for sounds of pursuit, but all she heard in the distance was the metallic rip of a tent being zipped shut.

• • • •

THAT NIGHT, ASHA slept in Willow's tent, not that she slept much at all. In the morning, she went to see Rowan, but he was already gone. With a lump in her throat, she undertook the lonely business of packing up their tent by herself. When they had assembled it the night before, she remembered thinking that the canvas and poles meant nothing to her, the tent was just a musty dome of space. But after that night, it would forever hold the memory of love. The tent collapsed under her hands, the reel of memories from their night together trapped inside as she finished packing it away, their bodies folded and rolled into a tight, misshapen thing.

What the heart wants

Chapter 33

Mala entered the unfamiliar pub and searched the crowded room for someone she knew. The student meet-and-greet had started about an hour ago. After checking in at her residence and dropping off her suitcase, she reluctantly decided to network a bit while she was at the conference, even though she was tired from her late flight and would have rather taken a bath and practised her presentation a few more times before turning in with her book. She was about to head to the bar and order a drink when she heard her name burst from the throng.

Ash was toward the back corner with a couple of people she didn't recognize, likely from another university. He wore a black corduroy blazer over his Christmas-ribbon plaid shirt, more formal than usual. Their eyes met, unblinking, for a long moment. She suspected the same wide-eyed trepidation marred both of their unsure faces. He waved her over cautiously. Her feet didn't budge. A couple of weeks had passed since their difficult conversation in the TA office. Ever since, they hadn't exchanged more than strained hellos and goodbyes in the most hurried of passings.

Mala dug a fingernail into the knuckle of her thumb and sluggishly made her way over to him. He excused himself and met her halfway, moving with footsteps as tentative as her own.

"Hi," she said with a stiff smile.

"Hi," he mirrored. "I was wondering when you'd get in. For

a second, I was worried you might've changed your mind and decided not to come."

"I waited too long to book my ticket, that's all. I took the earliest flight I could get." She threw a nervous look around them. "It looks like a lot of people are in town for the conference."

"Definitely a good turnout."

Mala couldn't think of what else to say, so she kept her eyes drifting through the crowd. The awkwardness was close to unbearable. She channelled her unease into the sway of her shifting stance.

"Do you want to sit down?" he asked at last.

This caught her off guard. "Are you sure?"

He shrugged one shoulder. "It would be good to catch up a little, don't you think?"

True. Besides, there was little danger of them overstepping boundaries, chaperoned by a room full of colleagues.

They ordered soft drinks and seated themselves at an empty table in a quieter corner of the bar. "I have to present tomorrow," he told her, more worried than enthusiastic.

"I know. I have a long list of questions written out already. I'm going to enjoy grilling you." She offered a small, teasing grin.

He laughed faintly, and so did she, as if for a moment the old warmth of their friendship was returning. She had missed him. And if the gentle sadness dangling from his crooked smile was any indication, there was a chance he had missed her too.

An hour slipped by. They chatted about their research—how far along they were with their analyses, how many chapters they had written, whether they needed more data, conflicts they were having with their advisers—the usual preoccupations of graduate students.

"Are you in for the long haul, Professor Sharma?" he asked. "A postdoc after you finish your Ph.D.?"

"Maybe. Although it's hard for me to think that far ahead." Since her father's passing, Mala tended not to plan the way she used to.

Why risk the disappointment, when roads could give way to sinkholes at any moment? "How about you?"

He sipped his Coke. "A postdoc, for sure. Although I don't know where. I've always wanted to live by the coast."

"East or west?"

"West. Definitely west."

"I can picture you sea-kayaking now. Not surfing, though."

"What? You don't think I'm cool enough for surfing?"

She wrinkled her nose. "Something like that."

He smiled. It was good to see him happy. Then, just as she had finished the thought, something shifted, and all the signs of their lighthearted banter vanished from his face. Mala was bemused by the sudden change.

"Come to think of it, moving back to Toronto would probably be best for us." He tried to dispel the tension with a light chuckle. "Too many Ottawa winters, I guess."

Mala observed him, still puzzled. "I don't mind the cold. In fact, if I could choose to live anywhere, I think it would be up north."

He tipped his head to one side. "I wouldn't have guessed that."

She pictured the land in her mind—sky and ocean and gently rolling tundra. "I don't know what it is, but whenever I'm up there, I feel free. Like I can just be myself. There's no one else to please."

"Almost like a new beginning."

Mala sparkled. "Exactly." She held his gaze and the chatter surrounding them seemed at a distance, as if they were inside the bubble of an impossible dream. *Would you ever want to live up north?* she asked him silently. *With me?* For an instant, she thought she saw an answer flicker back to her through the dreamy look in his eye, like a mirror catching the sun.

A server stopped at their table to ask if they wanted menus and the momentary spell was broken. As Ash spoke to the server, Mala raised her glass to her lips and swallowed a large gulp, bubbles sprinkling the tip of her nose. She considered leaving the pub. Clearly, it was still too soon for her to be spending time with him.

"It's strange to think about, isn't it?" he said, resuming their conversation. "What we might do next. Where we might end up. In some ways, I feel like I've only just settled into the routine. Soon, we'll be off doing other things." He paused. "Everything's about to change."

Peering into the fizz of her ginger ale, Mala drooped with sadness. She had felt this way after undergrad too. Back then, it shocked her how quickly her friends dispersed into the world, like the feathery seeds of a dandelion, carried away in all the varying directions of the wind. She had lost track of so many. Even more so after her father passed.

Was the same thing going to happen with Ash? she wondered. She couldn't bear the thought of not knowing what was going on in his life.

She looked up and caught him moping into his drink too. "What's the matter?" she asked.

"I'm a little distracted tonight."

"About your presentation? You're going to be fine. You always do well with these sorts of things. It's kind of annoying."

This time, her attempt at humour did nothing to chip away at his brooding. "Not your presentation, then," she said. "Am I supposed to guess?"

He reached for her with cheerless eyes. "Somehow, I don't think you'll guess this, Mala."

Something about the way he said her name made Mala squirm in her chair.

He stroked his bottom lip against the back of his front teeth and kept his gaze low. "It's fatherhood."

"You're right, I wasn't expecting that." She brightened, softened by the thought of him with children. "That's sweet."

"I've always wanted to be a dad."

Hearing this, she softened even more. "Well, when the time comes, I'm sure you'll be great at it."

"I figured it would happen somewhere down the road."

"After you're done with school, maybe? That makes sense. Thesis baby first."

"Right." He looked directly at her. A sudden, intense stare. "Not like this."

Mala retraced his last words. The logic that was supposed to link one word to the next failed her. Something was missing. "What do you mean?"

He didn't speak right away. Mala's unease grew with every mute second. Then his lips parted and words she never imagined him uttering slipped out.

"Laine's pregnant."

Mala sat motionless for several cold moments of disbelief, too stunned to even blink.

"It wasn't part of the plan," he continued, his face full of pain. "Although babies seem to decide when it's right for them to come."

Her head whirred as her heart twisted. She had heard that sentiment before. It was something her father would tell her around her birthday, or when she had trouble sleeping, or when she had done something to make him especially proud. That his rani beti had waited for everything to be perfect for her arrival—the house, the toys, the yard. That she had refused to come before the preparations were just so. His little queen. How he adored her.

A surprise, then. But also a life. One that—and this, Mala realized, was at the heart of what Ash was trying to tell her—he had devoted himself to, as he had committed to Laine. Maybe this was what he had been trying to tell her all along on that awful day back in the TA office. *We're trying to work things out. I have to believe that we can.*

Mala felt besieged.

Until this moment, she hadn't acknowledged the pixel of hope she carried at her core. That, in the end, they would find a way to be together. But her life wasn't a Victorian novel. She wasn't Jane Eyre, and Ash wasn't her Rochester. Well, perhaps he was as unavailable. Perhaps she was as tormented by desire.

Mala pressed her hands against the table and rose to stand on her shaky legs. "Congratulations," she managed to say despite her shock.

"Stay," he pleaded. "Let's talk."

But by then she was already striding toward the exit, *Laine's pregnant, Laine's pregnant, Laine's pregnant* booming against her skull with every unsteady step.

Back in her room, Mala cowered in the dark with her shoulder blades pressed against her locked door. The strength drained from her legs. She slid, collapsing on the cool tiled floor like a crumpled rag, as if under the weight of the news. Tears spilled down her cheeks. Effortless. Endless.

Would they ever stop?

Chapter 34

A short while later, Mala's mournful trance was interrupted by a reluctant knock on her door. She gasped from the surprise, and held her breath, without making another sound, hoping who-ever it was would leave her in peace.

"Mala?" she heard Ash call out.

Wiping her eyes with the edge of her sleeve, she clumsily picked herself up and faced the door. Why was he there? What more was there to say?

"Please, can we talk?"

She patted her cheeks to check they were dry, flicked on a light and cautiously opened the door.

"I don't want to leave things like this," he said. "Please."

Twisting her mouth, she stepped aside. He entered with a bowed head and quiet footsteps. He approached the loveseat, lowered himself and perched uncomfortably on the edge of a cushion.

She shut the door. "What do you want to talk about?" she asked as she walked from the partially lit entry into the shadows of the kitchenette, which faced the small living room where he was seated. Her legs still felt weak and light, almost feverish, but despite their shakiness she mustered what grace she could into her stride. Leaning against the counter in front of the sink, she crossed her arms and waited. His figure appeared dark against the backdrop of the soft blue night spilling in from the large windows behind him.

"I'm sorry about earlier. I didn't mean to shock you like that. We got to talking and I couldn't hold it in any longer. But I should have told you in private."

She spoke into his eyes. "How long have you known?"

He leaned forward, resting his forearms on his knees. "A while."

"Why didn't you tell me sooner?"

He ran a hand over his mouth, rubbing his stubble, as if wrestling with something he was embarrassed to admit.

"Because I was in shock. Because when we first found out, we weren't sure if we were going to keep it or stay together. We haven't even told our parents yet. You're the only person I've told, Mala."

Her mouth felt mealy. "You should have told me anyway. We're supposed to be friends." If he had been upfront with her, the Halloween kiss would never have happened. It would never have even crossed her mind to trespass on his relationship in the slightest way. She licked her lips. "I feel even worse about what I did now."

Ash averted his eyes. "I'm sorry. To be honest, you took me by surprise that night. I didn't think something like that could ever happen between us. I know how much your mom's opinion means to you, and I don't exactly fit her criteria, do I?" He raised his chin, his gaze a gentle beam cutting across the darkness between them. "I didn't mean to hurt you, Mala."

Thank God for the half-light. Otherwise he might have seen the flash of pain cross her face like a suddenly engorged vein. Heat flamed her cheeks, her forehead. She felt pathetic. "Why would I be hurt?" Her voice was hard and defensive.

The edge of her tone didn't make him flinch or recoil. He continued to peer at her openly, vulnerably, as if he knew that the time for hiding was long over. "You know why. Or was it all in my head?"

Mala clenched her hollowed stomach. So he had felt it too. The sparkle of the night sky. The convergence. But if that was the case, why wasn't he as distraught as she was, knowing they could never be together now, they would never have their chance? Or had the intensity of the nameless thing between them always been more one-sided? A bellow of her secret heart, a whisper of his.

Not that it mattered. Clearly, their connection wasn't deep enough. To make him leave Laine when he had the chance. To stop the two of them from being intimate even when they were close to separating.

Now he was humiliating Mala by bringing it up. Her chest rose and fell as her breathing became laboured. Anger rose from her belly like a column of fire.

"Don't feel sorry for me." She jutted her chin. "You aren't the only one with news." *What was she saying?*

He bunched his eyebrows. "What do you mean?"

"I'm marrying Sumesh," she blurted out, robotic. It wasn't true. She was just saying it. She wanted him to ache like she ached. Feel as besieged as she felt. Stab. Punch. Bruise. Was she having any effect? Was he bleeding? She searched him for signs of purple and red.

Stunned, Ash stared at her, open-mouthed. "I thought all that was over."

Was that what she looked like after he had delivered the baby news? Gobsmacked. "I met him for coffee the day after we . . . after Halloween. We talked. He changed my mind about things."

Ash gave her a deep, critical look. "I think you're making a mistake." His cadence was slow and grave. "I know you've been feeling pressured. But you can't marry someone you barely know to make your mom happy. You just can't, Mala."

She barked a laugh. "What do you care?"

His stoicism finally cracked. "I care, all right?" he said, raising his voice. He turned his head to one side and composed himself. "I care about you, Mala." He sounded downtrodden, drained. "I care about what happens to you. I'm just trying to do the right thing."

"Then go," she snapped, hoping the vehemence of her delivery carried enough force to shove him out the door. She needed him to leave before the next onslaught of grief assailed her and her legs gave out entirely.

With pain in his eyes, he rose to his feet, lingering for a moment as if waiting for something. Finally, he tore himself away and started walking toward the door.

Air barely passed her nostrils and seemed to go no farther. With every one of his steps, Mala wanted to call out, reach out, do anything that might freeze him in place, but she was paralytic, stapled, nailed.

The door creaked open and she cloaked her eyes, not wanting to witness his inevitable departure from her life, even askance. She braced herself for the metallic slam of the door.

Three seconds passed. Then five. Then ten.

The door should have shut by now. She glanced to the left. He was standing in the half-open door with his hand still on the handle, staring past the threshold at some middle ground in the brightly lit hall.

Pushing away from the counter, she advanced, tentative. "What is it?" she asked.

He let go of the door. They both watched it shut. Turning slowly, he faced her. His gaze streamed through the half-light, as if catching the gleam of the moon and reflecting it in a pair of silver dots. He approached her with measured footsteps. She didn't move. She wasn't afraid of him. Being afraid of him would have been like being afraid of herself.

Bluish light from the windows brightened half his face. She felt the warmth of his uneven breath brush against her mouth.

"You can't go through with it, Mala," he said, low and urgent.

Sadness pricked her eyes. Mala thought of Laine and their baby, and the family Ash was already a part of. Some things couldn't be undone. "It makes no difference now," she told him.

"This one choice could ruin your life." He pressed his lips together, fighting through pain. "Can't you see that?"

In that moment, what Mala saw was the two of them cloud-gazing and star-gazing and sharing a chaste kiss by the river. She watched at a distance as countless other daydreams burned away like melting celluloid, black and bubbling. A terrible thrust of grief wanted to pour out of her. "I have no life." Not anymore.

He hung his head in shame and sadness. "Neither do I."

They stood there as if in suspension, hearts beating slowly, breath barely flowing.

When he finally lifted his gaze, his eyes had lost their fierce-ness, perhaps weakened by the heartache she suspected was blooming in his chest, as it was inside her own. They were kind eyes. That was who he was—not perfect, but not cruel. Their eyes, Mala realized—like the rest of them—were the same, and she was going to miss him with a depth of longing she might not be able to endure.

Mala cupped the side of his face, not quite understanding how it had all come to this. She wanted to swallow but couldn't. She knew he was about to leave, the way she knew this was as close as they would ever be again, splayed along the separate paths where life had redirected them, like roads travelling east and south.

Mala told herself to lower her hand, release him. But her hand wouldn't obey. With a slight turn of his head, he pressed a dry kiss into the centre of her palm, sending a crackle of light along her arm and shoulder, right into her heart, as if wordlessly begging her to let him go, as if saying goodbye to what might have been, once and for all.

Later, Mala would look back on this moment, unable to tell how what happened next began: with her, or with him, or with the dark matter of loneliness within each of them. All Mala knew was that she felt the undeniable tow of the convergence again. As she sur-rendered to it this time, fully and completely, she veiled her eyes, and the darkness within her vanished into a warm burst of golden light.

THEY LAY ON her borrowed bed. Mala rested her head against Ash's chest and listened to the tune of his heartbeat, rocking to the gentle sway of his breath like ripples. Shifting, she gazed up at him. His eyes skittered beneath his pinkish eyelids. *Are you my love?* she asked his sleeping face. *Are you my destiny?*

Who could say? Life had brought them together before—although never this close—only to split them apart.

Was the decimating pattern going to repeat itself?

Had fate given her a glimpse of happiness only to have it disappear from her view like a receding train, a shrinking dot?

Was that what it meant to love? Was it not so much a fall as a hook through the soul? Not so much the offering of a heart but rather a promise to remain joined, come what may? Push, pull. Near, far. Life, death.

Mala lowered her head back over his heart. For the moment, the night, she decided it didn't matter. She reached out her hand and filled her palm with a resplendent moonbeam. Every one of his deep exhales drew her toward sleep, like waves gently tugging her away from a shoreline into a mer de rêves. Safety sealed itself around them like silence, like home. Lulled by such decadent intimacies, Mala softly closed her eyes, humming with love.

Chapter 35

The next morning, they woke in each other's arms, staring more than speaking, as if words might prick the golden dream that had formed around them in the night like a luminous bubble. Mala discovered something curious about being close to someone—this close to them. There was a gentle torture about it. She wondered, Who put these bodies between us? She wanted to tunnel down the dark centres of his eyes and not stop until she was on the other side of the window, in his house, where his soul dwelled. She wanted to know him, and she wanted all of him.

"I don't want to leave this room," he said, looking down at her, a film of sleep still clouding his vision.

She grinned. "There's a world outside this room?"

All peace vanished from his face. "I mean it, Mala. The thought of going back to our separates lives after this . . ." he trailed off, shaking his head.

Mala clutched him tightly. This was another perplexing reality, she was discovering, about being close to someone. It made you happy, more than you had ever known. But it also hurt. She was racked with fear at the thought of losing him.

"What are we going to do?" she asked.

He quietly traced the contours of her face. "I woke up in the middle of the night. You were fast asleep. You looked so beautiful with the moonlight shining on your face. All I could think to myself was, I want to be worthy of this person. I want to make things right out of the mess I've made."

Mala hooded her eyes. "I'm as responsible as you are. I feel awful."

The bump and gurgle of his swallow echoed in her ear. "Not worse than I do."

A long, brooding silence settled over them as they sank into the guilt of their own thoughts.

"I was wrong to think I could deny my feelings for you," he said at last. "There's no going back. At least, not for me."

Mala burrowed her face into the warm bend of his neck, wishing she could fuse their bodies together. Then nothing and no one—not even fate—could keep them apart.

"Not for me either." She had found her match. For her, there was no one else.

His arms fastened around her.

"We both have things to settle first. I have to tell Laine the truth. About what happened last night and my feelings for you. I'm committed to being the best father I can be. But she needs to know our relationship is over." Three strong beats of his heart. "What about Sumesh?"

"What do you mean?"

"When are you going to tell him the wedding's off?"

Mala shrank in his arms. She resisted the urge to hide her red face behind her hands.

"About that," she said. "I was completely sideswiped by your news. And I reacted. The truth is, after we kissed, I took your advice and talked to my mom. I told her that Sumesh and I weren't a good match and I wasn't going to see him again. Then we had a much longer conversation and by the end of it I convinced her to put off any talk about marriage until after I graduate." Having spewed her ramble, Mala stiffened, anticipating that at any moment, he would shove her away and jump out of bed, enraged.

He craned his neck to get a better look at her. She couldn't bring herself to meet his gaze, or to confront any change in the way that he saw her.

"So, you aren't getting married?"

Mala shook her head.

"You were *never* getting married?"

Mala shook her head again. She quickly pressed herself up, leaning on her elbow to face him.

"Please don't be mad," she pleaded. "I was upset. I lashed out."

He gave her a long, probing look. Then he fixed his eyes on the ceiling.

"I shocked you," he said slowly. "You wanted to shock me back. I guess that makes us even."

Neither of them spoke for some time. Mala continued balancing on her elbow, unsure of whether she was still welcome in his arms.

He shifted his eyes and regarded her, sombre. "No more secrets, all right? I'm sick of them. Nothing good comes of them."

Mala swallowed hard. "Agreed."

He drew her closer and she sank into his embrace, grateful, albeit flustered.

"What about your mom?" he asked.

Mala knew that telling her mother about him would be a much, much longer conversation than even the one they'd had about Sumesh.

"I'll handle it. I'll make her understand."

He stroked his fingers through her mussed hair and her breaths lengthened.

"Somehow, we'll find a way to make this work. We'll be honest with the people we've hurt. We'll face the consequences. And then, with a clear conscience, we'll be together."

Mala felt something bright kindle inside, like a candle, like hope. She raised her chin to look up at him and cupped the side of his face, as she had last night, feeling the same sparkle glittering beneath her skin, the same unstoppable convergence drawing them together. She felt calm, like there was nothing to fear.

"It was written," she told his beautiful face.

With a crooked grin, he echoed, "It was written."

They bent their heads together, foreheads kissing, and closed their eyes, sealing their promise as if it were a prayer.

HE STAYED FOR as long as he could, but the conference beckoned. They arranged to meet after his presentation later that morning. Now, as Mala dithered in bed, her earlier doubts surged back with triple the force she had used to silence them.

How was she going to convince her mother Ash was a more suitable match than Sumesh, or any other Indian boy who looked as good on paper, once she told her the whole truth? About his pregnant girlfriend, whom he had no intention of marrying.

Mala rolled onto her side and gnawed at her thumbnail. Her mother would never understand what she deemed dishonourable behaviour, regardless of background or culture. She would never approve of him under these circumstances.

Mala played out the conversation in her head. If he didn't marry the woman who was carrying his child, what made Mala think he would marry her someday? Her mother would call it a scandal. Fodder for community gossip. She would never be able to show her face at temple again. She would lose friends. She would be too ashamed to see any who might remain.

Mala sighed, listless. She would have to convince her mother times were changing. That people who found themselves in undesirable situations could still be good people. That it wasn't the lack of trouble, but the commitment to cutting a path through it, that made a couple strong. Wasn't that what her mother had taught her? Mala would have to remind her of the woman who had once thought she was an unsuitable match too. How her mother and father had defied that woman and her prejudice, staying true to their hearts. After all, it was in the heart, not the head, that these matters were written. Wasn't it?

Vines

Chapter 36

It took two sickening weeks for Rowan to answer Asha's messages. At first she was mad, but as the silent treatment dragged on, she felt more and more desperate to talk to him and work things out. Nothing so bad had happened between them, she told herself. They just needed to communicate better and be more careful, which was what she planned on telling him if he ever gave her the chance.

She missed him, especially since she couldn't lean on Willow like she used to. The shiver of the beast was fiercer than ever. She needed her warmth, her antidote. She needed Rowan back, even if it cost her a little self-respect. She wouldn't live through this otherwise. She nearly jumped when his text lit up her phone while she was sitting outside at the library picnic table, eating her lunch and reading *Jane Eyre*. He wanted to meet after her shift to talk and, she hoped, reconcile. The used bookstore a few doors down from the library seemed like the perfect place. It was never busy and had a little cafe where you could get a decent iced mocha, Rowan's favourite summer drink, which was why Asha suggested the bookstore in her reply.

Once she finished the last of the day's shelving, she scurried over to the bookstore to secure them a nook. Thankfully the corner spot, with the worn-in floral chesterfield and antique coffee table by the front windows overlooking Bank Street, was still free when she arrived. She set down her bag beside some fanned-out literary magazines and ordered their drinks. She imagined a pair of perfect iced mochas arriving shortly after Rowan did so there would be no awkward waiting before the barista; they could settle in and get to straightening everything out.

Instead the drinks arrived before Rowan, by a lot. Asha shoved away the idea that it was a bad omen, like she did twenty minutes later when the ice in the mochas had half melted, diluting the goodness of the coffee. He probably got stuck in traffic, she thought as she looked out onto the busy street, trying not to panic.

She was considering whether to order them replacements when Rowan glided past the window in his dad's Mustang. While he parked, Asha straightened up. A bell chimed as he stepped through the glass door.

He gave the bookstore a bland once-over. "Sorry I'm late," he said, making no effort to sound convincing. "I lost track of time."

"Oh." Asha blinked. She had been counting down the minutes since lunch. And he had lost track of the time. She had arrived early. And he didn't mind making her wait, like he had for the past two weeks.

Rowan finally sat down, so far from her on the chesterfield that he might have been more comfortable seated on the armrest.

"So," he said.

" . . . So."

He leaned forward, resting his elbows on his knees, and clamped his hands together. "Listen, I feel bad about how things happened. I got lost in the moment. I should have been more careful."

"I've been waiting to hear from you for two weeks."

"You're the one who stormed off."

"You're the one who thought it was no big deal. Rowan, you didn't even check on me."

"I might've if you'd stopped harassing me."

"How is trying to talk to my boyfriend harassment?" He twitched.

At what? The slowly rising volume of her voice? Or the word boyfriend?
"You know what's really harassing? The silent treatment."

"I needed time to think."

"You mean to post pictures online," she parried. "You knew I'd see them."

The door chimed as a middle-aged couple entered the bookstore.

"Rowan, just tell me, okay? What's going on with you?"

Stalling, he reached for his drink and took a deep gulp.

Every one of Asha's nerves sang in warning.

"Listen," he told her flatly. "We had fun together. At least, we used to. Then things got all intense with your adoption and your dad's accident. It's too much. I have enough drama in my life without having to be your everything through this."

"Rowan, I—"

"The truth is, when we started dating, I was just looking for something simple. Something fun." He wet his lips, fixing his eyes on her untouched coffee. "University's around the corner," he said, impassive. "I think we should break up."

A crimson flush swept up Asha's neck as she stared at him, open-mouthed, with a sudden ringing in her ears.

Chapter 37

Asha called in sick the next morning. Overnight, the love-sickness in her heart spread to the rest of her. The pounding in her head fused it to the pillow. Her body was a cold slab. And her stomach, the site of an uprising. After calling Agnes, she went back to bed, tenting the covers around her like a cave, hoping to sleep through the worst of it.

That afternoon, she woke feeling worse rather than better. She had never experienced heartbreak like this. Probably because she had never cared for anyone as much as Rowan before. Never entrusted someone with such a large part of herself. How could his feelings for her have changed so suddenly, so drastically? What was wrong with her? Maybe if she was prettier or more fun or less complicated he might not have broken up with her. Maybe if she hadn't been so distracted by her own life they would still be together. She agonized over these torments while fighting to convince herself she didn't need to throw up.

The convincing didn't work. And they had run out of Tums and Pepto. Asha thought a stroll might relieve her seasick wooziness, and while she was out, she could pick up the missing medicine-cabinet staples from the pharmacy.

While roaming around Shoppers, she passed the shelves of Always and Tampax indifferently at first. But by the time she reached the end of the aisle, it dawned on her: She was late.

But she was never late . . .

Salt water suddenly pooled in her mouth. She felt like she might be sick to her stomach.

Oh God, she thought, paralyzed with fear.

Then she scrambled for her phone, hesitated for a second and called Willow, not knowing what else to do or who else to contact.

"ATHENA?" WILLOW SAID through the washroom door. "Are you okay in there?"

After Asha phoned her, Willow rushed to the pharmacy. They sat on a bench and Asha told her everything. About how Rowan broke up with her, about how she was late, about how she was worried she might be pregnant after the accident on prom night. Willow listened with a clenched jaw, then threatened to mess Rowan up, which was exactly what Asha needed to hear. How badly Willow messed him up, though, depended on the test. Willow offered her house as a safe place to take it.

Asha read the instructions and followed them precisely. Now she felt too nervous to pace while she waited for the minutes to pass. Perched on the edge of the tub, she wrung her hands and flicked jumpy glances at the counter.

"Do you want me to wait with you?" Willow asked.

"Come in," she said, her voice fragile.

Willow gently opened the door and tiptoed her way over to Asha's side. She sat down and looped their arms together. "Don't worry." She rubbed reassurance into Asha's arm as if it were lotion. "Whatever it says, I'll help you figure things out."

Asha felt close to rupturing. "I'm not ready for something like this, Will."

Willow's fingers dug into her bicep. "I know."

They waited the rest of the time in thick silence. The minutes passed quickly—too quickly. Willow rose to her feet and approached the counter. Asha wasn't ready to face the verdict. Wasn't ready to confront the test Willow held out for her to see.

But she forced herself to look.

And then time stopped.

Chapter 38

Willow wanted to go with Asha for moral support, but she needed to face Rowan on her own. Over the past few days, she had gone through denial and shock and was now firmly rooted in fury. This was their problem now, not hers alone.

He entered the bookstore with disinterest stuccoed to his face. The strong scent of espresso, overwhelming in the air, made it hard to keep her nausea in check. She popped a mint into her mouth and watched him take a seat across from her uneasily, at the same table as last time.

"Asha, if you're hoping to get back—"

"I'm late," she said, blunt.

He gawped. "What?"

Asha didn't repeat herself but instead gave him a look that said, *You heard me.*

"Aren't you on the pill?"

"Not everyone is, Rowan."

He shook his head. "This is unbelievable."

"Are you saying it's my fault? You were supposed to use a condom, Rowan. That's what we talked about."

"I told you I got caught up in the moment. I thought you were on the pill." He ran a hand through his hair. "So what are you going to do?"

"What are *we* going to do, Rowan."

He looked at her like she was slow. "I'm not ready to have a kid. Are you?"

"No."

"It's simple, then."

"Even when you have options, it's never simple."

"What else is there?"

Asha faltered. "Adoption." She said it like a question.

"You're kidding."

"I was adopted, remember?"

He scratched his temple, taking a moment to think. "I'm not ready for anything like this. I'm off to college soon. My life is about to start, for real." He stood up. The dark eyes Asha had once believed held gentle love for her now glared with hard contempt. "You know what I want you to do. If you decide to go another way, fine. But it's on you. I want nothing to do with it."

In the years to come, when Asha reflected on this painful moment from her youth, the things she should have said to Rowan would flood her mind like a torrent of rage. But as a shaken girl of eighteen, all she could do was watch the first boy she had ever loved leave, without even a backward glance.

LATER THAT NIGHT, Asha languished in bed, thinking about what to do, when she got a text from Willow.

You have to tell them.

Dropping the phone to her side, Asha considered. Until recently, she never doubted the openness of her relationship with her parents. Now barriers stood in the way. She had promised to behave, to cause no trouble, to not add to their already mountainous worries. Her dad was still recovering at the rehabilitation centre. Her mom was frantic and overstretched with dashing between work and home and the centre. Both had enough to deal with right now without Asha adding to the mix.

Although it was hard to admit, part of her also doubted whether their love for her was absolute. Since finding out about the adoption, Asha was still shaken by the discovery that her family wasn't as close as she had faithfully thought. If she had been wrong about that, maybe she was wrong to believe that her parents would support her through anything. The people she trusted the most had let her down and her wounds were still jagged and raw. She struggled, not knowing who or what to believe in anymore.

What was she going to do? Who could she depend on?

But these weren't the only thoughts plaguing her.

Rolling onto her side, she drew her journal from the nightstand. With barely the energy to move a pen, she wrote.

What's wrong with me?

It's okay. You can tell me. I want to understand why it's so easy to let me go.

I used to think that Rowan was my anchor. Now I realize that he was also my shears. His love clipped back the vines. I would tell myself, sure, I was abandoned as a baby, but Rowan cares about me. I'm enough for him.

Now he's gone. Like "him." Like you.

And the vines are getting thicker. They're starting to whisper: It's not them. It's you.

Have you ever been betrayed? Did that betrayal eclipse the sun and convince you that your destiny was endless, endless night?

How do you escape from endless, endless night?

"Look up to the sky and you'll find me, always," you wrote to me.

But I can't see through the vines.

I can't see you.

I don't even know what you look like.

Asha

A silent howl

Chapter 39

The weeks following the conference didn't go according to plan. When Ash returned, Laine started bleeding unexpectedly. Panicked she might lose the baby, they rushed to the doctor, who told them there wasn't much they could do other than have Laine rest. Thankfully, the bleeding stopped on its own, but they were cautioned against putting mother and child under any undue stress. While early bleeding wasn't uncommon, if it returned, there was a chance it might indicate a more serious condition. Surviving their first terrifying experience as would-be parents made one thing frighteningly clear to Ash: he would do anything to keep his baby safe and healthy. As a father, this was his duty, and it must come first.

After the scare, he couldn't go through with confessing to Laine, not yet. He felt selfish enough already, but to endanger her health and the baby's seemed unfathomably so. The only choice was to wait.

At school, the semester passed with its usual rhythm—the quiet of reading week, the craze of midterms, the steady trudge leading toward the end of term. At home, Laine's condition vacillated but in the past couple of weeks seemed to stabilize.

Now it was the last day before the holiday break and more time had passed than Ash wanted without Laine knowing the truth. As the days flew by and Laine's belly budded, so did the black roots of doubt digging into his guts, but he tried his best to block out their dissenting whispers. Like he had assured Mala, somehow they would find a way to be together. He would set right the messes he had made.

He walked back to the Ph.D. office with a plate of gingerbread cookies, leftovers from the departmental Christmas party that afternoon. The halls were deserted, the office doors locked until the new year.

When he opened the grad office door, the lack of light took him by surprise. As he reached to turn on the switch, he was surprised again to hear Mala's voice from the dimness.

"Leave them off!" she ordered, her voice light and playful.

He cocked his head to one side, a grin slowly blooming across his face. She was up to something, although what exactly he wasn't quite sure yet. "Why are you in the dark?"

"You'll see. Come in and shut the door."

He entered, dubious, and let the shadows close around him. Faint light from the outside filtered into the office through the windows on the far side, offering barely enough to brighten the way to his cubicle. He found her seated on the tiles, ducked underneath his desk.

"Stop there!"

He chuckled, shaking his head. "Mala, what are you doing on the floor?"

The next moment, dozens of tiny white orbs lit up the dark, like bows of hovering souls, arcs of watchful angels. His spirits lifted and he was filled with awe.

"When did you do this?"

"Do you like it?"

He knelt and placed the plate of cookies on the floor. Looking up, he let the magic of the string lights dust his head and shoulders.

"I do." He grinned. "Thank you."

He took a full breath, indulging in the serenity of the silence, and the peace he only felt when they were alone, which they hadn't been for an age, it seemed. The taut cord of tension between his shoulders eased and released.

"The end of another year," she said. "I can't quite believe it."

Ash looked down at his lap, feeling unworthy of Mala's surprise, or of much of anything. They weren't on the other side of the winter solstice yet. For now, darkness reigned. She hadn't pressured him about moving forward. But he knew it must be on her mind. They wouldn't see each other again until after the break. If they were going to talk, now was the time.

"I think Laine's well enough," he said, earnest. Even though he and Mala might be together soon, it was impossible to feel anything but sick about the pain they would cause first.

He could tell by her wide open expression he had caught her off guard.

"Are you sure?"

He nodded. "I hate to tell her over the holidays. But too much time has passed already. She deserves to know. I'm starting to regret not telling her sooner."

"You couldn't risk anything happening to the baby," Mala reminded him.

"I know. But still." Shame closed around his throat. His heart had never felt heavier, blacker, like a lump of iron. How it stayed inside his chest rather than drop right out of him was a mystery.

They sat without speaking. He studied the patterns of light and shadow dispersed around them.

After a minute of quiet, Mala asked, "Do you still want to tell Laine?"

He looked up at her anxious face, half-lit from above as if by a halo. His poor love. He had to smooth away those crinkles of doubt. "Of course I do. It's just the circumstances. There's never a good time to tell someone terrible news, in this case especially." He felt the black roots of doubt burrow a little deeper into his guts. Why couldn't he shake the menacing feeling? What, if anything, did it mean?

"I'll talk to my mom too," she said. She reached for him through the dark and held his forearm fast. "We'll get through this. We'll come clean. We'll handle things as best we can. As kindly as we can. We'll find a way to make it up to the people we've hurt. And then we'll start the new year fresh. We'll be together." Her hopeful smile beamed brighter than any lantern, slicing through the moonless night that encircled him like a prison, an abyss. She believed every word she said. Their mistake hadn't changed who she was. She was still good. Inescapably human, but good. Which meant he might still have a chance at redemption too. Her light radiated. All he had to do was follow.

As he marvelled at the beauty of her kind face, marbled in soft light and shadow, the black roots of doubt ceased rooting and whispering. Mala reminded him that it was possible to atone for his mistakes. Possible to be a good person, a better person. Moving forward, that was who he would be.

Chapter 40

S eated at her desk, Mala waited for Ash to arrive, stewing. On the surface, she was still. Underneath, she paced. He hadn't replied to any of her emails over the holidays, and she didn't know his number, not that she would have had the nerve to call anyway.

Christmas had been quiet. Her house, cheerless—no lights, no tinsel, no tree. On Christmas morning, she and her mother exchanged a few modest gifts and that night ordered Chinese food, which they picked at while watching *It's a Wonderful Life* on the CBC for the hundredth time.

Mala had expected the week between Christmas and New Year's to be sombre without her father's big laugh like church bells, but what she hadn't anticipated was the gush of brine under her tongue that greeted her on Boxing Day morning. At first she thought the bug was a side effect of the egg fried rice. But when her nausea persisted for the rest of week, her mother convinced her to see the doctor.

"You aren't going to need antibiotics," said her GP.

"Is it a virus?"

"You're not sick, Mala. You're pregnant."

"That's impossible."

"Are you sexually active?"

They had only been together once. She would hardly call it active.

"What did you use for contraception?"

They had been blindsided by want. Neither of them had planned what happened that night, let alone planned for it. Perhaps he had assumed she was using contraception when she hadn't stopped things from progressing.

The shock of the news threw off Mala's plan to tell her mother about Ash, and she felt awful about it, knowing that he was following through as they had promised over the holidays. But she needed to talk to him first. As she jiggled her leg, overly conscious of her low belly, she felt like she was carrying a pearl and a detonator at the same time.

The office door creaked open. Mala recognized the sound of Ash's distinct walk. She rushed to his desk.

She wanted to throw her arms around his neck and dot him with kisses, but not having heard from him over the holidays gave her pause and she held back. Instead, she curved her lips into what she hoped was a compelling, relaxed smile while she played with her fingers behind her back.

"Hi," she said.

He was startled to see her, although she couldn't think why.

"Hi, Mala," he said, a touch ominous, as he pulled off his black parka. Underneath, he was wearing his Christmas-ribbon plaid shirt, her favourite.

A sickly feeling slithered around her belly. Not the warm reunion she had pictured during the holidays. Maybe he was picking up on her stress?

"You're here early," he said.

Could that be the reason for his coldness? He had anticipated having the office to himself, some alone time to settle in and shake off the post-vacation blues?

"What can I say? I missed seeing your face." She pinched the skin of her hand. "Why didn't you answer any of my emails?"

He wouldn't look at her as he hung his coat on the back of his chair. "Are we alone?" he asked.

"Yes. No one else is in yet. Tell me. How did it go?"

He shifted his bag from the desk to the chair, the chair to the floor, and back to the desk again. Then he unzipped it and started rummaging around.

The slither in her belly dug deeper figure-eights as the silence drew on.

"Ash?"

He finally stopped fidgeting and went still. He kept his eyes pinned to the floor as he spoke.

"I don't know how to tell you this."

"What is it?"

He wet his lips. "I didn't tell her."

The slither in her belly froze to solid. "Why not? What happened?"

"Laine's condition got worse all of a sudden. She started bleeding again before Christmas, but more heavily than last time. We had to rush to the hospital."

Mala clasped a hand over her mouth. "Oh God. The baby . . ."

"The baby's fine."

She lowered her arm with a sigh. "Thank goodness." She thought for a moment. "So we'll wait a little longer to tell people. That might be for the best, actually. Ash, I have something to—"

"No, Mala," he interrupted. His expression was crushed with anguish, and his voice meek with guilt. "You don't understand. I didn't tell Laine." He dithered. "And I'm not going to."

Was the air in the room suddenly thicker or were her nostrils compressed? "What do you mean?"

He lowered himself onto his chair like an old man. He still wouldn't look her in the eye. "We almost lost the baby. I've never felt more scared or helpless in my life. All I could do was sit by Laine's bed, begging the baby to stay put. Stay alive. I've never seen

Laine more devastated. I hope I never feel that useless again." He rubbed his chin. "When we got through it, I realized something. I'll do anything to save the baby. And I want to protect Laine from suffering like that ever again."

Mala eyed him, apprehensive. "What are you saying?"

He lifted his sorrowful gaze. His eyes were rimmed with water, glossy with pain. "I have to make a sacrifice, Mala. I have a responsibility to them. I always have, but almost losing the baby finally got through to me. I can't be selfish anymore. I have to do what's best for them. Lives more important than my own depend on it." He paused. "I'm so sorry."

Somehow, Mala managed to stay upright. She felt a sharp pang of neglect where the slithers had snaked. Her mind went cold. Her hand floated over her stomach. His words seemed to maul their delicate child in her womb.

"Mala?" he said gently. "Please, try to understand. We talked about making up for the pain we've caused. Well, this is how I make up for mine. If I left Laine and she lost the baby, I'd never forgive myself. I have to do the right thing. I hate hurting you—more than you'll ever know—but this is what I have to do."

Something inside her tipped. Water was sealing itself around her voice, drowning all the things she had planned on telling him. All the things that didn't matter anymore.

Mala turned away and faced the door. A part of her wailed mournfully as she put her feet in motion. Ash had made his choice. He had chosen Laine, like she had always secretly feared he would do. Laine and their baby would always be more important to him. They would always come first. Mala was on her own.

The hallway boomed with the sound of the office door slamming. Somehow her tube-like legs carried her along the hallway and around the corner to the washroom. A student was washing her hands at the sink. The disabled stall was free. Mala ducked inside, dropped her weight against the wall and slowly slid into a ball on the brown tiled floor, a wet patch and torn strip of toilet paper an inch beyond her shoes. As she hugged her knees, her grief seemed to octuple in mass. She let it slip down her cheeks, gather in her mouth, at her chin, on her sweater, all the while hoping no line was forming outside the flimsy stall door.

Chapter 41

L ater that evening, Mala pined in bed with her book. Jane knew all about life's disappointments. When Rochester betrayed her trust, she moved on because it was "of no use wanting anything better."

Before she set out, however, even Jane struggled with the matter of how.

"There are many others who have no friends, who must look about for themselves and be their own helpers; and what is their resource?"

Mala wondered, What is mine?

No easy choice

Chapter 42

Asha lay on her stomach in bed, brooding at her journal, glum and queasy. Even a few months ago she would have gone to her mom with this. Not that it would have been easy, but her mom had always encouraged Asha to be open, partly because she hadn't been able to talk to her own mom about relationships when she was growing up. Asha's heartbeat pounded at the base of her sour throat. She had promised her mom that they would talk if her relationship with Rowan became more intimate. Of course, that was before the secrets and broken trust and, most recently, the accident. Things had changed between them. Looking back, Asha saw with a blister in her heart just how much they had changed, how far she and her mom had drifted apart. Asha missed the closeness she had never questioned until recently, mourning it like a death. Willow kept trying to persuade her to talk to her mom despite the distance, claiming that the crisis might bring them back together. As well-meaning as she was, her best friend didn't understand the realities of their home life, or how overstretched her mom was already—because of Asha. Her mom's hands were going to be even fuller with her dad's homecoming in a few days. No, she was determined to handle things without causing any more stress in her parents' lives.

Asha flipped to a fresh page. Her birth mother had been in a similar position. This shared experience, at least, made Asha feel closer to her birth mother and her otherwise mysterious life.

How old were you when you found out you were pregnant with me? Did you wrestle with any doubts? Or were you always confident about what you wanted to do?

I know I made a mistake. But doesn't everybody when they're young? I realize I shouldn't have put so much faith in Rowan. I should have paid closer attention to what was happening that night. Which is another reason why I need to handle this on my own without bothering Mom and Dad.

How did "he" react to finding out he was going to be a dad? I like to think you were both excited. At that point, you didn't know what the future held. You didn't know you were going to get sick and pass away. I hope your pregnancy at least was a happy time for you.

Not a nightmare, like this. Rowan doesn't want anything to do with it, or me. Maybe I shouldn't let him off so easily, but to be honest, I can't even stand the thought of seeing him again.

So here I am, with an important choice to make, like you were at one time in your past. You chose to keep me. I want to thank you for that. Now I see how much it must have taken. Even when you want a baby, it takes everything, doesn't it?

The thing is, I'm not you. I don't know how old you were when you had me, but I've only just turned eighteen. I'm not ready to be a mom. And I'm not ready to have a baby either.

Somehow, I needed to tell you. Almost like a confession.

Asha

Chapter 43

Asha had arranged a consultation at a family planning clinic, but on the day of her appointment, she and Willow ran into one of her mom's friends on the sidewalk as they were about to enter the building. When her mom's friend asked, a little surprised, what they were up to in that part of town (mostly office buildings), Asha's mind went blank. Willow jumped in and said they were on their way downtown but she needed to use the washroom all of a sudden. They spotted a Starbucks from the bus, which was where they were headed. Her mom's friend declared that it must be fate. She had been thinking about Asha's mom that morning, wondering how her dad's recovery was going. She was on her break and insisted on treating them to a drink. While Asha updated her mom's friend, she missed her appointment. That evening, her dad was discharged from the rehabilitation centre.

Running into her mom's friend left Asha shaken and out spilled her worries. What if she had arrived a few seconds earlier and her mom's friend had seen her enter the clinic, and that news made its way back to her parents? It would have been a disaster.

That night, unsure of what else to do, Asha searched for alternatives online. She stumbled upon a recipe for an herbal concoction that claimed to be effective. She nearly burst into tears when she read the positive feedback in the comments section—it seemed like a godsend. If the concoction worked, she wouldn't have to reschedule her appointment or risk her parents finding out about her mistake. She had to at least give it a try.

Guessing that Willow would dismiss the remedy as folk science— or worse, that she might even tell her parents out of concern—Asha collected the ingredients on her own the next day, from health food stores, an apothecary and a Wiccan store she used to mill about in when she was younger, which sold certain plants and oils for rituals. According to the forum, she could expect some light cramping overnight, maybe a little bleeding, but by tomorrow morning Asha would be able to put this part of her life, and Rowan's betrayal, behind her.

Asha mixed the ingredients into a tall glass of water, aware of her parents sitting in the living room below her bedroom. Her breathing was uneven and her hands shaky. The smell reminded her of decay. Closing her eyes, she pinched her nose, brought the pungent drink to her lips and emptied the glass without stopping, knowing that if she paused even for a second she would gag. The concoction streamed from the corners of her mouth, staining her light T-shirt berry pink. She felt it burn along the column leading to her stomach, where it seemed to bubble and smoke.

Asha lowered the glass onto her dresser, sat on the edge of her bed and waited for something to happen. She stuffed a few pieces of mint gum into her mouth, hoping to overpower the bitter melon taste on her tongue. What if the remedy didn't work? she wondered. What if she took another pregnancy test in a few days and nothing had changed?

These were the thoughts that tortured her as a balloonish feeling swelled her lips. Her tongue inflated and overwhelmed her mouth. Her throat sealed itself. Her breathing became as thin as a wheeze.

The last thing Asha remembered was fighting to draw in a thread of air.

Then the world went black.

Who needs a heart?

Chapter 44

Mala followed a meandering line of moviegoers out of the darkened theatre. The ominous feeling she had harboured during the film descended upon her like nightfall, as every one of her reluctant steps brought her closer to the task she must now face. They entered the bright hallway and her eyes puckered sharply, adjusting to the light.

"Are you sure you don't want any of this?" Sumesh asked, shaking a half-eaten bag of popcorn under her nose. Mala suppressed a fierce gag as discreetly as she could while holding her breath with watery eyes and begging the bitter slime to slide back down her throat. Her nausea, she was discovering, worsened in the evening.

"No, thanks," she said quickly, then drew a long sip from her cup of ginger ale in an effort to rinse away the salty-sweet essence of popcorn painted to her palate.

Sumesh shrugged, thinking nothing of it, and tossed the rest of the popcorn into a trash can they passed on the way to the exit.

Cold January air, dry and lifeless, hit them like an icy shockwave as they stepped onto the sidewalk outside the cinema. Mala covered her head with the fur-lined hood of her parka and watched people trickle past them, in and out of the doors, sheltered beneath layers of their own winter armour. Funnels of amber light spot-lit the parking lot, casting a warm glow over the lightly falling snow.

She beheld the gentle cascade of crystalline flakes and enjoyed a rare sense of calm.

"Would you like me to drive you home?" Sumesh asked.

The reprieve didn't last. Mala shoved her hands into her coat pockets and shredded a balled-up tissue she discovered inside one of them to distract from the panic swiftly rising in her chest, like a charge building behind her breastbone. She could almost hear the electric hum of her nerves, sense the prick of their thin crackle. She observed Sumesh from the anonymity of her hood. The movie had been a way for them to get reacquainted. Now it was time for Mala to push forward with the rest of her plan.

"How about we get something warm to drink?" She pointed her chin at the Starbucks across the parking lot.

He grinned, amused. "Still thirsty?"

She forced herself to grin back. "It'll give us a chance to talk," she said, a serious note in her voice.

Sumesh nodded, suddenly sage, and they hurried across the parking lot, their boots streaking across the untouched layer of snow.

They entered the humid coffee shop and Mala's glasses fogged up in an instant. She slipped them off with a groan, fished out the remains of the tissue from her pocket and wiped away the cloudy film. Coffee shop jazz played in the background.

"I hate it when that happens," Sumesh said.

Mala looked up at him with a dimpled chin. "You wear glasses?"

"Contacts. Most of the time."

Contacts, she repeated in her head. She knew so little about him.

Once their drinks were ready, they carried their cups to a secluded table at the back, by the electric fireplace.

Mala took a sip from her steaming cup of mint tea, wincing as she singed the tip of her tongue. *When was she going to learn?* She silently scolded herself, irritated by this minor display of hastiness, although indirectly referring to her more reckless actions of late.

Where had her patience gone? Had it been it spirited away along with her good sense? These days she felt like her decisions were being timed. She could almost see the numbers counting down on a stopwatch in her head, almost feel time sneering at her as it dwindled, and her fate turned more dire.

Sumesh lounged in the brown leather armchair across from her with his legs loosely crossed. Mala tried to pay attention to his opinions about the movie, but her focus was cleft. Her leg bounced up and down. It was obvious from his casual manner that he didn't consider her attractive enough to be intimidating. Nevertheless, not long ago, he had thought they were a good match. This was the belief Mala needed to rekindle in him tonight. She only hoped he would still be open to the idea, if indeed he was still available.

Mala realized all at once that Sumesh had stopped speaking. She fidgeted in her chair as he surveyed her over the rim of his white mug, mildly unimpressed. "Are my film critiques that boring?"

"Not at all." She swept away a stray hair that was suddenly tickling her forehead. "What were you saying?" She leaned forward, feigning interest. "I missed the last part."

Her heart tapped in quick little beats. She smiled broadly and waited for him to reply, praying he wasn't offended and about to leave.

"It doesn't matter," he said at last. "It was a shitty movie anyway." He paused, his relaxed demeanour evaporating. "You mentioned earlier that you wanted to talk. So let's talk."

Mala broke eye contact. She fixed her eyes on the gritty puddle of melted snow around her boots, and her stomach coiled into a tight, strained mass. "I wanted to talk about us."

He sat up straighter, uncrossed his legs and set his drink on the table.

"Us," he said, like a statement. "I thought there wasn't going to be an us, Mala. You cut me loose, remember? I was surprised when you called the other day. Part of the reason I'm here is to find out why and, of course, why you ended things."

Her saliva tasted like consommé. "I'm sorry about that." She kept her face serene while her stomach twisted. "I'd never been through anything like that before. I guess you could say I got cold feet. It really wasn't about you. In fact, I enjoyed getting to know you when we went out for coffee." This was perhaps the one true thing Mala would say during their conversation.

He seemed unconvinced. "That's surprising. Because you didn't seem remotely interested in me. You were polite enough, but something tells me that's just your nature. I was sure you were only there to make your mom happy. When you ended things, I was disappointed, but I can't say I was surprised." He sniffed. "Unlike you, I've done this before. Too many times. You kind of get a knack for reading how things are going. But then"—he shrugged—"here we are. I guess I must be terrible at reading people."

Mala hid behind her cup and took a piping swallow, not caring that the tea scorched the inside of her mouth. Poor Sumesh. He *was* terrible at reading people. He had no idea how terrible. But she had to do this. She had no other choice. She needed to have an explanation for her condition and the only one her mother would accept was a husband.

"So," Sumesh continued. "Why the sudden change of heart?"

Mala nearly choked on her tea. The heart had nothing to do with what would happen next. Holding in a cough, she lowered her cup and composed herself.

"Like I said, I was always fond of you. It was more about having time to think things through." She paused. "And I have. You said something to me before. About how having an arranged marriage simplified things." She waited, the gruelling length of three long breaths, to keep from seeming needy. "Which is why, if you're still open to it, I would be happy to go ahead with the engagement."

Her insides writhed as if squalid with worms. Mala crossed her arms protectively over her midsection and waited for Sumesh to respond with feeble breath. So much of her plan depended on his answer.

"The engagement?" He cocked his head back. "I wasn't expecting that." Clearly unprepared, he leaned forward and reached for his hot chocolate. The shriek of the milk steamer sheared through the clouds of chatter hovering around them. The overpowering aroma of roasted coffee was giving Mala a headache, she could feel the pain building at her temples. The strained mass in her stomach throbbed in tandem with her rapid heartbeat.

"You've met someone else, haven't you?" She remembered how Mrs. Mishra had bragged about the long list of girls waiting to meet Sumesh. Something inside Mala plummeted.

He cradled his mug and appraised her with an undecipherable gaze. Mala knew, in the festering pit of her stomach, that her plan had failed.

"I stopped meeting women after you," he said at last. "Partly because no one likes rejection. Partly out of exhaustion. My parents have been pushing the marriage agenda for quite a while now."

"How did you get them to lay off?"

He gave a cynical laugh. "Exams."

Mala couldn't suppress her smirk. "What a coincidence. I used school as an excuse too."

"Not a coincidence at all, if you ask me."

They shared a muted, tragic laugh, and an understanding of sorts passed between them. Although they were as good as strangers, they could empathize with each other, knowing the cultural pressures of their upbringing. High marks, a prestigious career, a respectable marriage, children, children, children—these were the expectations their parents had drilled into them from a young age.

"Can I ask you something?" he said.

She nodded.

A tender sadness drifted into his eyes and lingered. "Speaking hypothetically, if we went through with it, do you think we could make each other happy?"

Happy? Mala wondered, taken aback. Of all the considerations whirling around in her mind, happiness hadn't occurred to her, not even once. Duty, obligation, survival—yes. But never happiness.

"I don't want to end up like my parents," he added, despondent. "Bickering all the time. I want a peaceful home. More than anything, I want the freedom to live my life."

Mala sympathized with his desire to flee a stifling home. Sumesh wouldn't be the first person to use marriage as a way out, a way of moving his life forward. At the same time, given his parents' relationship, she also understood his skepticism, and how it could co-exist with his willingness to consider an arranged marriage. "If it makes you feel any better, my parents didn't bicker. They had the best marriage of anyone I know. I like to think I've learned how to have a good relationship from them."

"What was their secret?"

Her heart brimmed with pride at the thought of her parents and the couple they had been. "They were friends."

Sumesh frowned. "You're lucky. I wish I'd been raised in a happy home. Mine's as dysfunctional as they come. My parents were doomed from the start. My mom's spent her life pining over what might've been. Of course, my dad doesn't make life easy either." He contemplated. "But I think you're right, Mala. Maybe the thing to focus on is friendship. Getting along."

Mala had heard the saying that at the core of every lasting relationship was the platonic ideal. That was what Sumesh was proposing, she realized, and so was she. Not the thrill of passion but the comforts of a peaceful household. The freedom to live one's life. A commitment to be respectful friends. Close to the offer St. John Rivers had made Jane.

"You should know," he said, "that even though I've agreed to these introductions, I fall on the more nontraditional side. My independence means a lot to me, and I would want my future wife to value hers as well. The last thing I want is to be a part of another codependent family. And I don't want to be my wife's entire world either. It's too much pressure. Which is probably why I've gone through so many introductions. It's been hard to find someone . . . unconventional."

"Well, my career's important to me. If my life is about anything, it's research. Family is important too, of course. But I have no intention of becoming just another self-sacrificing wife and mother, filled with bitterness by the end of her life because she gave up her dreams to raise a family. Which is probably why I've put off introductions for so long."

Another moment of understanding passed between them.

Then Sumesh fell silent.

Mala worried she had pushed too far, too soon, leaping over seeing each other to suggesting an engagement. The idea wouldn't have seemed strange to her parents' generation, of course, nor would it be unfamiliar to Sumesh, but it was a leap nonetheless.

She prayed Sumesh was tired of introductions and, based on their conversation, would see that their expectations were in line. It was clear they shared the same desire to have a modern marriage, regardless of its more traditional beginning. Mala was surprised to find herself seeing Sumesh as more than merely part of her plan, but also as a good match, under the circumstances.

There was nothing more she could do. Sumesh was free to make up his own mind. She hugged her belly and quietly awaited her fate.

She was lost in deep, mournful visions of her mother's stricken face when he broke the silence.

"Okay, Mala." His tone was measured.

She looked up. His expression was far from that of an enthusiastic groom. Instead, he appeared as level as his declaration, as practical as acceptance. Despite the lack of emotion, Mala was so surprised by his answer, so desperately relieved, she couldn't speak, only stare with an open mouth.

"Like I told you before," he said, filling the gaps in her shock. "When you meet the right person, you'll do anything to be with them. You'll make any compromise." He faltered, a twinge of pain flickering across his brow. "In this case, my pride."

Mala almost blushed from his adulation and her shame. "I'm flattered you think I'm that person."

He gave her a look, hooded and mysterious. *What did it mean?* She wasn't accustomed to seeing his face, period, let alone trying to decipher its etchings and twitches for meaning or tells. Perhaps he was having doubts, now that he had voiced his commitment.

As if remembering he wasn't alone, Sumesh softened his features and sent her a warmish half smile. "Our parents are going to flip. They'll probably start planning the wedding right away."

"The sooner, the better." Mala dug her nails into her palm. "What about next month?"

He smirked. "Funny." He sipped his hot chocolate.

Her solemn expression sobered him. "You aren't kidding." He licked cocoa from his lips. "What's the rush?"

A salty wave of nausea hurled into her with the force of the sea. She gripped the seat cushion to keep herself from pitching forward. Even if they were married next month, her delivery date would be off by several weeks. Mala whispered a silent apology to the face she loved in the clouds and readied herself for the last push.

With eyes downcast, she said, "Part of the reason is my dad's passing. It doesn't feel right to have a big wedding without him. My heart wouldn't be in it." She readjusted her glasses on the bridge of her nose. "And since his passing, it's been hard for me to catch up with school. I took off almost a year to mourn him, and while I don't regret it, ever since, I feel like I've been making up for lost time. I know how important your studies are to you too. Doesn't it make more sense to have a small wedding as soon as possible, instead of being distracted with plans for a year? I was hoping we could keep things simple, then move on with our lives. Together. That's what I'm looking forward to, not necessarily the wedding."

The final push drained the last of Mala's energy. She didn't even have enough to fidget anymore. While Sumesh rubbed his clean-shaven chin, deliberating over her request, she leaned back in her chair and rested her eyes on the electric fireplace. She was mesmerized by the false flames flickering behind the glass. While she observed them, a strange sensation came over her, as if her bones were losing density, dissolving like a tablet in water. Her body felt weightless as a tide of exhaustion washed over her, reminding her how much it took to tell lies. It took the body, and so much more. Mala wondered which parts of her were disintegrating. Whom was she transforming into?

"I've never cared much for the fanfare," he said finally.

She jerked her head in his direction. *What was he saying? Was he consenting? Was her plan about to work after all the sweat and worry?* "Are you sure you wouldn't miss parading through the street on a white horse?" she asked, tentative.

He gave her the same noncommittal half smile as before, regarding her as if from very far away. "I'll settle for a limo," he replied.

And the deal was done.

Chapter 45

Mala quietly entered the house. She hung her coat in the closet and heard the creak of the floorboards behind her, announcing her mother's approach. From the top of the stairs, her mother hummed with an excitement she couldn't downplay.

"How was it, beti?" she asked. "Did you and Sumesh have a nice time at the movies? I was expecting you a little while ago." She smiled. "I hoped you being late was a good sign. You should have invited him in for tea."

Mala's knees felt weak as she climbed the stairs. She entered the living room and collapsed onto the couch with a restrained sigh. The burden of her world seemed to crush her into the cushions. She thought she might never move again, not that she wanted to.

"It went well," she replied.

Her mother joined her on the couch, folding her hands in her lap. "He's a nice boy, isn't he? That's what everyone says about him. Good, respectful, honest. If a little picky. But he clearly likes you, beti. Otherwise he would never have agreed to see you again. You know how Indian men are with their egos, even the young ones." She gently patted Mala's hand a few times. "I'm so glad you changed your mind. We're lucky he didn't meet someone else in the meantime."

Mala didn't have the strength to respond.

Blind to Mala's preoccupation, her mother made herself

comfortable, placing a pillow under her elbow, like someone about to settle in for a long chat.

"Now, tell me what you talked about. When are you going to see each other again? Next weekend, maybe? Or we could have him over for dinner. You'll have to ask him what he likes to eat."

Her mother's hopeful voice pried something open inside Mala, and something else rushed out, a sort of madness that made her feel as if she were holding a scream in her throat. Perhaps it was the crazed voice of her conscience that she had locked away, deep below. The rims of her eyes shivered and the muscles along her neck tightened into ropes. Judging from her mother's unbothered expression, Mala was falling to pieces in ways only she could see. She flinched imperceptibly. It was sickening how good she had become at hiding.

"We talked about a lot of things."

Her mother gave her a light tap on the wrist, gently scolding her. "What kind of answer is that, hein? Don't keep your old mother in suspense."

What if, Mala wondered, she told her mother the truth, right now? What would happen?

Would she offer Mala a way of dealing with her predicament other than the plan Mala had devised on her own?

Would she be able to put aside her heartbreak and disappointment, and of course her deep shame, and despite all of that help Mala figure out the best possible option for her?

Once her eyes had dried, would she see the unborn child as innocent, a blessing, rather than a burden responsible for sinking their family's reputation?

"Mala?" she heard her mother say at a distance, yanking her back into the room and her reality.

Mala gazed into her mother's beautiful face, within which she saw her own, and was struck by an overwhelming instinct to protect her. From the judgment, the shame. The inevitable labels that would be attached to them both. *Pavan gone only a year and look at what happened to her daughter. Tsk.* Mala didn't want her mother to lose friends. She didn't want her to lose face. She didn't want people to see her as anything but the good mother that she was and had always been.

No, it wasn't fair or right for Mala's mistake to taint them both. She had been over this before. Nothing had changed. Whatever it was, madness or conscience, sank back into its oubliette.

Then, feeling like there was no more blood in her veins, Mala spoke the words her mother was hoping for, the ones that would bring her peace.

"We've decided to get married."

Chapter 46

Mala drove up the Mishras' long driveway, the kind she imagined Jane dragging her sensible granny boots along as she approached Thornfield Hall, although this road was paved, yet she, no less filled with apprehension. The expansive two-storey stone manor was nestled in the heart of Rockcliffe Park, one of Ottawa's more affluent neighbourhoods. Mrs. Mishra often boasted about their house's proximity to the official residence of the Leader of the Opposition, as though the short distance between trash cans somehow made her influential. After parking their car, Mala and her mother followed the slate path that led from the driveway to the Mishra's stately oak door.

They paused before announcing themselves. Mala's mother wore one of her best silk saris, cream-coloured with a maroon and emerald border. Heavy gold rings hung from her ears, stretching her lobes. Beneath her woollen coat, the matching necklace, a twentieth-anniversary present from Mala's father.

A keen midwinter gust pierced the delicate fabric of Mala's salwar kameez. Her mother touched her neatly bunned hair.

"You look great, Mom. Stop worrying. It's just the Mishras."

"Their house is very grand."

"It looks like a model, not a home."

"What they must have thought of our little bungalow."

"I would choose our house over some drafty manor any day."

Her mother frowned. "Not many would, beti."

Mala tapped the heavy iron knocker three times. Soon after, Sumesh opened the door and greeted them with a broad, if vaguely frightened, smile. He stepped aside to let them pass.

As she entered the vestibule, Mala smelled the earthy and familiar fragrance of sandalwood incense. Soft twinkling light rained from the ballroom-like chandelier, casting diamond shapes on the walls and pale marble floor. At the back, a spiral staircase led to the second level. To the right, there was an inviting sitting room with leather couches, floor-to-ceiling bookcases and a large fireplace that crackled with flames despite the room being vacant. Sumesh took their coats and Mala slipped off her boots, placing them to one side of the ornate hand-knotted rug, conscious of any grit she might have tracked in. She could hear the faint sound of a television somewhere toward the back of the house.

"There you are," Mrs. Mishra said as she emerged from a short hallway to the left, sauntering. "We were beginning to think you weren't coming."

"We got a little lost along the way," Mala told her.

"Yes, well, I don't imagine you visit this area very often, do you?" She waved a dismissive hand, her nails glossy with deep plum varnish. As Mrs. Mishra sashayed over, her emerald-green sari elegantly swept the floor and the clack of her kitten heels punctuated the air. Her hair was pulled back, her eyes thickly lined with kohl and her lips tinted a murderous shade of cherry. "Welcome to our little pied-à-terre." The woman showed the turmeric-stained yellow of her smile. Mala privately delighted in the blood-like smear across her front teeth.

"Kumari," her mother said, her voice low with admiration. "You have a lovely home."

"Oh, Veena, you haven't even had the tour yet! It's much larger than it seems from outside."

Mrs. Mishra turned her attention to Mala, scanning her from toe to crown with a pitiless eye. Mala felt as though the woman could peer into her bones. She flicked her tongue against the roof of her mouth, chirping disapproval.

Mala looked down at the teal-coloured salwar kameez she was wearing, an engagement present from the Mishras, along with a set of gaudy gold and ruby jewellery, complete with earrings, choker and forehead piece. Mala hadn't worn the jewellery today, thinking it was too elaborate for a dinner party, not that it fit her taste regardless.

"No bindi?" Mrs. Mishra scowled. "And why aren't you wearing your jewellery? Don't you like it?"

Mala felt an inner twitch. "Of course I do." She wrung her bare wrist with her hand. "I didn't want to ruin anything while we were cooking."

"Look at your dupatta." Mrs. Mishra reached for the long chiffon scarf draped loosely across Mala's neck and snatched it off.

Mala glanced at her mother, who had arranged the dupatta before they left home, expecting to see gall in her eyes, but instead, she saw her mother twisting her bangles while gazing at a diamond of light on the entry floor.

Mrs. Mishra draped the scarf over Mala's right shoulder. "It looks better like this. When we're finished cooking, I'll get you a bindi and some bangles." Pleased with herself, Mrs. Mishra led them down the hallway to the left, from where she had emerged.

"Ignore her," Sumesh whispered into Mala's ear. He placed a hand on her back, barely touching the dip between her shoulder blades, and nudged her along the hallway. Mala shuddered at his faint touch. She hoped he hadn't noticed.

They walked along the hall, cutting a path through the dense fog of Mrs. Mishra's rose perfume. Mala felt lightheaded. The volume of the television amplified. The living room was a comfortable size, neither too large nor too small, predominated by an L-shaped sectional and a wide, wall-mounted television. Sumesh's father was watching hockey and pecking at a cluster of pretzels held in his overstuffed hand. In appearance, he was round and bald and unlike Sumesh in every respect other than the deepness of their complexions.

"Turn that bloody game off!" Mrs. Mishra snapped on her way to the kitchen.

Her husband only had ears for the game. "Do you enjoy hockey, Mala?" He shifted his girth to make room for her on the couch.

"I'm a Sens fan, but only during the playoffs."

He made a display of laughing at her joke. "Come and sit." He patted the cushion beside him. "The second period is about to start."

Mala was in the midst of accepting his invitation when she felt Mrs. Mishra's bony fingers claw her elbow. "We have work to do," she said, stern.

Mala was led into the kitchen. She craned her neck and peered pleadingly at Sumesh, who was taking a comfortable seat beside his father on the couch, either ignorant of her plight or unwilling to do anything about it.

"Why don't they help us?"

"Nonsense," Mrs. Mishra clipped. She covered her sari with an apron. "Enough silliness. Today I'm going to teach you how to prepare my son's favourite meal: saag paneer, rajma and puri."

"Doesn't Sumesh know how to cook for himself?"

"Don't be ridiculous. I cook for him, I'm his mother. Now tell me, what dishes do you know?"

Mala reflected. With a flat stare, she said, "I make a fabulous lasagna."

Mrs. Mishra glowered for some seconds, then clacked her heels over to the white marble island at the centre of the kitchen, each clack like the slap of a ruler against Mala's palm. She rapped a large slab of butcher block with her talon of a forefinger, *tap-tap-tap*.

"Come here and chop these onions," she ordered.

More red lipstick had smeared across her teeth, but even that didn't have the power to lift Mala's mood. She dragged her soles to the marble island veined with grey and started peeling an onion. As she chopped, the smell stung her nostrils and salt water wept into the back of her throat from the sea of nausea in her gut, a fine trickle pooling in the well under her tongue.

All of a sudden, Mala wanted to stop everything—chopping, lying, twisting into an unrecognizable shape. The reality of the life she was choosing slammed into her. It wasn't surprising that Mrs. Mishra expected her to cook, like the women of her generation. What depressed Mala was finding herself under the pall of the same expectation, which she had always promised herself to avoid if and when she married. Yet here she was, a servant in training. Mala stilled the knife, relaxed her fingers around its handle and pictured herself running out into the cold winter night. Running and running.

Seconds passed. The saline well under her tongue spilled over her bottom teeth. She rolled her tongue and tasted the brine more sharply as it slipped back down her throat, the taste a reminder of the bud forming below her navel, the reminder like fuel, an injection of adrenaline into her barely beating heart. Not one heart—two. Mala heard their heartbeats—first her own, then the baby's—moving through her like an echo, her heart beating downward, the baby's bounding up. *I'm here*, the little heart was telling her. *I'm here, I'm here, I'm here.*

Regripping the knife handle, she continued chopping the pungent root. In the background, cheers as the home team scored.

As she fantasized about telling Mrs. Mishra what she thought of her, the way Jane had confronted Mrs. Reed, she heard Mrs. Mishra ask her mother, "Have you heard about the Patels?" Her mother was washing potatoes and Mrs. Mishra was retrieving pans from the cupboards.

"No," her mother replied. "I didn't see Sona at temple the other day. Come to think of it, I didn't see her the week before either. Strange."

"It's no wonder she didn't show her face. You remember Jothi, yes? The girl who was studying pharmacy?"

"Of course. She's a lovely girl. She and Mala used to play together when they were little."

Mala remembered.

"*Well*, not so fair and lovely, after all. The girl got herself pregnant."

Mala looked over her shoulder. Her mother stopped washing the potatoes, shocked. "But she's not married, is she?"

"No, Veena! The girl's not married! She isn't even finished her studies yet. Apparently, she's been living a double life. A good daughter at home and a floozy while she's away." Mrs. Mishra shook her head at the disgrace of it all.

Mala examined her mother's troubled face closely. "Her poor parents," she muttered.

Now was Mala's chance to challenge their outdated perception. "So Jothi's a single mother now. So are lots of women. It doesn't mean her life is over. A woman doesn't need a man to—"

"It's a complete disgrace!" Mrs. Mishra spat out. "I don't know how they will be able to face their family or any of us ever again. Thank God, I don't have a daughter. This is the kind of trouble you get when you have a daughter."

"Not all daughters behave that way." Mala's mother beamed at her, warm and proud.

"Well, you're lucky, Veena. I almost got Sumesh a girl from India, you know. They, at least, still know how to behave properly. Girls here don't listen to their parents. They run wild. They have no respect for themselves or their families. They have no shame."

Mala turned back and continued chopping the onions, the blade barely slicing or making a sound.

"What are they going to do?" her mother asked.

"I know what I would have done. But she's keeping the baby."

"So they are getting married, then. That lessens the family's shame somewhat. Eventually no one will remember what came before the baby."

"No marriage, Veena! Don't be so naive. The boy got what he wanted. And the girl got her lesson. You know"—lowering her voice—"he wasn't even Indian."

Mala froze, waiting to see how her mother would respond. "Oh," she said. That was all. Then she resumed scrubbing the potatoes.

Oh, Mala thought, beaten, diminished. *Oh*.

In that hopeless moment, Mala recalled what Helen Burns had told Jane: that it was better to endure the consequences of your actions than have those consequences extend to all connected with you.

Mala swallowed another gob of salt water.

All connected with you.

SOOTHING NOTES OF a bansuri flute lilted through the air, fine and graceful, as they gathered around the long oak dining table. At its centre, a slender crystal vase, ebullient with pink and yellow roses—dethroned, controlled, curated, like so much of the evening so far, like Mala herself. She felt an itch convulse against the adhesive of the crystal-like bindi that Mrs. Mishra had fixed between her eyebrows. The inches of bangles on her wrists were shackles. The heavy gold around her neck, a noose.

Mr. and Mrs. Mishra sat at opposite ends of the table, although Mala never doubted who was the true head of the household. Mala was placed beside Sumesh, and her mother across from her. She gazed at the vacant spot to her mother's right and pictured her father sitting there, but she couldn't hold the image for more than a few moments; it was too much to behold, it was too impossible.

Mala wondered, if he were alive, would they be there now, about to discuss wedding plans with the Mishras over an indigestible meal? If her father hadn't passed away, would she have fallen off track and lost herself to loneliness? Would she even be pregnant? Or would she have made better choices for herself? As the moments slipped past and the others filled their plates, Mala was alone with the thought of it.

Without appetite, she served herself a spoonful of rice, rajma and saag from the white dishes laid out along the middle of the table and pushed a soft square of paneer around her plate with her fork.

"Hmph," Mrs. Mishra grunted, critiquing her first bite. "Not bad for your first try at my recipes. What do you think, Sumesh?"

With one hand over his mouth, he mumbled, "Delicious," and smiled at Mala in appreciation.

Mrs. Mishra arched her clownish eyebrows. "Not as good as mine, of course. And it won't be as easy without me to help you next time." She smirked, appearing pleased by the idea of Mala's failure.

Mala reached for her tumbler of ice water, condensation dripping from its sides, and took a sip. A chill trickled down her throat as the woman's words slipped into her stomach, where they curdled like milk and lemon.

The conversation shifted to the wedding and reception. Mala leaned back in her chair and let the chatter hover above her. Mrs. Mishra had called around to various hotels and banquet halls in the city. Due to a cancellation, the Lord Elgin Hotel was available early next month.

About five weeks along, Mala thought. I won't be showing yet.

Mala felt a toe nudge her under the table. She looked up to find three pairs of eyes quietly judging her. "Sorry?"

Sumesh shared her mother's somewhat embarrassed expression. "Mom was telling us about the plans for the reception. Apparently, they can accommodate an Indian menu. Isn't that great?"

Mala nodded. "Great."

Mrs. Mishra frowned. "You know, I've always dreamed of having a daughter-in-law who I could plan my son's wedding with. Oh well, like everything else about this wedding, I suppose we will simply have to make do, hmm? With such short notice, it's doubtful that any of the family from India will be able to come. Maybe not even the cousins from the States, although I'll see what I can do. We're lucky the pandit was available! How about your family, Veena?"

Mala's mother shook her head with a kind of resigned disappointment. "All our family is back in India. The journey is too costly for them. But I will send pictures, as always."

Mrs. Mishra tore into a puri. "How about wedding clothes? Mala? Did you look through the copy of *Shaadi* I gave you?"

Mala mashed a kidney bean with her fork. "I flipped through it. It's all a bit extravagant, to be honest. I was planning on picking up a nice outfit from the mall. Something modern."

Mrs. Mishra stopped eating and glared. "Nonsense. You're an Indian bride. You need something proper. The wedding is the day we present you to our friends and family. We will not be embarrassed."

Mala looked warily across the table at her mother, who was grinning in agreement. She tensed her diaphragm. "What did you have in mind?"

"Well, it goes without saying we'll have to make a trip to Toronto. The selection there is good. Nothing compared to what you would find in India or the UK, but we will make do. We'll find you the lehnga of your dreams."

In her dreams, Mala envisioned herself marrying somewhere deep in the woods of Gatineau Park, barefoot, wearing a slip of a dress and a wreath of wildflowers in her hair. Nestled under the arching canopy of century-old maples and oaks, she would make vows of faithfulness to Ash, not Sumesh. These visions no one could touch, not even Mrs. Mishra with her suffocating grasp. Mala placed one hand over her low belly.

"I don't think I'll have time. Things are hectic at school."

"Too busy to choose your own wedding outfit?"

"You could always take my measurements."

Mrs. Mishra reclined in her chair, incredulous. "I have never met a bride who didn't care what she looked like on her wedding day." She rubbed her thumb and fingertips together, slick with puri grease.

Although Mala loathed to placate the woman, she knew just how to do so. She curled her lips into a synthetic smile and dipped her head in submission. "You know best. If what you're wearing tonight is any indication, you have lovely taste. I trust your judgment."

Mala watched Mrs. Mishra's hard features soften to her pandering. She felt something inside her detach and fall away, like rootless hair. How much more of herself would she lose with every lie she told? What creature would her baldness reveal? What new growth would take root in its place?

Mrs. Mishra sighed dramatically. "Well, I suppose you're right. I *do* have an eye for fashion."

Tilting her head to one side, she swept her eyes over Mala. Her future mother-in-law's disappointment covered her like primer, every stroke a promise to make a proper bride of her, a proper woman.

"When I'm done with you," Mrs. Mishra said with finality, "no one will be able to tell the difference between you and a girl from overseas."

Chapter 47

They almost collided as Mala was on her way out of the office
and Ash was on his way in. They stood in front of each other
like monoliths, goggling.

After a few awkward moments of silence, he said, "Hi," a little
breathless.

"Hi," she muttered back. Then she skirted around him and
marched into the hallway. He followed.

"Mala," he implored. "Wait."

She stopped. She wasn't sure why. She had succeeded in evading him until now, knowing his schedule as well as she did.

He loped toward her, his body blocking the way to the exit.
She glanced at him. He looked exhausted, ringed around the eyes,
gaunt in the cheeks. She fixed her eyes on his unshaven chin.

"How are you?" he asked.

Mala wanted to fill the empty hallway with her screams. "I'm
well," she lied, wearing her best false smile. "How are you?" She
tensed her core. "How's Laine?"

He slipped his hands into his pockets and stared at the floor,
shoulders rounding. "She's doing better. Thanks for asking."

"And the baby?"

"The baby's healthy too."

Mala stretched her smile so wide she thought the skin of her lips might split. "Then everything's as it should be." She commanded her feet to move and they carried her forward.

"How about you?" he said to her back. "How's everything? How's work?"

Mala halted, considered. Although she knew she shouldn't, she couldn't resist the opportunity to provoke him. "I'm a little distracted with wedding plans. But all of that will be over soon."

Her heart hoofed as she waited to see how he would react.

"What are you talking about?" She heard the shock in his voice.

She clasped her concealed hands. "Sumesh, of course. We're getting married in a couple of weeks."

The sound of his hurried footsteps, without a hint of shuffle or drag, drew toward her.

They stood face to face, eye to eye. "You can't do this, Mala," he said, alarmed. "You can't marry someone out of obligation. You'll find happiness on your own someday." His mouth twisted in pain. "Just not with me. Please don't let what happened between us be the reason you throw your life away. It's not a good enough reason, Mala." He exhaled. "I'm not a good enough reason."

She turned her face to the wall. Her heart wasn't hoofing any longer. Mala doubted it was beating much at all.

Just then, she felt the echo of the little heart below her navel ripple upward, sending a jolt of life through the dead muscle in her chest. *I'm here, I'm here, I'm here*, it whispered.

Mala faced forward and kept her gaze low. "Not everything's about you," she told him, matter-of-fact. Then she exited the hallway without another word.

Chapter 48

Mala suffered on the bedsheet-covered recliner in the living room, bored and immobile. Every time she made the slightest movement—to, say, scratch an incessant tickle or wriggle feeling back into a numb area—she shed tiny scabs. She surveyed the thick lines of mehndi drawn over her hands and feet. Eventually, they would make her beautiful for her wedding day, a rite of passage her mother insisted upon, but for now, as the mehndi dried and cracked, all the faintly herb-scented paste did was make Mala's skin itch. If it hadn't taken two hours of application, she would have given in to her slowly building urge and scratched it off, the mere thought of which made her eyes roll back with pleasure for a blissful instant. Mala gave an exasperated little sigh. She knew she had to sit for at least another hour before she could free herself from her casing and finally go to bed.

"The longer you keep it on, the better," the mehndi lady had told her earlier. "And no shower tonight." Apparently, when it came to mehndi and its fortune-telling powers, water was the enemy. The final instructions that the woman had given before leaving Mala to her tattooed prison was that after she picked off the dried henna, she slather a thick layer of Vicks VapoRub onto her hands and feet and sleep with socks on both. When Mala had asked the reasonable question—why Vicks VapoRub?—the woman had bounced her shoulders, conceding she didn't know, but why did it matter?

The important thing was *it worked*. Mala considered asking how the practice ever came to be, who was the first person to think to themselves that *of course* menthol rub was the answer to henna colour ripening to its fullest, but soon gave up, wearied by the absurdity of it all. The costs of beauty were often ridiculous.

Her mother approached with a plate of food in her hands. "How are you managing, beti?"

"I think it's dark enough, don't you?" Mala tried to sound persuasive. "I can probably take it off now, right?"

Sitting on the adjacent couch, her mother scrutinized the henna with a serious expression. "Not yet." She turned her attention to the plate on her lap and went about tearing roti into pieces. "Just a little longer. And try your best not to move."

Mala re-examined herself. Despite her best attempts at stillness, about a quarter of her mehndi had flaked off too soon, little brown flecks of failure scattered around her on the bedsheet.

"The darker the mehndi, the more blessed the marriage," her mother recited as she prepared a mouthful of cauliflower sabji and roti.

Wedding mehndi had a certain superstition attached to it. Was it a measure of a bride's forbearance? Mala wondered. Her ability to bear discomfort, quietly, while forecasting beauty to others? Underdeveloped henna peeked out at her between the scabby tracings of peacock feathers and petals, millimetres of burnt orange skin that were unlikely to deepen to the desired orange pekoe.

Perhaps the only thing more absurd than sleeping with Vicks VapoRub and socks on her hands was her own complicity in a plan Mala sensed with more and more certainty was doomed. Wasn't the mehndi telling her as much?

A parcel of aloo gobi waited inches from her mouth. Mala frowned. "Mom . . ."

"Come, you have to eat something. You need strength for tomorrow. You'll make less mess this way."

Her mother was right. Moving her arms would only cause more of her bark to chip off. The aroma of the food roused her hunger. She opened her mouth. While she chewed, her mother revelled in the quiet delight of feeding her child, as she never would again.

"Mala," she said. "I want you to know how happy I am for you, beti."

The blessing cinched the top of her esophagus. Unable to swallow, Mala kept chewing.

"I know this hasn't been an easy decision for you. But I truly believe you've found a good match with Sumesh. He is honest and kind. One day, he will make a fine husband, like your papa."

The top of her throat finally gave way to the pressure pushing against it and Mala swallowed.

"I know in this culture they say love comes first. And they are quite rigid about what that first looks like. This might surprise you, but in a way, I agree with them, about love coming first at least. After all, I believe it was love that led me to marry your papa. Love led me to a good person, a good man, who I could build a life with. I know relationships don't always work out so well, with arranged marriages or love matches, for that matter. So I've always felt blessed." Her mother placed the plate aside and lightly held one of Mala's hands, careful not to disturb the wedding markings. "I only hope you will be as blessed, meri pyar. That with Sumesh you are able to build as loving a life and home as I was able to build with your papa."

Mala couldn't bear to look directly at her mother, whose face she could tell, even out of the corner of her eye, was a muddle of joy and sadness. Of course, her father was on their minds. Although he was absent, his presence hovered over what had transpired so far and what was about to the next day.

An itchy heat rose across Mala's skin, as if she were reacting to the ornamentation that was slowly leaching into her, as if rejecting it. Without thinking, she scratched her left forearm.

"Careful, beti," her mother warned. "You'll ruin it otherwise."

The words echoed in Mala's head like conscience.

Careful.

You'll ruin it otherwise.

She had been given that warning once before, by Ash, on the night that love set them both on fire. Back then, marrying Sumesh had been nothing more than a meaningless threat, a way to gauge Ash's feelings and ultimately a way to hurt him. It was never meant to become her reality. It was never meant to be a choice Mala would actually make.

What was she doing? She would ruin more lives than her own if she went through with the marriage. She couldn't do that to Sumesh. Her mother was right about him, he was a good person, a good man who deserved more than to contentedly settle for a peaceful home. He deserved love—big, boundless, life-affirming. And Mala knew he would never find anything close to that with her.

She needed to free the truth. No matter how it might destroy her mother's hopes.

Mala was about to speak when a sudden bout of nausea clapped her mouth shut.

"Mala?" her mother asked, concerned. "Are you okay, beti?"

Her sickness was always worse at night. She forced down the salty slime. "I'm fine."

"Are you sure?"

She nodded.

"Let me get you some water." Her mother hurried to the kitchen, leaving Mala with the burden of her secret.

"Here." Her mother handed her a glass. "Drink."

Mala raised the rim to her lips.

"There's nothing to be nervous about, beti. Earlier I told you I was happy for you. But I'm also proud. I know Papa would be proud of you too, for honouring our ways. It's difficult to raise a child far from the culture you were brought up in. Many of my friends have children who don't respect their wishes and I feel sorry for them. I wish your papa was here." Her mother batted her damp lashes. "Thank you for taking our guidance. You make us feel like we have succeeded as parents. We have raised a good and respectful daughter. My heart is so full." Her mother bowed her head, overcome with joy.

An image of her proud father developed in the darkroom of her mind. She suppressed the uprising with a swallow, saltiness slipping down her throat.

Then Mala gazed distantly at the mehndi that covered her hands and feet, feeling disconnected from the artful patterns as they stained her skin, transforming her into a bride. And soon a wife.

Chapter 49

Mala heard a faint *tap-tap-tap* on the washroom door of the bridal suite.

"Mala?" her mother said. "Are you all right?"

She scrutinized her dazzling reflection in the wall-to-wall mirror, stiff and uncomfortable in her lehnga. She barely recognized herself under the ruby lipstick, kohl liner and gold Gopi dots arched over her eyebrows. Or the wedding jewellery on her forehead, neck and wrists, twinkling with light. Or the elaborate blood-red dress that sparkled with mirrors and golden thread. If Mala existed at all, it was deep beneath this artifice of her own making.

Her heavy skirts gathered against the tiles and whispered *swish-swish-swish* whenever she moved. The beaded top hugged her form, its sweetheart neckline leaving ample room to showcase the gaudy wedding jewellery the Mishras had given her. The dupatta, heavy and bejewelled, was pinned into her bun, tenting over her head and shoulders just so. All at once Mala felt a weight as heavy as tradition upon her.

"I'm fine," she called out.

"Five minutes and then we have to go."

Five minutes, Mala thought, her guts frothing.

The guests were a dozen floors beneath her hennaed feet, enjoying cocktails and appetizers, awaiting the arrival of the bride and groom so the lengthy Hindu fire ceremony could begin.

Five minutes. Less than that now. A familiar broth-like taste surged underneath her tongue. Heaving her heavy skirts, she hobbled to the toilet, the silvery jiggle of her payals sounding brightly with every quick step. Her eyes watered as she retched. Afterward, with her elbows resting on the plastic seat, Mala hovered, spiritless.

Another knock at the door woke her from her stupor.

"Mala, beti? It's time to go."

Go? she thought, panicked. Now? But they had five minutes! Was fate punishing her by clipping time, making minutes shorter than minutes, seconds shorter than seconds? That was all the time she had left. Seconds to be alone. Seconds to be herself. Seconds to tear away the finery and stop everything.

"Mala?"

She flushed the toilet, hauled herself up off the cool ceramic tiles and rinsed her mouth at the sink, patting her mouth dry with a facecloth. In the mirror, she saw the kohl had smudged underneath her eyes. Lifting one arm, adorned with red and gold bangles almost to her elbow, she swept away the tar-like smear with her orange-tinted fingertips.

"The darker the mehndi, the more blessed the marriage," her mother had repeated that morning, joyous and misty-eyed at how the colour had deepened overnight, taking it as a good omen, celestial confirmation of Mala's impending happiness.

Mala turned over her palm and probed the lines that were supposed to map her future like star charts.

Seconds to choose another river.

She looked up from her palm and held her own gaze in the mirror. Her dark eyes shone through her mask of adornment like beacons, urging her one last time to reconsider.

Seconds to make things right.

The silence was shattered by the most urgent knock yet.

Mala lowered her hand.

She had no seconds left.

The tinkle of bells as she approached the door. The cold touch of metal as she rested her hand on the handle. The delicate scent of rose as she inhaled deeply, siphoning courage from the air.

Then Mala slowly revealed herself. She found her mother—who was dressed in a champagne-coloured sari—seated on the bench at the end of the bed, knotting her hands.

"Oh, thank goodness," she sighed. "I was starting to worry you might not come out."

Little did her mother know that the time for turning back had passed. Mala curled her lips into a ravishing smile, the same smile she had been practising for days, and in a stranger's voice said, "I'm ready."

Chapter 50

Hours later, the newlyweds returned to the bridal suite. In the elevator, they made polite and awkward chitchat—about the tedious length of the ceremony, the number of guests, the quality of the meal, the flowers. Rather than look Sumesh in the eye, Mala fixed on the tilak marking his forehead, or the jaimala of red and white roses draped around his neck, the twin garland of which hung around hers. The flowers released a sweet fragrance that reminded her of the rosewater-infused kheer her mother had made on the evening that she first raised the matter of marriage, bringing Mala back to the beginning.

Sumesh trailed a step behind her as they walked through the empty hallway to their room. They lingered in front of their door for a few tense moments. Then Sumesh said over her shoulder, "You have the key."

His words repeated themselves inside her mind: *You have the key. You have the key.* As if she had power. The power to open doors and leave them barred.

Ignoring the whispers, Mala fished out the keycard from the small purse dangling on her wrist and let them into the room.

Sumesh flicked on the lights. When Mala saw the red rose petals scattered over the bed, her swollen feet forgot their function. On the side table, a silver bucket pearling with condensation held a bottle of champagne. Sumesh's breath grazed the back of her neck. A shiver shot down her spine like lightning.

"What's wrong?" he asked.

"Nothing," she said. "I just remembered something." She slowly stepped into the suite, although not nearly slowly enough.

Crossing the room, she took a seat on the bench at the end of the bed and unstrapped her shoes. "God, that feels good." She sighed, wriggling her toes on the carpet.

"At least you didn't have to wear Aladdin shoes." Sumesh smirked as he kicked them off. He unbuttoned his cream-coloured sherwani and tossed it aside. Underneath, he wore a kurta, thin and silky.

"Do you want a drink?" he asked. Mala heard the ice resettle as he freed the champagne from the bucket.

"Sure." A sip wouldn't hurt, while the lack of one might raise suspicion.

"I've never been good at popping these." He removed the aluminum wrapper with comical reluctance.

Mala smiled. "Just make sure you point it away from us." She covered her eyes.

The cork popped free and arced through the air, landing among the rose petals. Sumesh filled their glasses and handed Mala a slender flute, golden and lively.

He sat beside her on the bench. "What should we cheers to?"

Mala pressed her lips together, struggling to find something romantic to say, but came up with nothing. Neither could Sumesh, she realized.

Through the wall behind them, she heard the murmur of television and conversation, which made the mood in their room more uncomfortable. Staring into her flute, she watched the jovial bubbles of champagne skip and soar, thinking that was how a person should feel on their wedding night—effervescent—like a glass of champagne. Not fizzing with dread.

"How about we toast to finishing the bottle?" Sumesh suggested at last. She could tell by his overly light tone that he was trying to make her feel at ease, despite his apparent anxiety.

"And to raiding the mini bar as well?" she offered.

Sumesh held up his glass and she mirrored him. The *ping* of their glasses resonated through the air, clear and crisp, before silence girded them once more.

Sumesh guzzled his first glass of champagne, refilling it as quickly. Mala granted herself a third shallow sip. While she delighted in the tingles at the tip of her tongue, she thought of how desperately she wanted to relax, shed her heavy clothes, crawl into bed and drown the day in an ocean of dreams, a universe of them. But there was still so much to do . . .

"Want to see what's on TV?"

"Hmm?" she said, distracted.

He rose from the bench, stepped toward the television cabinet and grabbed the remote control. "Maybe there's a movie on."

Mala eyed him skeptically.

"Or how about room service?" He made for the desk by the window. "I don't know about you, but I barely ate a thing all night. Too many people to talk to." She continued studying him as he fetched the menu, then sat back down beside her.

He held the menu open between them. "What do you feel like? Pizza? Grilled cheese? I wonder if they do late-night breakfast. I could murder an eggs benny right now."

Mala didn't know what to say. Was Sumesh stalling? He sounded almost frantic.

Despite her doubts, she slowly rose to her feet and simpered. "I just need a minute to change first."

"Oh." He averted his eyes. "About that, Mala." He swallowed. "I've been meaning to talk to you. Listen, I know we're still getting to know each other. And we have time. I don't want you to feel . . . pressured. I'm fine with waiting for a while, okay? I just wanted you to know that. And I won't tell anyone either. It's none of their business."

Mala was stunned. While Sumesh rambled, her smile had flattened to a firm line. She hadn't expected him to need persuading.

She bent forward and placed a comforting hand on his knee. "It's okay. But thank you for being such a gentleman." She straightened and towed her heavy skirts over the carpet in the direction of the washroom. "I won't be long," she said over her shoulder.

"Take your time," he blurted. "Take a bath if you feel like it. Isn't there supposed to be a Jacuzzi in there?"

As she closed the door, Mala wore her best coquettish smile— not that Sumesh noticed, glued as his eyes were to the menu, although she doubted whether he had absorbed a word.

Splendidly alone at last, she flicked on the ceiling fan for an insulating layer of background noise and paused to luxuriate in the solitude.

Take a bath? she thought, frowning.

She raised her elbows and took a couple of self-conscious sniffs, but the only scent she found was tired perfume, like the wilted roses of her jaimala.

She stood in place, baffled. She had been so preoccupied with her own reluctance, she hadn't stopped to consider that Sumesh might be experiencing something similar. Still, there was no comfort—none at all—in knowing that he was more interested in ordering a midnight snack than he was in her.

Mala looked down at her elaborate lehnga, the most extravagant garment she had ever worn or would likely ever wear again. And yet she couldn't have felt less alluring. Her body flopped with fatigue, as though she had run a marathon in the unwieldy outfit, which in a way she had, although there were still a few craggy kilometres ahead of her left to tread. If she stopped now, she risked losing momentum and that wasn't an option. Mala didn't care if Sumesh never touched her again. In fact, she preferred that he didn't. But tonight he had to. Everything depended on it.

Mala thought of Mrs. Mishra—now her mother-in-law—and the smug way she took all the credit for the wedding, despite Mala's mother's contributions. Yet little did the woman know it was Mala, in fact, who was the architect of the evening. She wondered how Mrs. Mishra would have reacted if she knew the plans were nothing more than thin blue lines on Mala's drafting paper. That she had used them all to build a safe place for the little heart fluttering below her navel.

The little heart. *I'm here, I'm here, I'm here,* it reassured her.

Moving quickly, Mala undressed and tousled her hair free from her bun. She stood in her underwear and noted the unfamiliar marks of marriage she now carried on her body. Falling like a V between her breasts, the mangalsutra Sumesh had clasped around her neck, the necklace of gold strung with black beads, a sacred thread of commitment, which she was meant to wear for the rest of her life, or his. She unclasped the necklace and dangled it over the trash for a moment before finally lowering it onto the counter. The bracelets, anklets and silver rings on the second toes of her feet seemed more like shackles to her than treasures. She pulled them off and thrust them alongside the wedding necklace.

Finally, she peered into the mirror and inspected the red powder smeared along her parting line. There wasn't time to wash it off. Even if she did, Mala knew she would feel its stain, like a tattoo only visible to her eyes—the mark of her secret. As she beheld her reflection, a phrase from her bedtime reading the night before arose in her mind: "Worse than many a little heathen who says its prayers to Brahma and kneels before Juggernaut, this girl is a liar."

Mala blinked. A liar.

She shunned her shameful image and shifted her attention to the lingerie that hung from a hook on the back of the door. A lavender nightgown made of satin, simple and plain, sensual but dignified. Mala slipped the garment over her head and adjusted the straps to raise its sloping neckline. The satin felt cool and light against her skin, a relief after the heavy wardrobe of the day. Lastly, she refreshed her perfume, swirled a little mouthwash and faced the door. It's almost over, she told herself.

When Mala re-entered the bedroom, the television was playing loudly, although she didn't register what Sumesh had been watching in her absence. He was reclining in bed, resting against a few pillows.

He stared at her with alarm.

She glanced at her nightgown, smiling nervously.

He straightened against the headboard. "You look nice," he said, but without much effort or conviction.

She gripped the carpet with her toes. "Thank you."

The sound of the television cut off. She looked up. Sumesh set the remote on the nightstand. His eyes traced her frame—up and down, down and up.

She stepped forward and waited in front of the bench. For a few moments, they observed each other, a valley of silence between them.

Sumesh reached for the light switch and the room went dark. The naked windows revealed the nighttime glow of the cityscape. But there was no time to draw the blackout curtains. Momentum was fickle.

A dark figure, Mala crept over the bed. Her knees sank into the luxurious mattress as she crawled toward him, her movements as silent as her faint, faint breath.

"We can always order room service after," she whispered, placing a light hand over his chest. She felt his frantic heart patter against her cold fingertips.

He said nothing.

Then Mala shut her eyes and darkness closed around her.

Secrets and lies

Chapter 51

The roof's coming down, Nandini thought as the boom shook through the walls of the living room.

"What was that?" Prem said, startled awake from his post-physiotherapy nap while she kept him company, reading *Chatelaine*. He looked around with a perplexed expression it always wrenched her heart to witness, as if he were surrounded by a fog that showed no signs of lifting.

"I'm sure it's nothing," she reassured him.

He rubbed his ears. The ringing hadn't tapered off since the accident.

Nandini sighed on the inside. "Everything's okay. Go back to sleep."

Once he was resettled in the recliner, Nandini went back to wondering about the sound. Maybe a truck had passed or one of the neighbours was getting work done. She looked around the room, listening for residual noises, surveying for damage. When her eyes floated over the ceiling, it occurred to her that that was where the sound had originated. Not from outside or the roof, but from the floor right above her.

The magazine slipped out of her hands.

From Asha's room.

Chapter 52

Asha heard a voice shout her name. It sounded far away, like whoever was calling to her was on the other side of a canyon.

"Asha!" cried the voice again. It was closer now, bounding over the canyon in one leap. This time she recognized who it was.

"Stop yelling, Mom," she said. "I'm right here."

"Asha!"

"Mom?" Why couldn't she hear her?

Asha felt a pair of strong hands grip her by the shoulders and shake her.

"Asha, wake up!"

But she was awake. Wait, why couldn't she see anything? She tried with all her strength to peel open her glued eyelids.

"You have to wake up, sweetheart," her mom begged. "Please, angel, wake up. What have you done to yourself?"

A sliver of light. Her mom's anguished face. And back to black.

Chapter 53

The breathing tube lodged down Asha's throat made Nandini swallow uncomfortably. The IV line caused a sudden itch to prickle the back of her hand. She scratched it roughly. She never thought they would be back at the hospital again so soon. Prem was seated on the other side of Asha's bed with a worried scowl on his face. Without speaking, they watched their daughter's almost unrecognizable visage, its lovely symmetry distorted by swelling, although less so than a couple of hours ago. The doctor said whatever Asha had taken had caused a severe allergic reaction. Allergies? Nandini had wondered. Until then, she hadn't realized that Asha even had any allergies. After all, they didn't run in their family. That sensitivity, Nandini acknowledged with unease, must have been passed down to her by her other family, like the stunning grey of her eyes. Despite having raised her, they were discovering that their daughter still held many mysteries, not only within her body but also within the secret box of her mind, as the evening's events had revealed.

"What a mess we've made," she said to Prem. "I didn't know things were this bad."

Prem held Asha's hand. "Her issues weren't going to just disappear. First the adoption, then my accident. It was too much for her. She's such a mature kid, we always think she can handle anything. But we were wrong." A dense, shame-ridden silence descended upon the room like smog. "We let her down."

Prem suddenly winced, overtaken by a spasm. Nandini leaned forward, poised to help him. Raising one hand to calm her, he said, "I'm all right. It'll pass." Cautious, she retook her seat.

As Prem massaged the side of his head, Nandini thought back to the night of their confrontation. "I meant to call her doctor in the morning, so we could start addressing her sleep troubles. Then everything happened so fast with your accident. At first, when you were in the coma, I was terrified you weren't going to make it. Later, when you woke up, it hit me how severe your brain injury was. I worried you'd never be the same. I got distracted by it all. Your recovery. Trying to balance work and everything else." She paused. "But no excuses. You're right. I didn't pay close enough attention to Asha." Despite the breathing tube, Nandini wanted to hover over her daughter's bed and feel the gentle puff of her warm breath, like she had when Asha was a newcomer to their home, and she was hounded by her first raw parental fear: *Is she breathing? Is she breathing?* "Honestly, I thought she was handling things well."

Was that a sign of trouble? The way Asha had flipped from a state of turmoil to obedience, and the turmoil was never seen or heard again. Perhaps Nandini had believed too easily that the phase was over, that her Asha was back to herself, that at least one part of her life wasn't in upheaval because she needed to believe it, needed some sort of stability as the ground quaked beneath her small, beloved family.

Looking back, Nandini saw the signs. There had been something almost robotic about Asha's functioning, now that she re-examined it.

Nandini's stomach lurched. And she had forced Asha into it. Asha, go to prom even though you don't want to. *Yes, Mom.* Asha, work at the library. *Yes, Mom.* Asha, you'll have to cook dinner tonight, I'm going to be late again. *Okay, Mom. Yes, Mom. No problem, Mom. I'll take care of it.*

Asha, do this. Asha, do that. Never: Asha, how are you managing? How are you sleeping? Are you lonely? Are you scared? Then taking the time, however long, to probe past the quickly spoken "I'm fine" to see how her daughter was truly handling the changes in their lives. It was what Nandini would have done before the accident. Since then, though, the days didn't seem long enough to do everything she needed to. Nandini had inadvertently neglected Asha. She peered at her daughter's bloated face with a sinking heart. It was inexcusable.

Was this her punishment? Proof she was never meant to be a mother? She had been entrusted with a blessing, given a chance, and now she risked losing that precious gift because of her own insecurities. That was where it had all begun, wasn't it? With her inability to overcome her jealousy of Asha's birth mother. That was why she had withheld the letter, kept secrets and told lies, mostly to herself. And look what it had cost.

In that instant, Nandini gave up what she had held on to so tightly for too long. She relinquished her jealous heart. Tossed it away. Stomped on it. Along with her relentless need to claim all the good in Asha as a reflection of herself, and herself alone.

Nandini didn't care anymore that Asha had another mother, who had given her life and so much else, from her allergies to the grey of her eyes, to perhaps even her very goodness and inner beauty. All Nandini wanted was her daughter—her Asha—healthy and alive.

Nandini clamped her eyes shut and sent a prayer into the sky. One more chance to make things right. She could be counted on again. She could be trusted.

A sound as soft as an infant's waking murmurs reached Nandini inside the dome of her prayers. Her eyes flashed open. She watched Asha's eyelids slowly flutter up and down, up and down. She heard Prem call for the nurse, but she couldn't tear herself away from the miracle. She bent over Asha and cupped her swollen cheeks, probing her stupor for cognizance.

"Asha?" she said wonderingly.

The sound of her voice gave her daughter something to latch on to. Their eyes met, grey on brown. Nandini felt as if they were seeing each other for the first time. Her vision glistened with joy and gratitude. She covered Asha like a blanket, promising the sky to never leave her daughter unsheltered again.

Chapter 54

Asha was responding well to the antihistamines and other medications, although she still felt swollen and itchy, but thank goodness—she took a deep gulp of air—at least she could breathe. The threat of being strangled from the inside returned to her with a tremor.

Her parents re-entered the room cautiously. The staff had ushered them out when she regained consciousness.

"Hi," her mom said with a wide, nervous smile. Her dad stood a step behind her mom, stoic. "Do you feel up for a quick visit?"

"Come in," Asha croaked, her throat still rough from the breathing tube.

Her dad sat down gingerly on her right side, and her mom on her left.

"How are you feeling?" her mom asked, deep lines of concern scored between her eyebrows.

"Still pretty drowsy."

Her mom placed a comforting hand on her thigh. "We know you need rest. But there's something we wanted to say to you first. We promise it won't take long."

Asha's stomach roiled. She couldn't even fathom how much trouble she was in now. "Sure."

Her mom paused, hesitating. "Your dad and I just want you to know that we love you, Asha. So, so much. We're sorry for letting you down."

Asha didn't understand what her mom meant. She was the one who had let *them* down. Her mom looked like she was biting back tears, the very definition of putting on a brave face. "What are you talking about?"

"It's our fault this happened," her dad replied. "We knew you were struggling, you told us so the night of my accident, but we never followed through with you and we should have, regardless of the shape I was in." His eyes moistened with emotion. "I can't believe we almost lost you."

She finally understood her poor parents. They had it all wrong. She swallowed with pain. "I wasn't trying to hurt myself."

A confounded look passed between them.

"You weren't?" her mom said.

She shook her head. "I guess I have been feeling pretty low lately. But that wasn't what I was trying to do. I swear."

Her dad spoke next. "So that drink you took wasn't some kind of poison?"

She balled the covers over her chest. "Not exactly." Her empty stomach gurgled. She licked her swollen lips. "It was like a . . . remedy."

Her mom leaned in. "What kind of remedy? Something to help you sleep?"

Asha shook her head again. "It's supposed to . . ." She paused to capture the way her parents were looking at her so she would always have the image, captured moments before she changed the way they saw her forever. ". . . end a pregnancy."

Her mom's mouth fell open. "You were pregnant?" Her voice wasn't angry, just shocked.

Asha's heart sank to her belly. "I think I still am." She kept her eyes on the end of the bed. "Prom was the first time." A stab below her ribs as she prepared to say his name. "With Rowan. We talked about using protection, but he didn't. He made it seem like he did, but he didn't."

"Why didn't you tell us?" her dad asked.

Asha felt like weeping. "Because I've put you both through so much lately. If it weren't for me, you wouldn't have gone for a drive that night, Dad. And you just got released from the rehab centre. But you're still in rough shape, even if you don't like admitting it. I didn't want you to relapse because of me." The rims of her eyes quivered. She bit down hard on the corner of her mouth.

"None of that's your fault, kid," he said, tender. "You didn't force me out of the house. I chose to go for a drive, like I do from time to time. It was an accident. That's all. Unfortunately, these things happen."

Asha sniffled. "I just wanted everything to go back to normal. I made an appointment at a clinic, but I ran into one of Mom's friends right outside and I ended up not going. After that, I was scared about you finding out somehow. I didn't know what else to do. So I went online and found this recipe. It seemed like the answer I was looking for."

Her mom gently squeezed her leg. "That's not how you end a pregnancy, sweetheart."

"I know how stupid it sounds. But I wanted to believe it would work. I needed to believe it."

Her mom reached out and held her hand as if trying to pass strength through her fingers. "I'm sorry you went through that alone." She paused. "You must have been terrified."

Everyone sat in silence for a while, thinking. Asha dried her eyes on the bedsheet.

"We're going to figure this out," her mom said at last. "First, this. Then everything else. I promise. Okay?"

Asha looked up, expecting to see disappointment in her mom's reddened eyes. Instead she discovered something kinder, gentler, like sympathy. Asha nodded, as grateful as she was embarrassed.

Her mom pumped a last bit of strength into her hand and went to get the doctor.

Chapter 55

A short while later, Doctor Clarke entered the room. She was tall, with a long white coat and a mass of braids elegantly coiled into a bun that favoured the left side of her head.

Asha lurched upright. Her parents rose to their feet, their postures alert and ready.

"Well, Asha," Doctor Clarke said. "You've certainly been through the wars the past twenty-four hours, haven't you?"

Asha blushed, sheepish.

"I understand that the herbal remedy you consumed was taken as a method of abortion?"

She nodded.

The doctor shook her head. "And they want to cut sex education from schools." Remembering herself, Doctor Clarke smiled sympathetically at Asha. "You can't believe everything you read online. You could have died from your reaction. It was that severe. And, of course, whatever you took wouldn't have worked anyway."

Asha felt like her throat was closing all over again.

"Nevertheless," the doctor continued, "you aren't pregnant. In fact, from the test results, it's impossible to determine if you ever were."

Asha blinked, confused. "But I took an at-home test."

"False positives are rare, but they do happen. The other possibility is that you were pregnant and miscarried. That isn't uncommon for first-time pregnancies, especially in younger women. Your hormone levels are back to normal, which can happen quite quickly after miscarrying. Either way, I imagine I've given you the answer you were hoping for?"

Asha felt weak with relief. She nodded yes.

"Good. Well, while you're recovering over the next day or two, I'd like you to meet with one of our teen sexual health specialists."

Doctor Clarke finished by saying she would check on Asha the following day, then excused herself.

"Your boyfriend's the one who needs the talk," her dad said.

"Ex-boyfriend," Asha corrected. She felt defeated, as if one weight had been lifted only to be replaced by another.

"You and Rowan broke up?" her mom asked. "When?"

"A couple of weeks after prom. When I found out, I told him, but he didn't want anything to do with it. Or me."

Her dad sat beside her on the bed, his lips a livid line, although Asha knew he wasn't angry with her. Her mom remained standing, agitated and electric. Asha thought she might start pacing any second. Either that or thunderbolts might shoot out from her fingertips.

"Are you okay?" she asked Asha.

Asha shrugged a single shoulder.

After a short silence, her mom spoke. "I'm sorry about Rowan. Even though he clearly doesn't deserve you, losing your first love always hurts, regardless of the circumstances."

Asha's chest slowly rose and fell. She still couldn't believe that her relationship with Rowan had turned out to be such a catastrophe in the end.

Her mom crossed her arms and lowered her chin. "We can't carry on like this. With all these secrets and lies. Look at what it's done to us." She paused. "I'm sorry, Asha. We should have never kept the truth about your adoption from you. That's how all of this started. Can you ever forgive us?"

Asha stared at her mom in amazement. Hearing the words she

had been waiting for since the beginning left her speechless. All she could manage to do was nod her head. She felt a give in her chest.

Her mom responded with a faint smile of relief. "We need to start trusting each other. And it has to start with your dad and me. What can we do to make this better?"

There was only one thing that would make a difference. Asha needed to silence the phantoms once and for all. Who was she? Where did she come from? What happened to them? Why didn't they keep her?

"I want to know more about them," she blurted out. The desire burst from her so unexpectedly, and with such force, Asha couldn't tell how long or where she had been keeping it. "My birth family. I want to find them."

Her parents shared a look of belated resignation.

After which her mom said, "If that's what you want, we'll do whatever we can to help you."

Then her mom finally approached the bed and sat down. Without another word, Asha and her parents sought one another's hands, sealing their family circle around the promise held at its centre.

Chapter 56

Asha lounged on the back deck, enjoying the fading light as dusk slowly fell. After almost a week at the hospital, it felt good to be home. The clouds had sprinkled a little while ago, adding a glisten to the grass. The evening air was warm and misty, still holding the scent of rain, fresh and pleasing compared to the dead air of the hospital. The first twinkles of starlight were showing themselves. The moon wasn't in view yet. With her eyes on the darkening sky, Asha thought of her birth mother and wondered if they might be looking right at each other through the veil that hid heaven from earth. Dropping her gaze to her lap, she opened her journal.

I have my family back. God, it feels good to say that. It feels like such a relief. Mom and Dad finally apologized to me. It was the only good thing about being hospitalized. I guess it's true what they say. Sometimes you don't know what you have until you're about to lose it. That's how I felt after my dad's accident. My parents were just as shaken up after my mishap too. I feel like we're on the brink of a fresh, honest start. And for the first time in a long time, I have faith in us.

My mom asked me what they could do to make things better and I told her. The thing is, I write these letters, but I have nowhere to send them. I still have so many questions about you and what happened before my adoption.

I haven't wanted to face this, but with my parents behind me, I think I'm ready. If there's anyone left who has answers, it's "him."

I wish there was another way, but there isn't.

I'm going to have to find the man who let me go.

Asha

Choices and everything after

Chapter 57

Among the food court's sticky tables, with the lunchtime thrum packing her ears, Mala found a spot and set down her shopping and milky Tim Hortons tea. The air was oversaturated with competing odours—fast-food meat, battered fish, the sulphurous reek of stir-fried cabbage. Even a week ago, the smells would have triggered a reaction like two fingers prodding down her throat. But oh, the bliss of the second trimester, her nausea sailing away like a stretch of bad weather. Mala opened her shopping bag. The miniscule clothing inside seemed too small to cover a human of any age. Did they truly arrive so tiny? She admired her selections: a yellow onesie with an elephant on the front, a snowy lamb comfort toy, impossibly miniature socks.

She had purchased doubles of everything, but not only for little bean. According to the departmental gossip, Ash was having a girl too. Betty, the matronly graduate administrator, had told her when she dropped by the office to inquire about leave of absence forms. Mala recalled the airless feeling that had overwhelmed her after Betty broke the news, as if the air had been booted right out of her lungs by a sudden fall. Compounding the shock was the fact that Ash hadn't told her about the baby's gender himself, which exemplified with heart-rending clarity the canyon now between them, to the point that it pained Mala to remember a time when they were close, closer than anyone.

She hadn't spoken to him since their run-in in the hallway. She chose to study in the library rather than the Ph.D. office, only venturing to the department to teach her class. She even switched her office hours to online or by appointment, to reduce the likelihood of them crossing paths. She hadn't shown much during her first trimester, nothing that couldn't be disguised by bulky clothing, so the few times they had glimpsed each other in the hall, he hadn't suspected anything about her condition, nor had she given him much of an opportunity as she sped away.

Now, while she sipped her tea, Mala reminded herself that what had happened between them didn't matter any more. Nothing mattered, apart from little bean. Something about seeing the grainy green ultrasound image had aged her a decade in an instant. Any resentment she had gave way to acceptance of her new path, her new role. The shift felt like an unclenching of her heart as something was let go, maybe hope, maybe wishing. Which was why Mala bought duplicates of the baby things today. As a final goodbye and good luck to him. She would drop off the gift at the office after hours, then continue along her path while wishing Ash well on his.

Mala placed the shopping aside and reached for her purse, drawing out the letter she had received from the Faculty of Graduate Studies that day. She tore open the envelope, unfolded the paper and began to read.

Dear Ms. Sharma,
We are writing to inform you that the Faculty of Graduate Studies and Postdoctoral Affairs has approved your application to take a leave of absence for the period of . . .

Mala lowered the letter. The air around her seemed thin, like in the mountains. Insufficient, no matter how hard she tried to fill her lungs. The invisible walls slowly rose from the floor and surrounded her, separating her from the rest of the world. She had first encountered them after her father passed away, and now they surrounded her again as she wrestled with this most recent loss. Grief was a glass prison no one else could see.

Mala remembered standing by the river's edge, marvelling at the current, that chameleon, that wizard. How she felt like a leaf tangled in the reeds. How she wanted so desperately to rejoin the flow of life. She had a plan back then. School was going to be her canoe. But she paddled too close to the rapids, and the rapids became a waterfall. Now her life was in pieces, and once again she found herself bobbing in the reeds.

This is just a detour, she thought, to calm herself. A pause. And all pauses are temporary.

To prove it, she went over her plan, imagining she was writing on the glass prison walls with a marker. Now that she was starting to show, she would work from home as often as possible. If she pushed hard, she could finish most of her analysis by July, the month before her real due date. After the birth, she would take four to six weeks to recover and then go back to school. She wasn't naive enough to believe in the covert misogyny of *having it all*. But staying on track to graduate next summer seemed feasible. She would spend the fall writing, the winter revising and defend her dissertation next spring.

Mala looked to Ash for further proof. After all, they were in parallel situations. If anything, the prospect of parenthood spurred him on. Nothing compromised his goals or ambition, least of all himself. Why should it be any different for her?

Of course, Mala knew there were differences; she had encountered some already. She wondered if his adviser told him he probably wouldn't finish now, like hers had. Did Laine's father expect him to abandon his thesis, the way Mrs. Mishra expected Mala to drop her degree now that she was pregnant?

Never mind the disbelievers, she told herself.

She remembered the time and glanced at her watch. Sumesh wouldn't be back from his rounds for another few hours. We can do stats in our underwear if we want to, she thought, grinning at her belly.

Her mother had been right about him. He had turned out to be a good partner. Somehow, she would figure out a way to repay him.

Bag in tow, Mala exited the food court through a set of double doors, stepping out into the oil-stink of Rideau Street. As she approached the bus stop, she wondered if they had any gift bags at the apartment that she could use for the present.

Chapter 58

The creaky elevator carried Mala to the tenth floor. She stepped out and made her way to their apartment at the end of the hall. The air smelled pleasantly of home cooking—fried onions and jeera; the unmistakable scent of curry; the sweet, warm steam of basmati. Her mouth watered. She would have to fix herself a snack before settling into her work.

Inside, she placed her shopping bag and purse on the pale tiles, then slipped off her sandals. She noticed Sumesh's black brogues in front of the closet. He's home early, she thought, surprised.

"Sumesh?" she called out.

She heard the sound of distant voices but assumed it was the noisy couple who lived next door. She walked to the kitchen and found Sumesh standing at the entrance of their bedroom, blocking the way like a sliding door. Her eyes slowly moved up the length of his body, pausing at his boxers, his bare chest and finally his wide, fearful eyes.

"Mala," he said, startled, as he held his elbows. "What are you doing home? I thought you were going shopping this afternoon."

Was it her imagination, or was he trying to sound casual and failing? "It didn't take as long as I thought. What are you doing home? Are you feeling okay?"

"I'm fine." He paused. "I have a migraine coming on, that's all. I came home early to sleep it off."

"Oh no. That's awful. I'm sorry for waking you."

He grinned stiffly.

"You won't even know I'm here. I'll just be working in the office." She took a step forward. "All I need is my lab book. I left it on my bedside table. I'll grab it, then you can go back to sleep."

Mala took another step forward. Sumesh's body tensed, the muscles in his neck taut. He placed his hands on his hips and pushed his elbows out to either side, blocking the doorway even more.

"What's wrong?" she asked.

"Nothing," he said, relaxing his face, his voice. "Actually, the truth is, I'm worried I might be coming down with something. In your condition, I wouldn't want to expose you. You probably shouldn't go in the bedroom until I've had a chance to sterilize everything. Why don't you get settled at your desk and I'll bring your lab book over, okay?"

Something wasn't right. "Sumesh." She frowned. "What's going on? You're acting strange." Mala thought she saw a flash of terror cross his face. Then again, the spasm was so quick and slight, she couldn't be sure.

"Nothing." There was a defensive undercurrent to his nonchalance. "I don't want you to get sick, that's all."

"Then it must be my imagination. Because it feels like you're trying to stop me from going into the bedroom for some reason."

He chuckled, nervous. With a bounce of his shoulders, he said, "Why would I do that?"

She saw what she could over his tall shoulders and through the portholes of his bent arms. "I don't know. But if that isn't the case, can you please let me by?"

Sumesh remained unmoving, a wall in front of her, a slab. His complexion paled with the passing seconds, like jute left to bleach in the sun.

"Mala," he said at last, lowering his arms to his sides in defeat. "I didn't want you to find out like this."

She stared at him, perplexed. His words held no logic. "What are you talking about?"

The next moment, a tall man stepped out behind Sumesh from his hiding place around the corner. Mala let out a short, sharp cry of fright.

"It's okay, it's okay." Sumesh reached out to steady her. He looked racked, the way a person looked when they were about to cause someone else pain but wished there was another way. "This is Adam. He's a . . . friend of mine from school." The man gave Mala a quick, embarrassed smile, then pinned his dark eyes to the parquet floor.

These words held no logic either. They ricocheted around Mala's addled brain in unison with her pounding heart. She wriggled free of Sumesh's grasp. What was happening? Her eyes darted between him and the stranger. Who was this man standing in her bedroom? Her eyes travelled down his body. Wearing nothing but grey briefs?

. . . Nothing but grey briefs . . .

The answer was slow to form in her mind. Until she finally registered what she had stumbled upon. She suddenly felt very lightheaded.

Her heels inched backward. She held Sumesh in a stark, dumbfounded gaze.

"Mala," he pleaded. "Please don't leave like this. Let me explain."

She rushed to the front door. On the way, she heard them talking, distraught voices figuring out a plan. She slid into her sandals, grabbed her bags and let the door slam behind her.

Then she slipped out to the stairwell. Loose-jointed, she gripped the metal railing and trundled down the echoing cement stairs. With her other hand, she cradled her underbelly protectively, fearful she might trip, tumble, hurt her precious little bean.

What do I do? she thought, tremulous, as she descended. Where do I go?

Chapter 59

Mala teetered by the river disoriented, as if a haze were slowly lifting from her blood. Her feet must have moved ahead of her jumbled mind, shepherding her to the safest place she knew. The water, high and fast, twinkled in the afternoon light. With the sound of draining eavestroughs in her ears, she fixed her gaze on a rock that pierced the rush. As gallons streamed past, the rock, like a pillar, held its place. Mala wondered, Was she the river or the rock? Was she destined to flow with the current or be weathered by it?

Withering, she knelt in the sun-warmed grass, still clutching her purse and the shopping bag. She closed her eyes and raised her chin to the strong afternoon sun. She felt a warm beam against her third eye. She imagined the ray unlocking this locus of wisdom within her. Maybe then she would know what to do next.

Sumesh is gay? she asked the open sky that always withheld its sage counsel.

Sumesh is gay.

Mala knew she had no right to feel betrayed. And yet, there it was, the sharp sting. Was it that Sumesh had cheated? Was it that he had lied? No. Mala had done those things too.

The insult came from knowing she hadn't been the only architect, the only one drafting blueprints. It came from knowing Sumesh had used her as completely as she had used him.

I don't know him at all, she thought. But by her next breath, she knew she was wrong about that. She knew Sumesh better than ever. There was a part of him, at least, she knew as well as herself. The part that was as old as life. The part that knew sometimes life wasn't about living at all.

Mala cradled her belly, her little bean, and listened for the ripples that always had the power to calm her, remind her that she wasn't alone.

I'm here, I'm here, I'm here.

Mala unveiled her eyes. She knew something else now too. The shape of her marriage, if you could call it that. Dark and deep. A cave. A place of blackness where they could hide their transgressions, their truths, their secret selves. Maybe she and Sumesh were a perfect match, after all.

Mala envied him. True, he had been exposed, and that exposure had left him vulnerable. But it also meant he was free. He no longer bore the weight of his secret as far as she was concerned. His truth was out. Mala, on the other hand, was still caught in a lie.

She shuddered in the spring afternoon. That was who she was now, a liar. Discovering the truth about Sumesh was merely a consequence of the karma she had put into action by marrying him with a dishonest heart. Bearing the punishment was her duty. This was how cosmic scales rebalanced themselves.

Or was it? Her father always said that life spoke first in taps, then in shoves, then in open-handed slaps that left behind red fingermarks.

Was life trying to slap Mala awake now? Show her the wrongness of her ways? Remind her that other ways were possible? Truth was possible.

Given that Mala was now the keeper of Sumesh's secret, could she be honest with him too? Tell him she was pregnant with another man's child? Could she count on there being solidarity between deceivers? As she ruminated, two outcomes played themselves out inside her mind with fast-forward speed. Outcome 1: Sumesh accepted the baby as his own and they resigned themselves to bear the inconveniences of their arrangement for the sake of its advantages, namely that they kept each other's secrets, and their lives carried on separately yet together. Outcome 2: Sumesh rejected the baby, dissolved their marriage, exposed Mala; she lost her mother's respect and her life as a shamed and friendless single parent began. Even if Mala exposed Sumesh in retaliation, she knew the Mishras wouldn't believe her word over their unimpeachable son's. They would simply dismiss her as spiteful and her accusations as vengeance. Then they would slander her. And her mother would be ruined.

Probabilities rolled inside Mala's head as she calculated the likelihood of each scenario. Then, abruptly, they stopped. The results glared at her with statistical certitude. If she confessed, Mala knew, either way she was sure to lose.

The fact remained that even if she let go of one secret, she would still bear the burden of others. Even if she told Sumesh the truth, she would still be lying to her mother, to Ash. Shedding one secret without also peeling back the duplicitous self she had become would be incomplete and unsatisfying.

A thought occurred to her as the river washed her careworn gaze. If life was in fact trying to slap her awake, perhaps that meant going all the way . . .

Perhaps she didn't have to live the life of secrets she had resigned herself to at all.

I am not an oppressed woman, she thought, her veins shaky with a sudden injection of power. I have choices.

She could tell the truth. Blow up her life. And Sumesh's. And Ash's.

She could change the way her mother looked at her forever. Lose her.

She could be a single mother. Raise the baby. Survive on her meagre stipend. Finish her doctorate. All on her own.

She could live in a shelter. Go on welfare. Apply for subsidized housing.

Women did these things every day. Women could do whatever they wanted.

She could be good again.

She could start over.

Chapter 60

Her mother's voice inside her head: *Mala, beti?*

She could tell the truth. Disappoint her. Change the way she looked at her forever.

Mala?

Lose her.

Mala?

Lose her forever.

Come, make me some tea.

Lose her. Leave. Start over. Alone.

Mala? Where are you?

Leave her alone.

Her father's body slumped on a snowbank.

Her father's face in a cloud, watching.

Watching her.

Watching every disgraceful thing she did.

Watching what she would do next . . .

The river coursed in the background. Mala remembered standing in the same spot last fall, marvelling at its fluidity, envying the water, identifying with a caught leaf. The river coursed and coursed.

No, she couldn't. She couldn't blow up their lives. She couldn't risk being exposed. She couldn't do it alone. Most of all, she couldn't abandon her mother to loneliness and shame.

"It is far better to endure patiently a smart which nobody feels but yourself."

She couldn't start over.

"This girl is a liar."

She couldn't make herself good again.

"It would be your duty to bear it, if you could not avoid it."

No, she would never be good again.

"It is weak and silly to say you cannot bear what it is your fate to be required to bear."

But there was still a chance that she could be a good mother.

A gust of wind wove itself around her like a braid. Her shopping bag crinkled, reminding Mala of what was left to do.

Chapter 61

From the riverside, Mala cut across the campus to the Ph.D. office. The bag felt heavy in her hand. The handle, a hot line brandishing her palm.

Now's your chance, a voice inside her whispered. *Tell him the truth.*

Mala entered the building and veered left for the stairwell. She climbed to the second floor with purpose. *That wasn't part of the plan*, she replied to the dissenting voice firmly. Ash had already made up his mind. He had chosen his path. That wasn't why she was doing this.

Only because he doesn't know about little bean. Now's your chance to make things right. There's still time. Tell him the truth. Tell him everything.

Mala exited the stairwell, panting. She stood to one side, caught her breath and stared down the hall in distress. The office was no more than ten paces away. The department seemed unusually deserted. Then she remembered. It was Friday afternoon, seminar day.

Mala cursed the dissenting voice. She had made up her mind at the river, and before. She had done the hard work of accepting her circumstances, and Ash's too. Now she was harrowed with doubt. Not only that, she felt something deep inside her shift, like the sliding of a latch. The truth fluttered inside the oubliette, probing for a crack to slip through.

Mala fumbled around her purse for her office keys, disheartened to find herself revising what should have been a simple, concrete plan.

If Ash wasn't at his desk, she considered, she would leave the gift like she had originally intended and delete this shameful footnote from her life once and for all. That was what the gift was meant to be, an ending. A goodbye and good luck.

The drum in her chest boomed. Slow. Strong.

And if he was there . . .

She would tell him. Everything.

She would unburden her heavy heart. Stop hiding and lying and finally confess the truth, come what may.

A mere glimpse of that freedom made Mala want to weep—deep, silent, tormented sobs. Oh, how she wanted to let it all go. How she wanted to see him, talk to him, like she used to not so long ago, when they were still friends and confidants.

If destiny was at play, as she had once believed, fate would intervene now. She would find Ash seated at his desk, and by that sign she would know their story wasn't over. That truth was indeed possible. Perhaps fate was responsible for the sudden uprising of her conscience. Perhaps it had sown the very plan in her mind.

Mala took a short, bracing breath. She approached the office door. It made not a creak as she entered. Her heart went from booming to racing as every step brought her closer to his cubicle.

She held her breath as she peered around the wall, her eyes reaching far, in search of the broad T of his shoulders.

When her eyes settled on his empty chair, Mala felt a column inside her begin to weaken and run, like a spill of mud in the rain, a pearl of wax down a candlestick.

There was no fate. There was no destiny.

Her despairing gaze drifted over his desk, pausing on a framed black-and-white sonogram. Mala beheld the image, breathlessly, achingly. She revised her earlier pronouncement. Fate did exist.

Destiny too. Only not for them. Ash's path would carry on without her. And hers without him. If anything was meant to be, it was that.

Mala had done the hard work of accepting this reality before, hardened herself to it, because she knew thinking twice could lead to a bad place. Now, as she shook and her teeth began to chatter, she saw all her hard work unravel, and it was her own absurd fault. The column inside her, that thing keeping her upright, melted another foot, burying her feet and ankles. If she stayed much longer, soon the rest of the column would liquify and she would finally collapse into a mess of her own misery. She had to move fast.

Mala removed little bean's clothes from the shopping bag, dropping it in the centre of Ash's desk, without a card or even a hastily written note on scrap paper to let him know who the gift was from.

Then she fled, scurrying out of the office, along the hall and down the dank stairwell, as skittish as the mice that lived in the walls of the building when the weather outside turned cold.

Chapter 62

The apartment door whined open. Mala saw Sumesh standing by the large bay window with his arms crossed, watching the sun sink below a magenta sky.

He shot a frantic look over his shoulder. "Mala," he said, spinning around. He took a few quick steps forward, only to halt, as if respecting this boundary of personal space might make up for the earlier ones he had breached. "I'm so glad you're back. I've been worried about you."

Mala freed her swollen feet from her sandals and set down her things. With a lumbering gait, she brushed past him and slumped on the couch. Her whole body groaned with relief. "I wanted to be alone for a while. I went to Bridgehead."

They remained silent for half a minute. Mala stared straight ahead out the large bay window, taking in the unreal beauty of the Caravaggio skyscape. "You don't have to worry," she said finally. "I'm not going to tell anyone." Not his secret, or her own.

He crossed the room with trepidation, sat rigidly beside her and kept his eyes forward, locking his hands in a tight grip. "I wasn't expecting you to say that. I had a whole speech planned out. About how it was the first time, the last time . . ."

"But it wasn't, was it?"

He paused. "No," he admitted in a deep, guilty voice.

"How long have you been together?"

294 / Anita Kushwaha

"Since our first year of med school."

Mala thought back to something Sumesh had said to her the first time they met for coffee. "So he's the one you'd make any compromise for. The one you'd do anything to be with." She gave a quiet, cynical laugh. "I can't believe I thought you were talking about me."

"Mala—"

She raised a hand to forestall his speech. "Why haven't you told your parents?"

"You know why." His tone lacked inflection, like someone who had moved beyond the highs and lows of hope and disappointment and resigned themselves to the flat indifference of acceptance.

"Why does it matter what they think?"

"I don't know. But it does. You know, I could ask you the same question. Why didn't you defy your mother and refuse an arranged marriage?"

Mala looked at him curiously. "You make it sound like I didn't want to marry you."

"I know you didn't, Mala," he stated plainly. "Not at first anyway. Then something changed."

Mala felt a twinge in her womb.

"I figured you came to the same conclusion I did. You didn't want to disappoint your family or risk losing them. So you decided to make the best of things."

Sumesh's summary bore an eerie likeness to the truth, although he had misunderstood the reason she had pursued their relationship. Mala supposed that for him a sham, arranged marriage was inevitable, knowing that his parents would shun him if they discovered the truth about his sexuality. Mala could relate to this fear. She risked losing so much if she couldn't find a way to keep the sham going now.

"And he's okay with it?" she asked. "Adam?"

"I wouldn't say that, but he understands. His parents are as ignorant as mine."

Still, Mala considered, Sumesh and Adam had options because they had each other. "He clearly loves you a lot to put up with this. You two could start over somewhere else." What was she saying?

Sumesh bristled. "Why should we run away? We've built our lives here. Our careers, our friends, our families—it's all here."

"You could have a fresh start." Mala knew she was tossing her shattered fantasies at Sumesh. "You wouldn't have to hide anymore."

"Fresh starts are just another kind of hiding, Mala."

The colour of the sky lost its loveliness, devolving from magenta to a sickly, orange-tinged grey.

"Like marrying me," she said. Why did that still sting so sharply? Why was she encouraging him to reconsider his options? Maybe because part of her envied what he and Adam had together. Real love. The kind that was open and honest, at least with each other, the rest of the world be damned.

Mala fiddled with her nails. She needed to refocus on her plan. Any more talk like this and Sumesh might bolt out the door into Adam's loving arms.

"Mala—"

"It's okay. I probably would've done the same thing." She *had* done the same thing, not that Sumesh would ever know.

Like a strip of tape being slowly pulled away from a wall, Mala felt herself split in two, the way she always felt whenever she told lies, her true self sinking below to safety while her other self pushed through her pores like a numb second skin. Today's covering looked as saintly as Sita.

He eyed her, dubious. "You should be furious with me. But you haven't even raised your voice."

"The brownie I ate at Bridgehead helped," she said, deflecting.

"I lied to you. I cheated. You should hate me."

"Okay, two brownies."

"Mala."

She sighed, depleted. "I *was* mad, all right? I felt cheated. But then I tried to see things from your perspective. It can't be easy. Especially these days, when more and more people live out in the open."

He peered through the window again, resigned and remote. "I'm not above envy." He swallowed with difficulty, as if vulnerability had closed around his Adam's apple, and he fought to dislodge it. "I'm sorry, Mala. For involving you in this. For hurting you."

"I'm not hurt," she blurted out. Then she went rigid. Those were the wrong words. A real wife would have reason to feel hurt right now. "What I mean is, I understand your reasons." She gnawed the inside of her cheek, hoping she sounded convincing.

He lowered his chin. "I don't deserve your kindness. I'll call my parents in the morning and tell them everything."

An inner sigh. He believed her. She counted to three. "There's no need," she told him.

He turned his head slowly and beamed at her with disbelief. "You want to stay together?"

Little bean broadcast her beacon: *I'm here, I'm here, I'm here.* Mala had lost parts of herself—the honest parts, the good parts. But what she did now was to preserve the parts she had gained, namely little bean. And the parts she still hoped to earn, like the role of a good mother.

"I'm still pregnant, Sumesh." The other Mala's voice was toneless, it gave nothing away. She suppressed a chill.

"Of course. But even so, most people would find this situation unlivable. Most women would demand a divorce." His surgical gaze cut into her as if searching for cysts. "So why haven't you?"

A good question. Sumesh was right. It was what anyone in her place would have demanded—a divorce, child support, alimony. Unless, of course, they also had something to hide. Mala knew the survivor in Sumesh was tingling because the survivor in her was prickling along her veins too.

She hugged her stomach. "It's not your fault," she said, hedging. "You are who you are. You shouldn't be punished for it." Mala believed this. She didn't want Sumesh's family to disown him, which would undoubtedly happen if he told them the truth about who he was.

For Mala, however, this was about more than keeping a secret. It was about penance. She would carry Sumesh's secret forever in the hopes of making up for the lies she had told, and the dark business she was conducting even now. It wasn't enough to clear her debts, perhaps. It wasn't gold. But it was payment, nonetheless.

"This isn't just about you," she continued. "I have no desire to raise a child on my own. I also haven't given up on my dreams. I want to finish school. That would be a lot harder to accomplish as a single parent. When we first talked about getting married, we mentioned focusing on friendship. Despite everything that's happened, I still think we can be friends. We can find a way to make things work for us, if we want to."

Sumesh's expression relaxed and he resumed his stoic watch of the dusky evening. "I can understand if you want me to stop seeing Adam."

Mala tossed another coin at her debts. "I would never ask that of you." It went against her atonement, the rebalancing of the cosmic scales. "But I'll settle for a bed in the office for now." She had never wanted to share his bed, and now she would never have to again. "Once the baby comes, we can see about getting a bigger place." With a strained voice, she added, "Who knows, maybe we'll end up having the most honest marriage in history."

Sumesh turned toward her and cradled her hand between his cold, moist palms. "Thank you, Mala," he said earnestly. "You're unbelievable."

The corners of her lips lifted into a faint smile. She tucked her chin, demure, like so many self-sacrificing depictions of Sita. From somewhere deep below, Mala imagined her true self glaring up at her in disgust. A look that said, *He has no idea.*

Chapter 63

Mala wakened, gasping. Her front side still felt plastered with mud and guano from the spelunking dream. She touched her belly, then sighed. She lingered on her stomach, gripping it gently. The dome was absent in the dream, as if the thirty-nine weeks it had taken little bean to sprout and swell were a figment. This frightened her more than the shapeless thing that had chased her through the labyrinthine tunnels of humid blackness, so unrelentingly lightless, so endless they might as well have been the human mind. She had woken with the chilling memory of the thing clawing at her middle, like it was tearing something vital away from her. A dream so real she remembered the stab of its talons, the loss. She pressed her belly a millimetre against some part of little bean and felt the nudge of an elbow—maybe a heel?—against her palm. Breath seeped back into her tight lungs. Nothing was wrong. They were safe. Another nudge. *I'm here, I'm here, I'm here.*

Her neck ached from holding her head up. She rested against her pillow, relaxed her grip on her belly and took in the charcoal greyness of the ceiling, which hung over her like soot. As she lay on her side, her damp cotton nightshirt clinging to her skin, it seemed like the tropical humidity of her dream had rolled into her bedroom. The August night was sweating and covering her in dew. Her thighs slipped against each other as she readjusted.

The clock on her nightstand glowed the lonely hour of 3:00 a.m.

Her bladder had wakened too. She shifted herself up with effort. At first she thought the wetness underneath her was nothing more than sweaty sheets. A few confused seconds later, she realized she was lying in a puddle.

Lovely, she thought. Apparently she had already relieved herself, and yet the cruel joke was that she still needed to use the washroom. She lurched to her feet. The next moment, her belly seized up, stripping her of breath. Stabs of pain like in the dream. She doubled over. This felt different than the false labour she had been experiencing for the past couple of weeks. This pain spiked her lower back and spread forward in throbbing tentacles. She knew she wouldn't be able to breathe it away or walk it off or hide it. She knew these contractions would only end with the song of little cries.

Wetness trickled down her inner thighs. Cradling her underbelly, she waddled to Sumesh's room and shook him awake.

"What's wrong?" he said, half asleep.

"I'm in labour."

"You aren't due for weeks." He rubbed his eyes, more drowsy than alarmed. "It's probably just Braxton Hicks. I know it hurts, but it'll pass."

With trembling hands, she gripped the end of her damp nightshirt. "My water broke."

Now he was alert. "When was your last contraction?" He pushed away the sheet and leapt out of bed.

"I just had one."

He checked his wristwatch. "When? We need to track them."

"About thirty seconds ago. Should we go to the hospital?"

"Normally, I would suggest waiting, but preterm labour can come on fast."

Mala twitched at the mention of early labour. Quickly, she reached for her excuse. Speaking with her eyes lowered, she said, "My mom delivered early too. But I didn't think I took after her in that way, so

I never mentioned it. Since I didn't have trouble conceiving like she did, I didn't think this would be an issue either." She tipped her head up to see if he believed her.

Sumesh gave her a flat look. "Okay. Well, that would've been good to know before, but it's too late now. I'll tell the ob-gyn when we get to the hospital. Now, come on. Let's get ready and go." He touched her shoulder and smiled at her reassuringly, exuding his best bedside manner. "I can help you change if you'd like."

"I'm in labour, Sumesh," she snapped. "I'm not an invalid. I can get dressed on my own." Mala hobbled back to her bedroom. She couldn't understand why the welter of fear grinding in her chest had made her lash out at him. He was just trying to be helpful. He followed her into her bedroom despite her harsh tone, averting his eyes as she pulled off her nightshirt. She was halfway into a summer dress when another violent contraction besieged her. Crying out in anguish, she doubled over and clutched her belly.

"Mala." His voice was controlled. He steadied her by the shoulders. "Just like in Lamaze, okay?" Through pursed lips, he huffed a breath pattern into her ear, giving her a sound map to follow through the staggering pain. Finally, she remembered how to breathe. She channelled all her focus and effort into that one task and soon the strangle of hyperventilation passed. When the thorny fist around her middle let go at last, she was streaming with sweat.

"Was that more intense than the last one?"

She nodded, then threaded herself through the rest of her dress, exhausted by the thought of what was to come.

"Things are progressing faster than I thought." He fetched the overnight bag from the end of her bed and tried to usher her out of the room with care, but Mala had turned from flesh into rusted, jointless metal. "Come on, Mala," he said. "We need to go."

In vain, she thought of ways to stall them. "I have to call my mom."

"I'll call her once you're admitted."

"I haven't brushed my teeth."

"That isn't important right now."

"Let me just fix my hair."

He peered at her with a sympathetic frown, like he was sorry for her. "Everything's going to be okay," he said gently and with confidence. "But we can't delay any longer. It isn't safe."

Not safe for little bean. Mala felt an unexpected swell of courage. She braced herself with a short, stiff breath. She knew another contraction was gathering strength inside her like lightning bundled inside a cloud and there was no hiding from it in doorways. She was going to have to face the storm, urged on by the promise of sunlight, the promise of finally holding a green little bean.

Chapter 64

Short, quivering cries cut a slit through Mala's exhaustion, calling to her from beyond the blackness that surrounded her, the sound like a distant flashlight flickering a message in the deep, deep dark: *I'm here, I'm here, I'm here.*

Mala's eyelids felt weighted as she slowly opened them to the blinding light of the delivery room. The nurse leaned over her bed and placed a wet, squirmy, unhappy little bean on her chest. *Little bean,* she marvelled, here at last. Tiny, trembling, topped with fine hair. Mala felt a burst of elation and exhaustion hum throughout her body. She had done it. She had brought her daughter safely into the world.

Then she was gone, swept away by the nurse, who had matters to take care of. Mala let her eyelids drop, lifting them again when the nurse returned, this time with a clean, silent, swaddled bundle, which she carefully placed into the dip of Mala's chest. Happiness sparkled in her eyes. She took in every detail of the baby's face. Then she pressed a soft kiss on the infant's wrinkled forehead. She had been waiting so long to meet her.

Soon the grandparents hurried into the room, all gasps and smiles, as they gathered around the bed. Her mother stroked away the tiny rivers of perspiration that had wept from her hairline during labour.

"She doesn't look premature to me," Mrs. Mishra said. "Aren't preemies supposed to be smaller? She seems just the right size."

"Seven pounds and three ounces," Sumesh said. "I was surprised too."

An explanation burst from inside Mala like instinct. "I might've had gestational diabetes. It can go undetected." She glanced up. Sumesh rolled the possibility around his clinical mind. How easily the lies spill from me, she thought, dismayed. Soon, she remembered, there would be no need for deceit. Soon she would be able to shed the weight of her second self entirely and start anew.

"It's possible," he said. "Remind me to ask your doctor."

"Oh, Sumesh," his mother clucked. "It doesn't matter now, does it? She's here and she's healthy." Mrs. Mishra reached for the baby with her too-long fingers. "Now give her over, Mala. We all want a chance to hold her."

Mala resisted. Everyone was watching. Full of reluctance, she passed the infant to Mrs. Mishra, who immediately started bouncing her knees and rattling off lines of baby talk in Hindi. Mala had never seen the woman look happy until that very moment, the angular symmetry of her unpleasant face sanded down by the child's softness.

"I see so much of our Sumesh in her." A smug grin curled her dark painted lips. "Daddy's little girl."

Mala agreed but for different reasons. Where Mrs. Mishra saw her son, Mala saw hints of Ash: in the tone of her daughter's complexion, in her wispy brown hair.

"She's looking at me! She's looking at me!" Mrs. Mishra squealed. "What stunning eyes. They're blue, I think. Or grey, maybe?"

Mala froze.

Grey eyes?

Sumesh investigated. "Let me see." He peered into the infant's puffy face. "Well, she didn't get those from me."

His manner was joking, but Mala found no humour in the discovery. She kept very still. This was it, she reasoned: karma. The coppers she had tossed at her debts hadn't been enough. The cosmic equalizer had come to collect greater payment. Of course it had. No one could outrun consequences. It was universal law, like gravity. The lies and plotting and manipulation she had flung into the world were now falling from the sky in a storm of hellfire. Any moment, they would blow up and scatter her life. Any moment, the others would see the truth. It was calling to them through a pair of newborn eyes: *I'm here, I'm here, I'm here.*

Mala's mind went white. She had no lies left to tell. If this was the end, let it come.

"You know," Mr. Mishra said, deliberating, "a cousin on my mother's side had grey eyes."

"The baby will grow up to be as beautiful as Aishwarya Rai," Mala's mother cooed.

"She already is," Sumesh asserted with a proud grin, stroking the baby's delicate cheek.

Mala's eyes were large with shock. Unblinking, she looked from person to person, scrutinizing their content, unsuspecting faces.

"I'll call the pandit and get her rasi chart made," Mrs. Mishra said.

Breathing faintly, Mala could scarcely believe it, but the moment of danger appeared to have passed, like a brief twist of wind that threatened a tornado but in the end held no greater fury than a momentary rustling of debris. A blue wave of relief swept down the back of her neck. Her shoulders eased a fraction. She had done it. Her plan had worked.

"Then we can choose her name," Mrs. Mishra went on.

Only then did she fully register her mother-in-law's overbearing presumption. "I've already chosen her name," she said.

Mrs. Mishra showed her displeasure. "Nonsense, it's tradition."

In a sudden display of husbandly solidarity, Sumesh took the baby from his mother's arms and handed her back to Mala. "Don't be superstitious," he said, although he seemed too enamoured of the little one to sound very cross about his mother's overreaching.

Mrs. Mishra raised her absurd eyebrows half an inch.

"We've already discussed it." He gave Mala a discreet wink. "The name Mala chose was better than my entire list."

Mrs. Mishra's bangles chimed as she made a show of unhurriedly crossing her arms. "Well then, Deviji," she said, mocking. "*Do tell.*"

Mala forgot about the others and she focused on her daughter, whom she hadn't dared to call anything but little bean until now, wary as she had grown of fate. The secret of the name, however, unlike the other secrets she kept, carried no weight. Rather, it fluttered against the arch of her mouth like something winged and lovely. She enjoyed the sensation, holding it back a few seconds more.

Then, she spoke into the infant's familiar grey eyes. "Asha," she said softly. A radiant smile set her face aglow. "Your name is Asha."

From the outer rim of her awareness, she heard Mrs. Mishra bark, distant and harsh, "What? Like the playback singer?"

But no vinegar, judgment, or harm whatsoever had the power to penetrate the brilliant sphere of love she emanated around herself and her daughter.

Her Asha.

"It means hope," Mala told her.

Chapter 65

A leaf-crisping, late October breeze shifted the bedroom curtains with ghostly grace. Cooler nights usually meant easier sleeping, but not for Mala, not for weeks. She looked around the walls of her shadowy bedroom, which no longer resembled a room of her own. There wasn't space for her desk once the crib, glider and changing table were moved in, so it was stored in the closet, along with a few crates of her papers and books.

The avalanche of baby things would have been enough to squelch her. Everywhere she looked there was kiddy clutter, as though every room in their apartment had been pelted with grenades custom-made by Toys "R" Us. Motherhood was burying her, bottle by bottle, burp by burp, diaper by diaper. Soon no one would be able to find her. Would they even try? Mala wondered. Did she even matter anymore? Or was she like her desk and papers, those relics of her goals and ambition, those things that were moulding over in the dark of the closet, like the parts of herself she had pushed aside to make room for her new role?

Asha stirred in her crib. Mala listened to the familiar whimper and rustle. She felt the warmth slowly drain from her face, chest, legs. Please don't wake up, she thought. Please stay asleep, little bean.

The first six weeks were a death-march struggle. The colic, unrelenting wails, haunting memory of sleep. The growing sense of uselessness metastasized a little more each time Mala failed to keep her daughter happy. Wasn't every woman born a natural mother? Wasn't that the message she had been fed her entire life? The reason little girls were given dolls that soiled themselves to play with before they could even read? Why couldn't she figure this out? She was an educated woman, a researcher. Solving problems, answering questions, this was her livelihood, or at least it used to be. What had become of the mind she relied on more than talent or beauty? What was happening to her?

"It's just the baby blues," her mother had said. "It happens to some women. Things will improve when Asha starts sleeping through the night. Have patience, beti. Motherhood is about sacrifice." But how would her mother know? She had never felt like this before.

Asha continued to squirm in her crib, stretching out her arms and legs. Mala sat rigid in bed, wringing her wrist, anticipating the cries that would soon pierce the dormant night air. The clock read 3:00 a.m., as if her daughter knew the night's loneliest hour.

Stone-faced, Mala listened to Asha's cries build up and up, like sirens speeding closer. She asked herself why she felt so cold. Was it possible to be both inside a room and outside of it at the same time? She mined her insides for the nurturing instinct that was supposed to be a building block of her DNA, supposed to make her leap to the rescue. But all she found was cold. Thick, dense ice impervious to Asha's cries. Mala wanted to pick up her daughter and soothe her, but she had tried that before, so many times, and it never worked, not like it did for Sumesh. Something looped and tightened in her chest. The truth was, her baby didn't like her. Mala shuddered. And it was her own fault.

The lactation consultant at the hospital had warned her against the bottle, coding into her psyche the importance of breastfeeding to the baby's immunity, growth and development, leaving Mala with the acute impression that mothers who chose store-bought milk over their own were in effect abusing their children. She didn't want to be a child abuser. She wanted to be a good mother. A natural mother. A mother as natural as breastfeeding was promoted to be. But no matter the number of attempts, Asha had only latched successfully a few times.

"The breast is best," said the consultant, reciting her brigade's motto. "Don't give up. You'll have a stronger bond. It's all worth it in the end!"

The fabled bonding experience never happened for them. Asha got used to bottle-feeding in the hospital. When Mala started pumping, her breasts were dry as empty bladders, so she had to use formula, feeling decimated each time she mixed the off-white powder with water, the colour an unconvincing imitation of the real milk, the better milk, that she was incapable of providing. On the rare days that Mala ventured outside of the apartment, as she pushed her stroller around the park, she envied the milky breasts of the other mothers she sometimes saw, feeding on benches, beaming their Mary-like glow, natural mothers.

Maybe it was worth another—

Her bedroom door swung open with a thrust. Sumesh tromped to the crib. "Why haven't you picked her up yet?" he snapped. Mala watched, speechless, as he leaned over the crib, lifted Asha and rested her small, mewling body over his heart.

She sprang to her feet. "I was about to." She reached out. "Here, let me take her."

He blocked her with his shoulder and bounced Asha in his arms. "Just get her bottle ready."

Mala left the room, carving a rut into the floor with her guilty stare. In the kitchen, she hurried to prepare Asha's bottle. When she returned, Sumesh was gently rocking a peaceful Asha in the Band-Aid–coloured glider by the window while the baby sucked contentedly on her fingers.

Mala handed Sumesh the bottle and sat across from him on the edge of her bed, tugging at the sleeves of her pyjamas. Soon she heard the reassuring sound of Asha suckling, like the rhythm of an easy heartbeat, and took quiet pleasure in this lullaby.

Sumesh fed, burped and changed the baby. She watched him with envy, noting his tenderness and care. He was as natural a father as she was unnatural a mother.

Once Asha was settled in her crib, Sumesh paused. Mala could feel him smoulder. "Can we talk?" he said, biting back an angry tone. Then he padded out of the room without waiting for an answer.

The knot in her chest tightened another centimetre. She followed him into the living room. They swept aside the baby things to make space on the couch. Mala slouched with her hands underneath her thighs. Sumesh leaned forward, resting his elbows on his knees, his hands clasped in front of him. His eyes were fixed on the parquet.

"We've been over this a million times, Mala. When Asha cries, you need to pick her up."

"I told you I was about to."

"Well, I don't believe you."

"What are you saying?"

"I'm saying that if I hadn't come in, I think you would have let her cry."

"Some people would call that ideal parenting."

"I'm not joking. You couldn't see yourself. When I walked in, you were just sitting there, staring at her. You looked so . . ."

Mala pinched her leg. "What?"

"I don't know." He tilted his head away from her. "Detached."

Mala pinched herself harder. "You're overreacting, Sumesh."

"No, I'm not. The truth is, Mala, you haven't been yourself for weeks."

She felt a flash of irritation. "Taking care of a newborn might have something to do with that. Of course I'm not myself. Nothing's the same. And it's easy for you to judge. You're not the one who's stuck here every day. You still have school and Adam and a full life away from all this."

"Maybe you just need to get out of the apartment and meet some other moms? You know, take a yoga class with Asha or something?"

"She would never settle down for long enough, you know that."

"Well, maybe she would, Mala. Maybe if you were happier, she would be happier too."

Mala glared at the back of his head, appalled and ashamed.

He cooled himself with a deep breath. "I'm worried about you," he went on, his tone softened.

"Enough to switch places with me? Or to quit school for a while? How about postponing date nights with your boyfriend?"

He sniffed the air and wiped the end of his nose with a pinch, as if cleansing away an unpleasant smell.

"I didn't think so."

He opened his mouth to speak, then resumed his hushed pose a while longer. "I think you should talk to someone."

"The last time I checked, you were a GP, not a shrink."

"I've been reading up on postpartum." He hesitated. "You're very symptomatic."

"I don't need antidepressants, Sumesh," she said, dispassionate. "Or therapy, or Mom and Baby Yoga. What I need is a bit of normalcy. A shred of my old life." Her plan of going back to school after four weeks was as unsuccessful as her attempts at breastfeeding. The semester was half over already. Instead of registering, she had filled out another leave of absence form. She was in no shape to return to her studies.

"We have a child now, Mala. Our old lives are gone."

The knot in her chest loosened into a whip. "Really, Sumesh? Because your life seems more or less unaffected."

"You think it's easy being at the clinic all day?"

"At least you get a break."

"Work is work, Mala."

"Well, at least you'll finish your residency on time. All my plans are on hold." She had revisited her analysis half a dozen times since Asha was born, but the baby never napped long enough for her to rediscover the story she was trying to tell and how she wanted to tell it. The longer she left her work to idle, the more it seemed like a stranger to her, less like her story and more like someone else's.

Sumesh rubbed his hands together. "So what do you want to do?" he asked.

Wanting wasn't allowed anymore, was it? Only selfish women wanted anything other than their children's happiness. Nevertheless . . . "I want to be able to think straight. And get back to my thesis. And feel like there's more to my life than diapers and spit-up." *I want my life to be about more than sacrifice,* she quietly admitted to herself.

He rested his eyes on one of Asha's toys on the floor. Then he wrenched a hand through his dishevelled hair and sighed. "We'll work something out," he said at last.

Mala's eyes shot to his face. "Really?"

He rose to his feet. "We have to." He looked worn, pale. "We can't keep going on like this." He limped toward his bedroom. "But let's talk about it tomorrow, okay? I think we could both use some rest. If Asha wakes up again, let me know. I'll put her back down." And with that, Sumesh took his leave.

Mala listened to the receding sound of his footsteps and the soft latching of his bedroom door.

Alone in the living room with her eyes unfocused on the floor, she felt something inside her ice slab of a body begin to shimmer, the way the river did whenever it caught the sun. As the shimmer spread its light, it cleared away the nameless grey substance that had been hardening in her veins for too long. A soundless tear slipped along her cheek. Far too long. Maybe it was a sign that she could be like water, after all. Maybe she was about to shift phases from solid into something fluid, something free. Maybe the dark whispers that told her nothing was ever going to get better were wrong.

Mala rose to her feet, tiptoed to her bedroom and leaned against the door jamb. She listened to the comforting sound of her daughter's quick breath and wondered what Asha saw in dreams on the backs of her tiny eyelids. Someday, would Mala look upon this troubled time as though glimpsing a nightmare, something that had happened in another place, to another version of herself? Someday, when she and her beloved daughter were living happier lives, would this all seem as temporary, distant and meaningless as a bad dream?

Outside, soft rain fell. An earthy scent rose from the wet pavement, cleansing the air of the room. Soon the charcoal clouds would part, having shed their weight, and daylight would herald a fresh start for everything that it set aglow, even Mala.

Bloodlines

Chapter 66

The thick August air was so plump with humidity, Asha wouldn't have been surprised if droplets materialized right in front of her at any moment, thanks to the belligerent sun and fatiguing heat of the day. The AC in the car was cranked to its limit, but even so, the skin under her thighs felt soggy against the back seat. In the background, classical music played, which her mom insisted would soothe the jangle of her nerves, but of course it didn't.

Their silver Mazda pulled up alongside the curb. According to her mom, the contemporary design of Sumesh Mishra's house was "hardly in keeping with the neighbourhood's colonial appeal." To Asha, his house felt impersonal, resembling a slate-coloured shoebox mounted on a concrete slab. Instead of grass, the front yard was a garden of bowling ball–sized rocks. At the centre of the rubble stood a shiny metal sculpture of a tree trunk, without any branches or foliage, that split sunlight into beams. Asha wondered how a lungless column of chrome could ever compete with the beauty of an actual tree. As she scrutinized the yuppie garden art, it confirmed something Asha already knew deep inside: she wasn't going to like him.

"Are you sure you don't want us to come in with you?" her mom asked. She watched Asha in the rearview mirror with a hopeful look in her eye.

But Asha hadn't changed her mind on the drive over. She clenched her stomach.

"I'm sure," she said, trying to bolster a note of confidence into her voice.

Her mom narrowed her eyes, her reluctance reflected in the mirror. "Really sure?"

"*Mom.*"

"Okay, okay." Her mom raised her palms in surrender, then dropped her hands onto her lap. "In that case, we'll be at the Bridgehead on Bank Street if you need anything. Call us when you want to get picked up, okay?"

As if her parents would actually make it to the coffee shop. More likely, they would meander through the neighbourhood for a while, only to park in the very same spot they were now, and spend the rest of the time anxiously waiting for her to re-emerge from Sumesh Mishra's ugly grey house.

Asha stepped out of the car. "Sure thing." She wore a tight-lipped smile as she swung the door shut and waved her parents a lazy goodbye, watching as their car receded down the quiet, tree-lined street with a shaky breath.

Once they were out of sight, she made the slow journey up Sumesh Mishra's driveway, the twist in her stomach tightening with every foreboding step. When she reached the glossy ebony door, she paused, took a deep breath and pushed past her nerves to ring the doorbell.

While she waited, she scanned her outfit for any straggling lint, tweezing away the few pale strands she came across. Black felt like an appropriate colour to wear despite the equatorial heat, a shade to match her mood.

Through the door, she heard the scuttle of approaching feet. Then a pause. And lastly, the restrained clearing of a manly throat.

She sucked in a breath and held still.

The door opened. A slender man towered in front of her. His

commercial-worthy smile exposed too many of his teeth. His neatly styled hair was a few shades darker than her own, as was his complexion. She was disappointed to find no hint of grey in his eyes. He wore khakis, a navy polo shirt and flip-flops. The uniform of someone trying hard to look casual.

"You must be Asha," he said. His voice was low and careful, a listener's voice.

Her mouth twitched an involuntary smile. "Hi."

He stepped aside, held the door open for her and with his other arm made a grand sweep of the air. A welcoming gesture. "Please, come in."

Asha crossed the threshold and entered the foyer. She slipped off her ballet flats and took in the space—open, high ceilings.

He stared at her while she stood in her stocking feet, not in a sinister way but how Asha imagined people looked at each other in heaven when they were reunited with their loved ones. Was he seeing her, she wondered, or her birth mother?

She held one wrist and peeked into the living room, setting her eyes on a striking pair of Dutch-orange antlers mounted above the fireplace.

"Forgive me." He gave his head a slight rattle, as if shaking off the awe of her being there. "Please, come in, come in. Have a seat."

He ushered her into the living room. The conversation area was made up of a glass coffee table flanked by a lime green couch and two ivory-coloured leather sitting cubes. The antlers were mounted on a white brick wall. Neatly arranged along the mantel was a line of photographs encased in mirrored frames. Asha's eyes slid from picture to picture in search of a face like her own. Most of the photos, though, were of Sumesh and another man.

He approached the couch and she dove for the nearest cube.

As she took a seat uneasily, he asked her, "Would you like some lemonade? It's homemade. Well, technically, it's not lemonade, it's made with limes. What do you even call that? Lime-o-nade? That doesn't sound right." He smiled, embarrassed. "In any case, it *is* homemade."

His jumpy prattle almost made Asha smile back. "I'll have a little."

While he poured them each a glass of the cloudy drink, she admired the artfully curated treats that adorned the coffee table: a cake pedestal spilling over with a bouquet of pastel macarons, a bowl of fresh strawberries slathered in whipped cream, a teak board topped with wedges of unrecognizable cheese.

He handed Asha her glass and took a seat. "Are you hungry?" he asked.

With one hand pressed against her knotted stomach, Asha looked guiltily at the extravagant spread. "Not really," she confessed.

He appeared a little disappointed. "I knew I went overboard." His dark eyes hopped between the items on the table. "I wasn't sure what you might like. Anyway"—he shrugged with a timid grin— "please, help yourself, okay? Make yourself at home."

"I will." Asha was surprised by how polite and considerate he was being. She hadn't expected that. "Thank you."

They sat in silence for a while, sipping limeade, avoiding each other's gaze. The tartness of the drink made her mouth pucker and her tongue feel bumpy and dry.

"Asha," he said, his voice rising. "I'm happy you're here."

She looked up from the dust-free hardwood. "You are?"

"Of course. I can't imagine it was an easy decision to make, following up with the adoption agency. But I'm glad you did. And I'm so glad you called me." He paused for a beat. "I want you to know you can ask me anything. You must have a lot of questions."

Yes, she had questions. A journal of them. But now that she was seated across from Sumesh Mishra, and he wasn't at all as she had presumed, Asha didn't know where or how to begin. The glint of the mirrored photographs caught her eye again. That was a place to start.

"Who's the man in the pictures?" she asked.

He glanced at the mantel. "That's my husband, Adam. The lemonade was his idea. He wanted to be here, but I thought it would be best for us to get acquainted first. You can always meet him next time, if you like."

Next time, she thought transiently. "How long have you been together?"

He held back the answer for a long moment. "Almost twenty-two years."

Asha wrinkled her nose as numbers played across her mind. Wait, she wondered. How could that be?

"Your mother knew about him, in case you're wondering," he said, guessing her thoughts.

"She knew you had a partner when you got married?"

He hesitated, his mouth pinched. "No, not then. Shortly after."

Asha stared at the spread in dismay. None of it made sense.

"We came to an understanding. I suppose you could say we both entered our marriage with secrets. Which isn't surprising, really. We barely knew each other."

Asha looked up. "What do you mean?"

He sat back and crossed his legs. "We had an arranged marriage."

Just like Asha's grandparents, although they were so perfect for each other, it was a detail she usually forgot. Somehow, she associated the custom with older generations, maybe because her own parents, in comparison, had done things in reverse—gotten to know each other, lived together and then married.

More secrets? she thought dismally. She'd had enough of those with her parents. Now she was learning that her birth parents had them too? What could her birth mother's have been?

"You can live your entire life with people and still not know everything about them," she said, then blinked with surprise. That had gushed out unexpectedly. "I only found out that I'm adopted last spring," she added.

"Ah." He nodded. "I was wondering." He watched her closely. "That must have come as quite a shock."

Her face suddenly felt very long. "The past few months haven't been the smoothest, I'll admit."

"Do you know why they waited so long to tell you?"

She considered. "Fear, I think."

Tugging on his bottom lip, he lowered his glass onto the coffee table as if the limeade had lost its appeal.

Asha glanced at the mantel. "I noticed you don't have any photos of her on display."

"I thought you might ask about that." Leaning forward, he reached under the coffee table and pulled out a black leather album. "Would you like to see some pictures of your mother?"

Asha went rigid, clutching the glass in her hands. She stared at the album with a pulsing, terrified gaze. "Birth mother," she blurted.

He lifted the cover of the album, squinting. "I'm sorry?"

"Birth mother," she repeated. "I already have a mother."

"Right." He reddened, sheepish at his mistake. "Of course. I apologize."

"It's a subtle yet important distinction." Her eyes stayed glued to the album now open in his lap. "To me, anyway."

"I understand." He flipped a page. "Let me try again. Would you like to see a picture of your *birth* mother?"

Dread spasmed in her belly. "Sure," she told him without feeling remotely so. The moment had arrived. The woman made of mist who had hovered in Asha's mind for months was about to materialize on glossy paper. Was she ready to face her ghost? Ready to meet the stranger who had pushed her into the world, then disappeared? A face she had been longing to see. A face she would never forget.

Through half-closed eyes, Sumesh peered at one of the pictures with an expression Asha couldn't decipher. "Unfortunately, there aren't many to show you." He placed the album between them on the coffee table. "This was taken at our wedding."

The photograph burst with extravagance. Colour, sparkle and bloom. Five people stood next to one another dressed in dazzling finery on a beautifully decorated mandap. Asha leaned in for a closer look. Her eyes narrowed on her birth mother. She wore a maroon lehnga. Her dark hair was covered by a shawl so elaborate that Asha could feel its weight pulling at the crown of her own head. Her full lips were painted maroon to match her dress and her almond-shaped eyes were striking, bold with dark liner. She looked as lovely as the wooden dolls Asha's naniji displayed on her hutch shelves. And yet neither the sparkle of her birth mother's dress nor the splendour all around her appeared to reach her deep, mournful eyes. Those, Asha was certain, had no bottom. A gathering place for sadness.

"She's beautiful," Asha said, feeling weak.

"You look so much like her. That's why I couldn't stop staring at you when you first arrived."

"Do I?" She probed the picture. *Where? Where was she in the beautiful stranger?*

"I see her in the shape of your face and your nose and even your wavy hair, although hers was darker. You're about the same height too. She might've been a little taller, but then I suspect you've got another inch or so in you."

Why was Asha riffling inside? Why was she smiling stupidly at the saddest wedding photo she had ever seen? Could these similarities truly mean that much to her? She touched the photo. Yes—she quietly acknowledged—they could, and they did.

"I don't even know her name," she admitted, her smile faltering.

"You don't?"

She shook her head. "I've been too afraid to ask my parents, and they've been too afraid to tell me." *Naming things made them real.*

"Would you like to know?"

Asha looked up, her eyebrows slanting upward. She nodded. More than anything at that moment, yes.

"Her name was Mala."

The silence cracked with a new sound. "Mala," she said, the name rolling strangely off her tongue.

Your name is Mala, she repeated silently, peering deeply into her birth mother's woeful eyes. A garland of flowers. A rosary.

She kept her eyes glued to the photograph, wrestling with a commotion of conflicting emotions, elation and despair. The longer she stared at the picture, the more disheartened she felt, as if absorbing the tar of her birth mother's wedding-day gloom. Sumesh didn't disturb her. Eventually, she became curious about the others in the photo. "Who are they?" She pointed at the stern-looking couple standing beside Sumesh.

He craned his neck for a better view. "Those are my parents. And the woman on the other side of Mala is her mother. Your birth nani."

Asha saw something of her grandmothers in the short, round woman, and this recognition made her heart beat with warmth. She noticed the odd number of people in the wedding party and realized someone was missing. "Where's her dad?"

A deep furrow wrinkled his forehead. "I'm sorry, Asha. But he passed away the year before Mala and I were married. I never met him either. She loved him very much."

"Oh." Asha swallowed, unsure of how else to respond. Something else they had in common, their deep love for their fathers. "Well, will I get to meet the others?"

He took a longer pause, his expression closed and unreadable. "I don't think so. You see, Mala's mother passed away shortly before Mala passed away herself. You were still an infant at the time. You were still living with us then, actually."

The sudden loss thundered in her like an encyclopedia slamming shut as another part of her history closed to her. "What about your parents?"

He shifted, uncrossing his legs. "I don't see them very often. They're . . ."

"Old-fashioned?"

"Making your own lemonade is old-fashioned." He reached for his drink, swallowed a mouthful and held the glass in his lap.

"They're prejudiced. Fortunately, I stopped seeking their approval a lifetime ago." He squeezed his hands around his drink. After a brief silence, he asked, "Do you know how Mala died?"

Asha nodded, solemn. A terminal illness. Sudden and unfair.

He held the base of his neck with one hand, gazing downward. "I still have nightmares about the accident."

Wait, she thought. "What accident?"

The look on his face could only be described as petrified. "I don't know why I said that," he stammered. "I meant her illness. It was . . . brutal to see her like that." He gazed to one side as if glimpsing the past with sudden anguish. "By the end, I didn't recognize her."

Clearly, thinking of her illness had unsettled him. Asha dismissed the slip. She had more questions, but reasoned they could wait until their next meeting. There was too much to talk about in one afternoon.

She gave him a moment to recover and examined the photograph, disappointed to find no trace of grey in any of their eyes. She looked up. He seemed calmer. Maybe a slight change of topic would do him good. "I was wondering," she said. "Do you know where my light eyes come from? No one else seems to have them."

He kept his face turned away. "We used to think you got them from my side of the family."

"But I didn't?"

He shook his head.

Asha waited for him to go on. She didn't understand why he had gone so quiet, so serious, over something as insignificant as eye colour.

He swallowed with effort. "You have your father's eyes," he told her, stoic.

Asha blinked three times in quick succession. "Wait. I don't follow."

Without a word, Sumesh reached for the album, flipped it over and withdrew a white envelope from behind the back cover.

Asha had seen an envelope like that before. On the morning after her eighteenth birthday. This time, though, she recognized the handwriting across the front. Not just a name, a full address.

"She wrote other letters?"

"She wrote three. One for you. One for me. And this one."

"Who is it for? Why do you still have it?"

"Mala mailed it to the wrong address and it was sent back to me." He waited a moment. "Before I tell you more, I need you to understand something, Asha. When Mala died, my world was devastated. Her death alone would've been enough to deal with. But there was so much more to it than that."

Asha's heart pounded against her ribs as if warning her, giving her a beat to follow out of Sumesh Mishra's house and down the street to Bridgehead.

"Mala's letter changed everything I knew. She wasn't the person I thought she was. Neither was I." A reluctant pause. "And neither were you."

"What do I have to do with it?"

He finally looked at her with large, regretful eyes. "Everything, Asha. All of this is about you."

Something felt very, very wrong. *Go, go, go,* hammered her heart.

"Why did you give me up?" she blurted, suddenly bold. "After Mala died, you looked after me for a while. But then you put me up for adoption. Why? What was it about me that was so horrible you couldn't stand it anymore?"

An incredible look of pain washed over him. "There was never anything horrible about you, Asha. There never could be. Mala wanted me to raise you, but I couldn't. Not after I found out about her secret." He rubbed a tickle from his nose. "And because of her secret, when the letter was returned, I was so livid, I decided to keep it. I kept it for you."

"What secret?" she demanded. "And why would you keep that letter for me? I already have a letter from Mala."

Sumesh tongued his cheek and passed her the envelope. Although it was paper, it carried weight, the burden of secrets.

Asha read the name of the addressee out loud. "Ash Groves." She looked up. "Who is he?"

"A classmate of your mother's."

"Birth mother," she corrected. The similarity of their names couldn't go unmentioned. "But . . . my name is Asha."

"I think Mala must have named you"—a wince of pain crossed his mouth—"after him."

Asha thought her hearing must have played a trick or faltered for a second. "What?"

Sumesh lowered his forehead, offering Asha no further explanation. His words boomed against her skull.

After him. After him. After him.

Then, all at once, the booming stopped, and she finally understood. After him. Ash Groves. Her birth father.

"That's why you didn't want to raise me," she said slowly. "Because I wasn't yours to begin with. And that's why no other family members offered to take care of me, either. I'm guessing you told them I wasn't your real daughter."

He didn't speak at first, rubbing the smooth leather of the album with his thumb. "Mala's mother was gone," he began. "But I still had my parents to deal with. You might not believe me, but I did try to raise you on my own, even though I felt like I'd been railroaded into it. I loved you. You *were* my real daughter for a while, Asha." His face seized with pain. "But Mala robbed me of that. I still tried, though. Then my mother started pressuring me to remarry, saying that you needed a mother to raise you properly. After the last fiasco, I wasn't about to jump into another arranged marriage. But I wasn't out back then. So instead of telling my parents the truth about myself, I told them the truth about Mala's affair." He grunted. "They wanted nothing to do with you after that. And it got my mother off my back for a while, although not for as long as I had hoped." He scratched his neck.

If this was meant to offer consolation, it had failed entirely. Asha managed to pluck a thread of sense from the tangled mess of information unspooled inside her head. "If Mala told you about my birth father in your letter, then she probably told him about me in his, right?"

"I would assume so, yes."

"But his letter was sent back to you. And you never tried to resend it?"

"Like I told you, I was livid. I was through doing Mala's bidding. But despite my anger at her, and at him, I didn't throw the letter away. I kept it."

"Because you felt guilty," she muttered. "At some level you knew what you were doing, or not doing, was wrong." An incredible weariness passed through her. She felt beaten, diminished, by all their secrets and lies. How could her birth mother have endured them? Asha looked across at him. "Does he even know that Mala died?"

Sumesh reflected. "I don't know. Maybe not."

They sat for a while, not speaking. Asha thought and thought.

"You didn't want to raise me," she said at last, her voice calm and intimidating. "But my birth father might have. Or at least I could have known him. He might have wanted some kind of relationship with me. Or maybe not. But at least if he had known, he could have decided for himself. I know Mala didn't explicitly ask you to deliver his letter, but you knew she had things to straighten out, otherwise she wouldn't have mailed it to begin with." Asha sagged. "My entire life could have been different."

In that instant, she didn't consider whether a completely different life was something she wanted. All she felt was robbed of something that should have been a part of her story, and would have been if Sumesh Mishra had made a different choice. A vast loneliness poured out of her, flooding the room, the house, the street. She was the centre of her own friendless sea.

"I was trying to protect you," he said. "Nothing I knew about him led me to believe that he would want you or that he even deserved you. For all I knew, he had gotten Mala pregnant and abandoned her, leaving her to marry the first guy who came along, which ended up being me. I thought the last thing you needed was another reluctant parent. So I placed you for adoption, knowing that the right people would find you. People who wanted you more than anything."

A fierce anger chewed through her. Protect me, she thought. Could he still believe that? When it was now clear that all his inaction had done was cause her harm. She was sick of people thinking—worse, believing—that they knew what was best for her. Why couldn't they be open? Why couldn't they let her make her own choices? Why couldn't they see it was her life, not theirs, that kept bearing the brunt of their withholding?

"You could have given his letter to the adoption agency when you gave them mine. At least then I would have known about him. I could have decided for myself whether I wanted to find him."

He opened his mouth, then pressed his lips into a tense line. He looked to the side, appearing to weigh an option, and an outcome, that had never crossed his mind.

Asha considered flipping the table, belting him with the album, tearing the tacky antlers right off the wall. But there was nothing she could do—no assault was vicious enough—to hurt him the way he had hurt her by doing nothing.

"Asha," he said, leaning in with a tortured expression. "Please let me help you figure this out. We can track him down together. I can explain to him my reasons for not delivering the letter when I should have. You don't have to face this alone. Please, I want to make things right. That's why I was so relieved when you called. It's haunted me, Asha. You've haunted me all these years."

Asha shot to her feet, loped to the door and wriggled into her flats.

He rushed after her. "Please, don't leave," he begged. "Let me at least call your parents to come and get you. I can wait in another

328 / Anita Kushwaha

room until they arrive. I won't say another word to you. Please, just stay."

Asha ran out the door and down the driveway, half expecting to see her parents' car parked at the curb. A waterfall of disappointment rushed through her at not finding them. Bewildered, she stood in the street, looking blankly from left to right, unsure of which way to go.

"Asha!" he cried. "Please come back inside!"

Then, like a whisper in her ear, she heard her mom's voice, reminding her where they would be waiting.

Asha pointed herself in the direction of the coffee shop and ran. Her flats slapped against the pavement, her elbows and knees pumping fiercely, as she barrelled away from the hurt and confusion, toward her parents. The ones who had wanted her more than anything.

Chapter 67

Asha sat upright in bed with her journal open to a fresh page, unsure how to start her letter. This wasn't exactly true. In fact, of all the letters she had written lately, this was the first that would have a proper opening. Ever since the name slipped into her ear at Sumesh Mishra's house, it had been circling inside her head like a butterfly trapped under a cloche. And yet, she couldn't bring herself to tip out the four letters, send them along her arm, into her pen and release them onto paper. She couldn't yet catch the butterflies and pin down their wings.

After leaving his house, she ran three blocks to Bridgehead with the letter clenched in her fist. She found her parents at the back, sharing a coffee and an untouched slice of carrot cake. Surprised to see her, when they asked why she was finished so early, she couldn't explain, there in the coffee shop, with strangers embarrassingly close to her misfortune. All she could manage to utter was, "Please, can we go home?"

The solitude of the car was no better for revealing long-kept family secrets, silence stuffed around them like the thick heat of the day. At home, she numbly climbed the stairs to her bedroom, closed the door and slipped into bed, frozen and mute. Willow texted her half a dozen times throughout the afternoon, wondering how the visit went, anxiety building with every new message, but Asha's temporary speechlessness made replying impossible. She decided to patiently outwait the syndrome. Hours passed, and evening fell without a sound.

Nothing hindered her ability to think, though, or the speed of her thoughts. Now she was considering the similarities between herself and her birth mother, other than their heart-shaped faces, warm complexions and tendency to love boys who didn't love them back enough to stay.

That is, they had both lost their mothers to early deaths. They were both orphans in a sense. Asha wondered if that was how her birth mother had felt. Homeless. A plant with no soil to anchor itself.

She wondered if her birth mother's hungry roots had veined themselves around Ash Groves, mistaking him for good earth, a good home. True, Asha didn't know anything about him other than what she had learned from Sumesh Mishra. But it seemed to her that if he had been a good home, then her birth mother would have told him about her pregnancy. Something had prevented her, though, to the point that an arranged marriage had seemed like her best option.

Then again, maybe Asha had it all wrong. Meeting Sumesh Mishra was supposed to give her answers, and while it had provided some, it also doubled her questions.

Asha's eyes flitted toward the soft tapping at her bedroom door. A second later, a sliver of her mom's worried face appeared through the inch of open doorway.

"Can I come in?"

Asha nodded.

Her mom entered and lowered herself onto the bed. "I waited as long as I could. Can I bring you up some dinner?"

"No, thanks."

"Dad made chicken soup. It's only going down to twenty degrees tonight, but he made soup." Her mom strained to laugh, then turned serious. With her head bent forward, she played with her fingernails, chipping away at the nude polish. "I knew meeting him was a mistake."

"You couldn't have stopped it."

"That's what I hate about all of this. I can't stop any of it."

"Not now, no."

Her mom looked up from her lap, her eyes pink and moist. "I'm sorry your birth father was such a disappointment. But now you can put it behind you."

Asha readied herself with a deep breath. "He's not my birth father."

Her mom's face was a portrait of disbelief. "What do you mean?"

Instead of repeating herself, Asha pulled out the letter she had been concealing at the back of her journal and placed it on her mom's lap, a strange reversal of events leading back to the morning after her eighteenth birthday, when her mom had played postman.

Her mom picked up the letter, etches of disbelief deepening on her forehead. "Who's Ash Groves?" she asked.

Chapter 68

Once her dazed mom left to tell her dad the news, Asha started her journal entry.

Mala,

It feels strange to use your name. My name feels strange now too, but we'll get to that.

So did you watch the whole catastrophe unfold while hiding behind a cloud? Did you see the last bits of your plan come undone, and me along with it?

I agonized about meeting him—Sumesh—for months. He was supposed to answer my questions. But he isn't even my birth father.

I know that isn't your fault. You tried to set things right before you passed away. You couldn't have known that the letter would be returned, or that Sumesh would choose not to deliver it on your behalf.

You know what this means, don't you?

My birth father is still out there.

You left me a clue. In your letter, you said that Asha means hope and a wish. But it means so much more, doesn't it? Can an entire love letter be whittled down to a name?

So many secrets. How could you live with them?

I thought Rowan had disappointed me, and don't get me wrong, he has. But at least I have my parents and Willow to lean on. Even though what Sumesh did—or didn't do—was horrible, I guess I have him to thank for that. He said that when he gave me up for adoption, he knew the right people would find me. He was right.

But what about you? Was there no one who understood? No one you could trust to stand by you? Not even my birth father?

Asha

Chapter 69

"You can't make this stuff up," Willow said, shaking her head at Asha. They strolled around the block, enjoying the mild evening, reunited at last, since Willow had apologized to Asha's parents and Asha had promised not to keep secrets from them anymore. Everyone was getting another chance.

Asha kicked at a twig. "It's been shock after shock from the beginning."

"What are you going to do?"

"None of this has been up to me, Will. It's been happening *to* me."

"You chose to meet with Sumesh, didn't you?" Willow challenged. "Well, you can decide whether or not you want to look for your real birth father. I mean, it might not be easy based on an old address, but that's beside the point."

Asha walked a short distance, considering. "Mala wrote him a letter," she said. "I think he deserves to receive it." It was the right thing to do. It was what Asha wished her parents, and Sumesh Mishra, had done years ago.

Willow shrugged. "So then, once you find out where he lives now, drop it in a mailbox."

"Oh," Asha said, unblinking. "I guess I could do that."

Willow gave her a little shove. "You hesitated, Athena."

"Did I?"

Willow nodded with a smirk. "It's good. It means that deep down you know what you want to do."

Deep down, all Asha knew was cold, quivering fear that threatened to split across her like a fault line.

Willow gave her a look. "I know you're scared. But really, what's the worst that can happen?"

The worst wore the mask of many monsters. Her birth father could call her a liar, accuse her of fabricating the letter. He could reject her, make her feel even more unlovable.

He could turn out to be the kind of man Asha despised. The kind who lied and cheated and abandoned pregnant lovers. After all, there was a reason her birth parents hadn't stayed together. And it was possible that the reason was Ash Groves himself.

"If he turns out to be an awful person," Willow said, "would you even want to know him? Wouldn't that make it easier for you to walk away?"

Asha thought about this, and as she did, ripple by ripple, the cold, quivering fear started to still. She had done it just a few days ago: walked away. She could do it again, if she needed to.

Willow reminded her of something important. Something that fear had tricked her into believing she had lost.

Asha remembered she had a choice.

In another time, another life, Mala had put letters, and Asha's welfare, into other hands. But that was the past. This was Asha's time, Asha's life. And while she found herself lost somewhere in the pages of the book her birth mother began, it was a story they were writing together. The story may have started with Mala, but Asha would be the one to continue it, to the end, whatever end she chose.

Chapter 70

After their walk, Willow biked home and Asha went back inside the house, thirsty for a glass of cold water. On the way, she checked the mail, stuffing her hand in the letterbox, tickling around with blind fingers. Not much that day, just one thin envelope. She gave it a bored glance, thinking it was probably junk or another bill for her parents.

When, a second later, it registered that the letter was for her, Asha's heart hitched. Her eyes flicked to the top-left corner and she read the return address. Her heart hitched again.

Sumesh Mishra had found out where she lived and written to her. Her chest heaved as she stared down his name. What more could he have to say?

She rushed to her bedroom, then tore open the envelope, uncovering two single-spaced pages of tiny print. She read as fast as she could, her eyes darting from left to right, devouring line after line. As she made her way through the story Sumesh Mishra had neglected to tell her face to face, she was transported back to his living room—specifically, to a slip he made that she dismissed at the time as nothing more than nerves.

And since she had dismissed it, there was never a reason to reconcile the words *accident* and *illness,* or to raise questions about conflicting information related to Mala's death. Never a reason to wonder if it was one or the other. Or, in this case, as Asha discovered by the end of the letter, both.

Be good,
I'll be gone

Chapter 71

Mala lumbered into the apartment, clutching Asha snuggly to her chest. The baby's warmth was her body's only source of heat since the numbness set in, after she had emptied herself at the cremation service.

She lay Asha gently on the couch and removed her snowsuit, reflecting on how many of her mother's friends and acquaintances had attended. How many had approached her with stories about her mother she had never heard before. How many had told her how proud her mother was of having such a modest, respectful daughter. How full of purpose her mother's life had felt again since becoming a grandmother.

At one point, Chitra Shah—Chitra Auntie to Mala—her mother's closest friend, pulled her aside, taking it upon herself to reassure Mala that her mother had passed a happy woman. She had been so worried about Mala's future after her father's passing. But once Mala was married, according to Chitra Auntie, a peace had befallen her. An ease that made her last days among the most joyful of her life. Chitra Auntie knew because her mother had told her the last time they met for tea, the week before she passed.

Chitra Auntie had caressed Mala's dimpled chin with her fingertips then, in the manner of Indian mothers, pausing to admire her face, as if it were a rare and beautiful portrait, despite Mala's streaming tears. Mala was a good daughter, Chitra Auntie said one last time before spiriting herself away as the tide of her own sorrow rose.

"Here," Sumesh said to her with his arms outstretched. "I'll put Asha down for her nap. Go and get some rest in my room. That way you won't be disturbed. You haven't slept properly in days."

Mala straightened and lifted Asha into her arms, pressing her closely to her heart, so she could feel her daughter's quick, steady heartbeat, the rhythm of which had often been Mala's only comfort during other recent times of turmoil. *I'm here, I'm here, I'm here.*

"It's okay. I think the drive calmed her down. I could use some quiet time with her."

Sumesh nodded, frowning. "Mala," he said sadly. "I'm so sorry about your mom. She was such a sweet person. I was really enjoying getting to know her. She was the polar opposite of my mother. I was growing very fond of her."

Mala said nothing. She had found her mother lying in bed earlier that week. That day, they had made plans to go shopping for Asha, only her mother hadn't picked them up when she was supposed to. Looking back, that was the first moment Mala knew instinctively that something was wrong. After calling her mother for an hour to no avail, Mala bundled Asha into the carrier, fastened the carrier to the stroller, and rode the bus to her parents' house. The second moment Mala knew instinctively that something was wrong was when she entered her mother's bedroom and saw her sleeping face. It occurred to Mala that she looked altered, as if something vital were missing, as if her mother were both present and not. She set Asha's carrier on the floor and approached the bed. Then Mala touched the cold skin of her mother's face, and in one horrific, life-changing moment, she knew her mother was gone. A heart attack, they found out later, like her father. Dying alone, like her father. But perhaps, Mala considered, as Chitra Auntie had said, also dying happy and at peace. Mala hoped so. As she felt herself going to pieces, she prayed her mother was above it all now.

Mala bowed her head, acknowledging Sumesh. She slowly turned away from him and walked rigidly toward the nursery, feeling part of herself lift away, as if the only way to survive the heartbreak was to sequester her pain in some attic of her being and give control to the part of herself that felt nothing so that she might function.

Mala lowered herself onto the glider and started rocking with Asha, back and forth, back and forth, falling into numb hypnosis with the rhythm of the sway.

A good daughter, Chitra Auntie had called her.

And so what?

What difference had it made?

Mala would have lived with the shame of breaking up Ash's relationship and conceiving his child, but it was her love for her mother that stopped her from revealing the truth.

So she married a man she didn't love—a man who had deceived her about who he was—so she could give her mother what she always wanted: a married daughter and a grandchild.

Mala made every choice and sacrifice, denied every whisper and howl of her conscience, bore the weight of every secret, all to keep from being cut off from her mother's life. And in the end, she had lost her mother anyway.

What was it all for?

Mala didn't know anymore.

All she knew was that she felt deathly tired, her life was an unfixable mess and she wanted to be with her parents again. All she could hear was the dark voice, once a whisper, now a roar. It was right. Nothing was ever going to get better. She was trapped. There was only one escape.

Asha snored in her arms. Mala gazed upon her with deep love and sadness, wishing they had known more moments of peace and closeness like this. Wishing she had been able to transform herself into the good mother she wanted to be in her heart, the good mother Asha deserved. Oh, her beautiful daughter. She warranted so much more, so much better, than the nameless black void Mala had to offer. There was no chance of the lead leaving her veins now. There was no shimmer left inside her to break through it. Mala clamped her eyes shut against a crippling pang. It was all too hopeless.

Chapter 72

Thick, downy snow fell outside the balcony window as Mala signed her last letter. Once she was finished, she folded the page in three, tucked it inside an envelope and wet the glue with a slide of her tongue, grimacing at the acrid tang that gummed up her taste buds. She flipped the envelope over and paused. She hoped she had the right address.

She checked her watch. It was nearly six o'clock. Sumesh and Asha would be home soon. Where had the day gone? Preparing the baby food—Asha was going through an avocado and sweet potato phase—and tidying had taken longer than she anticipated. Mala gathered the letters, rose to her feet and walked to Sumesh's bedroom, placing two of the envelopes on his pillow. The other she would mail on the way out.

An ache beat through the numbness of her heart. Sumesh would be angry. Ash too. Someday, though, she hoped they would understand her side of things and, maybe after some time had passed, remember her as she once was. A good friend. An ally.

Mala bent to pick a stray sock of Asha's off the floor and grinned; her little feet wriggled them off everywhere. She held the sock to her nose and inhaled deeply. It still carried a hint of Asha's sweet milk scent. Her daughter did love munching on her toes.

Her brief grin fell, like her heart, all the way to the floor, the basement, the centre of the Earth. She dipped her heavy head and stared vacantly at the parquet. The one person who wouldn't remember her was Asha. While there was no comfort in this, there was at least some in knowing she had passed on the greatest lesson of her own tragic life in the hope that Asha's story might have a different outcome.

Like the women before her who had gently cast their precious baskets downriver, Mala knew that letting Asha go was the unselfish thing to do. Real love was an act of surrender. Mala pulled Asha's scent deeply into her lungs one last time, luxuriating while she imagined kissing her sweet feet. Then she let go of the breath, the dream and stuffed Asha's sock into her pocket. Turning on her heel, she clenched her fingers around the last of her letters and made for the door.

The rest happened without ceremony. She put on her winter clothes, held Ash's letter in her hand and left the apartment without a backward glance.

She exited the building, stepped out into the thick snowfall and raised her fur-trimmed hood. They were forecasting another twenty centimetres before sunrise. At least half of that had already shaken from the light grey sky. The powder glittered under the orange glow of the streetlights as she trudged along the sidewalk. At the corner, she stopped in front of the mailbox and dropped Ash's letter into its open mouth. She felt nothing as she walked away.

Resuming her path, Mala turned her attention back to the snow. The stuff was pure magic. *How could anything so beautiful be deadly?* Her father's last words to her mother. What had her mother's last words been? Dear God, how she missed them. She knew they would understand. She knew they would forgive her.

In the distance, by the intersection, Mala heard the angry blare of horns. Fresh snow like this, the fluff that soon turned dripping wet, was often more dangerous than black ice. Slippery. Hard to brake on.

Squinting as she approached the traffic lights at Bronson and

Carling, she saw the silver glow of the walking man and slowed her pace. By the time she reached the corner of the busy four-lane intersection, the signal had changed to the red hand.

The shriek of tires spinning in the snow, digging for asphalt to grip, ripped through the air, followed by the slow chug of acceleration. No matter the weather, people always drove more recklessly at the end of a workday, anxious to get home, eat something.

Mala looked to her left, spotting a dump truck, heavy with a load of snow. Before her eyes, the road transformed into a river, and the truck into her parents. Her vision shimmered at the pleasing sight of their smiling faces, their loving outstretched arms. They were flowing toward her, faster now. Ready to catch her.

One. Two. Three.

Step.

And they carried her away.

Letters

Chapter 73

Asha plodded, catatonic, to her desk and sat down. She blinked at the pages of Sumesh Mishra's letter, her light eyes despairing. Then she reached for her journal.

Mala,

When I first saw his letter, I wondered what more he could have to tell me, but I never imagined something like this. I've wondered about how you died for so long. Now I know, and I wish I didn't. He told me about your depression. Did you really feel so utterly alone even when I dozed in my crib? Or when you fed me or rocked me to sleep? That makes me sadder than I can say . . .

He reassured me that I wasn't to blame. That your problems started before I was born. I don't know if I believe him, but it was nice of him to say.

Now here I am. With the whole truth. What I've wanted from the beginning.

And one more letter that still needs to be delivered.

Asha

Chapter 74

Ash stood looking at the river from his office window and sipped a passable cup of coffee. Students strolled along the river path, like he had decades ago, and still did, any time he needed to clear his head or, more often, feel close to Mala. He searched for the spot, to the left, and saw a younger version of himself seated on the grass, pointing at clouds, trying to make the loneliest girl he had ever known smile.

He shuddered as he remembered the awful day he found out about Mala's death. By then he had graduated and started a post-doc at UBC. They were back in Ottawa for a few days to celebrate a cousin's wedding. While in town, he dropped by the department to pick up the bound copies of his dissertation. As he walked the custard-coloured halls for the last time—or so he thought—with the hardcovers digging into the crook of his arm, he ran into her adviser. Desperate for any news, he asked about her.

Dead for weeks. Hit by a dump truck. Hadn't he heard? Weren't they close?

The copies slipped from his weak arms, filling the hallway with a resonant boom. A deep, racking, silent pain overwhelmed him, too vast for him to make a sound or even to flinch. When he got back to the hotel, he couldn't conceal his grief. Elaine didn't understand why he was so inconsolable over a classmate. It all gushed out then, his shame, his secrets. Elaine ended their relationship shortly after that, and rightly so. Ever since, he had battled to remain a part of Ruby's life.

A noisy group of students passed by his office. His tongue felt rough and dry. He gulped a mouthful of coffee.

When he accepted the faculty position at his old alma mater, he wondered whether it might be a mistake, knowing that for him the hallways of the department would always be incurably haunted by Mala's memory. Nevertheless, he felt an undeniable pull and couldn't resist it. What he hadn't expected was how much comfort he would derive from the haunting. While their time had passed, this would always be their place. Every year, when the leaves burned with such beauty, he thought of Mala and the autumn they fell in love. Their love that could never be. The greatest of his life.

He was startled from his thoughts by a knock on the door.

He glanced over his shoulder, expecting to find one of his students hovering at the threshold.

Instead, he gawped at a ghost.

Mala? he thought, chilled.

His mug slipped from his hand.

Chapter 75

Asha wakened with wolfish dread biting at her heart. Today was the day. In the end, finding him wasn't as difficult as she had anticipated. Ash Groves was an uncommon enough name. When she googled him, a list of scholarly articles on wetlands and climate change popped up in seconds. She got his contact information from the bottom of an abstract. It seemed unbelievably lucky that he not only lived in Ottawa but also taught biology at Carleton, where she was studying English.

Now, as she waited at his office door, she took a moment to observe him. He was standing and looking out the window, holding a cup of coffee in one hand, with the other at home inside his pocket. He was sturdy but not very tall. He wore a navy sweater, khakis and, unexpectedly, a pair of red Converse. He dresses like a prof, she thought. He dresses like a dad who still wants to be cool. The afternoon sun highlighted his auburn waves. She had always wanted red hair.

A noisy group of students walked by. Asha flinched as he came to life, terrified he was about to look in the direction of the racket and discover her before she was ready to be seen. But he just raised his mug to his lips, took a sip and returned to his statue-like pose, never pulling his gaze from the window.

She reached inside her satchel for the letter. The back of her hand grazed the notch in the cover of her well-loved copy of *Jane*

Eyre, which Agnes had retired from circulation and given to her as a belated graduation gift, knowing how she had connected with the heroine. She had brought the book with her today as a talisman. The very book she had picked up in search of escape and in which she instead found a hero in Jane. Asha reminded herself that if Jane was true to anyone it was herself—not fear. If she believed in anything, it was her own ability to persevere, no matter what ghosts might be howling in the attic.

With the letter in hand, Asha took a bracing breath and knocked on the door.

His shoulders twitched. She must have startled him. He turned around.

His eyes widened with alarm. She kept very still. He mouthed a single word. He dropped his mug.

As he looked down at the mess splattered around his feet, she ran.

She didn't stop until she was outside the building. She stood off in a corner and caught her breath. The autumn afternoon cooled her burning cheeks. She touched her face. And in a frozen moment of terror, Asha realized what was missing from her empty hand. She stared at the cinnamon-coloured lines of her palm, slack-jawed.

He had dropped the mug.

She had dropped the letter.

Chapter 76

B y the time Ash looked up from the spray of coffee and broken porcelain, the young woman was gone.

But she had left something behind. He walked over and picked up the envelope, surprised to discover it was for him. The mailing address, however, made no sense. He had never lived anywhere with that street name.

He tore into the envelope and unfolded the letter. He recognized her handwriting right away. The voice he had thought was lost to him forever.

Ash,

I have something to tell you. I'm afraid it's long overdue. I'm sorry.

Do you remember that day in the office after the holidays? You told me you couldn't leave Laine and the baby. Well, I had news to share with you too. You see, I hadn't followed through with our plan either. And my reasons weren't that different from your own.

Her name is Asha. And she's yours. Your daughter has a sister.

I didn't tell you about her because I was hurt. You made your choice and I felt abandoned. I didn't think telling you would make any difference. So I married Sumesh and spared my mother from having to bear the shame of my mistakes.

I have a feeling that once you look into our daughter's eyes, you won't be able to look away from her again. The only reason I'm able to leave is because I know she's better off without me. I'm unworthy of her perfect, spotless gaze. I've told Sumesh everything. His number's below. Reach out to him. He loves Asha to pieces. I hope you'll be able to work something out.

My mother was also spared the heartbreak of receiving a note like this. Did you know she passed away? I found her resting peacefully in bed. She's with my father now. By the time you read this, I'll be with them too.

Tell Asha about the good times, will you? Tell her about who I was back when I still believed in old sayings like "It was written."

Mala

The letter shook in his quaking hands. There was too much to process. For now, he could only focus on one thing.

Her name is Asha. And she's yours. Your daughter has a sister.

He dashed into the hallway, jerking his head from left to right as he searched for her with panic in his eyes. But she was nowhere to be found. Fear seized his heart.

Asha. His daughter. Where had she gone?

Chapter 77

Asha stood rigid, lost. She didn't know where to go or what to do.

A distant gleam caught her eye, the bounce of metallic light off rippling water. As if called by a gentle whisper, Asha was drawn toward the river. She descended the building's concrete steps, crossed the street and knelt in the grass.

Reaching into her satchel, she pulled out her copy of *Jane Eyre* and stroked the notch in the cover, dejected. She had thought she was ready to face him. Thought she was brave like Jane. But she was wrong.

Asha stared at the river, listened to the rush of the water and wondered what to do next. Should she go back to his office? She hadn't given him a way of contacting her. Unless Mala had told him in his letter, he wouldn't even know her name. Asha hung her head, miserable. She had made such a mess of things . . .

Chapter 78

A sh went to the river, crestfallen.

How was he ever going to find her now? He exited the building, walking with his head down, his feet knowing the way.

He stumbled upon the ghost, kneeling in the grass, gazing at the water, as Mala had so often done. He didn't breathe. Only watched her. Asha. His daughter.

He wiped his eyes and approached her with a fiercely beating heart. Her face was turned away. She hadn't noticed him standing beside her. He spoke her name for the first time and waited.

And then she looked up.

And their grey eyes met.

And in that moment, Ash knew Mala was right.

These eyes he could never deny. Eyes in which he saw the beginnings of something wonderful, a second chance. Eyes that shone so faultless, so true, they made his full heart burst with every warm, glittering colour of love.

Chapter 79

In long strokes and gentle curls, the balmy spring breeze wafted the tempting aroma of roasted corn throughout the yard. Asha stood to one side of the deck leisurely sweeping her gaze from left to right, taking in the small gathering of loved ones who had come together to celebrate her nineteenth birthday.

There were her grandparents, bent over the patio table, taking extra care to dress the roasted corn with ample squeezes of lime, shiny slatherings of butter and heavy pinches of salt. She heard snippets of their bickering, as harmless as it was habitual, each claiming to know the ideal ratio. An unstoppable smile lifted her cheeks.

There was her Willow, plucking her way through an unrecognizable tune on Asha's dad's guitar.

There were her parents, standing shoulder to shoulder at the barbecue, talking easily like they used to, her dad now restored to full health.

And there were Ash and Ruby, looking more at ease than when they first arrived. Asha's relationship with them was still new, they were still getting to know each other, but she had wanted to invite them today, so they could meet the people who meant the most to her in the world.

Since her birth mother's letter entered her life, she had often felt cursed. Now, with fresh eyes, Asha saw that she had always been fortunate.

Long before she ever knew Ash, Ruby or Mala even existed, she already had a sister, a father, a mother. She already had a family. With them, she belonged. With them, she was home. And they belonged with her too. She kept them safe and sheltered. She was their home, and she was her own.

She had her birth mother to thank for that, in part. When Mala had let her go, she unknowingly gave to Asha the things she wished had been given to her. A family who would stand by her through anything. The freedom to choose her own life.

Asha's eyes sparkled. They hadn't gathered like this since her eighteenth birthday, the day before she found out she was adopted. At one point, she might have considered that night her last happy memory because it marked the end of a time of innocence for her, a time of not knowing.

Yet, despite the turmoil of the past year, given the choice between leaping backward or standing firm, she would choose the Asha she was today. She would always choose knowing the truth.

A warm glow swelled her heart. She beamed affection over them all.

Happiness wasn't behind her, she knew.

Happiness was all around, like the far-reaching roots of a tree, linking her to a forest of others.

Look to the sky
and find me

*T*his is where we meet. I know it was a special place for the two of you. Now it's a special place for us three.

I've been waiting for him at a picnic table under a shady oak. It's a warm autumn afternoon. I can hear the wind in the trees. Leaves are raining all around me. One just drifted onto my journal.

And another, into the river. I can't see it anymore, but I know it isn't gone. Nothing ever is. I can hear the river tinkle a song. It's telling me that things don't end. They flow.

He just arrived. He's sitting cross-legged on the grass, staring at the river. Now he's looking at the sky. Now he's smiling. At what?

The clouds. A shape. A face, backlit in white gold.

I see it too.

Is that you, in the clouds, where birds don't fly? Have you been watching over me like you promised in your letter? Did you know we would find each other?

Yes, I can see you now. Your lips curved in a gentle smile. Your spirit glowing with sacred light.

I can see you now, Mom.

And all I see is love.

Acknowledgements

Heartfelt thanks to my wonderful agent, Stacey Donaghy, for being an enthusiastic champion of this story. Stacey, thank you for your feedback, the time you've taken to edit and read multiple drafts, for always being available to talk, and for helping the book—which will always go by a different name to us (wink)—find a good home.

I'm grateful to my editor, Iris Tupholme, for the enlightening discussions, thorough editorial notes and encouragement throughout the revision process. Sincere appreciation as well to Helen Reeves, Jennifer Lambert, Natalie Meditsky, Heather Sangster, Allegra Robinson, Karmen Wells, Laura Dosky, and Lisa Rundle for their valued contributions at different stages.

Thank you to the talented Lisa Bettencourt for designing a lovely cover and to Kathy Youssef for the author portrait. My deepest gratitude to everyone at HarperCollins Canada who contributed to this book and helped bring it to the world.

Thanks also to Sherrill Wark and my dear friend Sam Bailey for feedback on early drafts. Kendra Ayers, my book sister, what would I do without you? I appreciate your constant support and enthusiasm, which never dwindles no matter how many manuscripts I send your way. You really are the best. Many thanks to my family and friends for their support throughout this process. Especially grateful for my parents, Nim, Kiran, Neena, Michael, CT & Co., Jacinth, Sonia, the London crew and Noodles.

Last but never least, my dear husband, Daniel, I appreciate your support more than I can say. You're a huge part of this book and my writing. Thank you for being my first reader, my plotting partner, my therapist, my cheerleader. Life with you is a splendid thing.